SHADOWS

Peter J. Manos

ISBN: 978-1-953735-98-0

Melange Books, LLC
White Bear Lake, MN 55110
www.melange-books.com

Published in the United States of America.

Cover Design by Ashley Redbird Designs

For Ingrid

CHAPTER ONE

A blinding white light. No sound. No mushroom cloud.
Just a searing, unearthly, excruciating light.

Edna O'Hare's first nuclear war dream occurred on October 22, 1962, during the first semester of her sophomore year in college where she'd met her future husband, James. President Kennedy had ordered a blockade of Cuba because the Russians had brought missiles to the island. The world was on the verge of nuclear war. Such dreams began again after James's death, almost a year ago.

Before the pandemic had ended, both she and James had been vaccinated, but he got sick none the less. They'd spoken on the phone until he was intubated and then he became delirious. A nurse had sent her videos, but they were terribly disturbing.

Adding to her torment, she'd been to the gravesite only

once, on the day he was buried. She couldn't face him, so to speak, because she'd failed to take up his campaign as she'd promised him she would.

She stared at the moon as she did after each awakening from one of her nightmares. A lunatic, she thought, that's what she would become if she continued awakening in a panic to stare at the moon. What was the purpose of these dreams, she asked finally. To overcome her inertia? Must she pick up James's banner and do something bold to prove to herself that she could face angry people?

Faced with a patient with crippling acrophobia, what would a therapist do? Take that person to the top of a skyscraper and make them look down until the dread of high places burned itself out. She knew where her skyscraper was, though it was underground.

CHAPTER TWO

Edna O'Hare in a black short-sleeve blouse, black jeans, and black boots, her mourning outfit, had also brought her wooden cane in the event she felt unsteady.

She drove her small black pickup truck on U.S. 52, through Velva, onto 46th Street North, then south on 12th Avenue North, parking near the entrance to the B-02 missile silo access road. The expansive flat countryside seemed forlorn. Distant swatches of smeared out clouds hovered motionless, all color washed out of them as the morning sun had risen.

Skyscraper, here I come, she thought, trying to joke with herself to ease the tension. And now that she thought about it, it was indeed a skyscraper in its own right.

No sign of Amy Haugen, Minot Daily reporter, who'd promised to be there to take pictures of what might happen, though Amy herself was not in sympathy with Edna's protest. After all, Amy's husband worked on the base. On the other hand, Edna was no stranger, having been a friend of Amy's mother and quite solicitous of the family after she had died.

Though there was nothing of particular interest to see, she scanned the land for ten minutes before recognizing procrastination. How much easier it would be to give up this half-baked idea and go home. Yes, she wanted attention, but suddenly she was frightened. Once she started down that access road the situation would be out of her control and there was no guarantee that she'd get the kind of attention she'd envisioned. But there was nothing for it but to do it, not if she wished to maintain any self-respect, put an end to the dreams, and complete the work of mourning.

She climbed out of the truck. With her crook-necked cane she walked to the access road. Fifty or sixty yards ahead, the installation waited for her. She began toward it, glad she'd brought the reassuring cane, which felt like a companion. Why was she scared? Because she was being *bad*? And if you were bad, you were punished?

She forced herself to keep walking until she reached the imposing chain-link fence surrounding an area a little larger than a basketball court. The assemblage of hardware in a corner—metal boxes, antennas, access hatches and the cap over the silo—was the size of a small gas station. A sign on the fence read:

WARNING RESTRICTED AREA
IT IS UNLAWFUL TO ENTER THIS AREA WITHOUT
PERMISSION FROM THE INSTALLATION
COMMANDER.
USE OF DEADLY FORCE AUTHORIZED

The response to this sort of incursion was supposed

to be quick, but Edna paced back and forth for forty-five minutes before the gray vehicle, an oversized rhinoceros, grumbled its way up the gravel access road toward her. She faced it, paralyzed. When it was twenty feet away, the raspy grumbling ceased. A woman with a megaphone and man with an assault rifle stepped out.

"Drop your weapon," boomed the woman. Uncomprehending and scared, Edna, still gripping the cane, raised her hands overhead, the "weapon" now inclined toward the airmen.

Kak. Kak. Kak. Kak. Kak. A burst of rifle fire. Petrified, Edna only stood more stiffly.

"Drop it," said the woman.

A man jumped from the vehicle and addressed the airman with the rifle.

"Goddamn it, Forster, are you completely nuts? That's an old lady with cane. What the fuck you thinking, you trigger-happy idiot. Get back in the truck."

Sergeant Caulfield walked up to O'Hare, who by now had dropped her "weapon."

"You can put your hands down. What do you think you're doing here?

"Protesting," she said weakly.

"Hernandez," called Caulfield to the woman. "Pat her down."

In searching Edna for weapons, Hernandez also removed from a back pocket Edna's small, red leather wallet. Together Airman Rita Hernandez and Sergeant Caulfield examined her driver's license.

Hernandez picked up the cane, hesitated, then gave it back to its owner. They walked Edna to the vehicle, not even bothering to hold her by the wrist. She was so obviously harmless.

She sat in back, Sergeant Caulfield on her left, Hernandez on her right. Charlie Forster drove. As the Humvee turned left onto 12th Avenue North, Edna peered out the window. There on the side of the road, leaning against her white sedan, Amy Haugen took pictures. So she'd come after all.

"What are you protesting? Nuclear weapons?" asked Caulfield.

"No, sir," said Edna. "Land-based missiles."

"And why's that?"

Prudently, Edna made her presentation brief, then added, "I respect and admire you all for serving our country and I want to offer an invitation to you and your fellow airmen on the base to come to my house for coffee and cake any time. Well, anytime between two and four in the afternoon. But will they let you?"

Airman Forster turned for a second to Caulfield. Without a hint of irony he said, "You're fraternizing with the enemy."

"Eyes on the road," said Caulfield.

For the next mile or so, no one spoke. Edna sensed the tension between Caulfield and Forster, who, after all, had unnecessarily fired his rifle, scaring the bejeezus out of a harmless old woman.

His beef was with anyone who was anti-nuclear, anti-air force, even anti-war. He lumped these all together as treason and, in some indefinable way, as personally insulting to him as a spit in the face.

To break the silence and reduce her anxiety, Edna talked

about growing up on the farm, how hard-working her father and mother had been, and how loving.

"My father was always warning me about the danger of agricultural machinery. He'd let me ride with him on the tractor but wouldn't let me shift gears or anything. So one day when I was about nine or ten I climbed out the window and took the tractor for a little drive."

"You were a bad girl even then," said Forster, again without irony.

"I suppose so. Anyway he was waiting in front of the shed when I returned. He looked like he'd hit his thumb with a hammer. We sat down in the living room. I folded my hands on my lap and waited for it. He was making me stew. I dared not say a word. I pictured being whipped, but he'd never hit me. I thought I might be housebound until I was eighteen. I pictured all sorts of things but didn't want to cry. All of a sudden laughter came pouring out of him like Niagara Falls. He laughed so hard he buckled over. That's when I cried. From that day on he showed me how to operate everything. Even the jolly green combine when we rented it. Nothing bad ever happened."

They drove to the Ward County Sheriff's Department in Minot, and handed her over to Sheriff Bjorn Andresen, a short, heavyset man in his fifties, with a pink, moon-shaped face, a man everyone in town knew, including Edna. Caulfield summarized the situation and left.

Andresen, in his turn, took her to a booking office where she sat on a hard, cold steel chair, the memory of her once fulsome buttocks flashing through her mind. The booking officer, Shirley Johansen, a middle-aged blonde, looked like a powerlifter. No buttock shrinkage there, thought Edna.

"What were you doing there?" asked Johansen.

7

"Just standing."

Johansen shook her head.

"What was the purpose of your trespass?"

"I was there because I want to educate the public about the expensive, useless, unnecessary and dangerous new missiles that are supposed to replace the expensive, useless, unnecessary and dangerous old missiles."

Johansen, needing to hear no more, efficiently photographed and fingerprinted her charge, before asking if she wished to make a phone call before going to her cell.

"My cell? What do you mean 'my cell?'" asked Edna alarmed. "I didn't do anything. I didn't take anything. I didn't hurt anyone."

Johansen shook her head in disbelief.

"You trespassed on a Minuteman missile site. Do you want to make that call or not?"

The only one she could think to call was Amy Haugen.

"They're arresting me."

"Oh," said Amy. "I'll come on over." She seemed uncertain.

"Please do. Talk with Sheriff Andresen. Thank you."

As efficiently as she'd been booked, she was escorted to a changing room where, Johansen looking on, she took off her clothes and changed into an orange jumpsuit, her personal belongings put into a large plastic bag.

The windowless, dank concrete, twelve-by-fourteen foot holding cell housed a bunk with a blue-plastic-covered mattress against a wall and a toilet and a small sink opposite.

A pretty but weary-looking young woman also wearing an orange jumpsuit, sat in the middle of the bunk. Her shoelaces had also been removed.

"What are *you* in for, grandma?" she asked sneering.

Standing with her back against the bars, Edna felt like having a conversation about as much as she felt like dancing. But she didn't want to be rude, and the woman frightened her.

"Trespassing."

"Trespassing on what?"

"A missile site."

"What?"

"Oh, it's not important."

She wanted to sit, but the woman occupied the middle of the bunk. Raising her hands to cover her face, Edna began to cry.

It seemed like quite a while before the woman moved to one end of the bunk and said, "Sit down."

Wiping her eyes and nose on the sleeve of her jumpsuit, she sat on the opposite end of the bunk. The woman, surprising her, scooted over and put her arm around Edna's shoulders, which released a fresh outburst of crying. Minutes went by before Edna's crying diminished to sniffling. When it stopped the woman asked, "What's a missile site?"

Edna brought her sniffling under control, wiped her nose on her sleeve again, and forced herself to look at her cell mate. The woman removed her arm from Edna's shoulders and moved away slightly.

"It's a deep underground silo holding a Minuteman missile."

The woman looked puzzled.

"What's a Minuteman missile?"

"It's a rocket that can travel six thousand miles with an atomic bomb on the top."

"Oh, like for the air force."

"Yes, it's an air force rocket."

"And it's underground and you walked over it?"

"There's a fence around it. I walked next to it."

"It's against the law?"

"Yes."

"So why'd you do it?"

From the looks of this woman and her situation, it was unlikely that she was about to take up the cause and she seemed woefully ignorant. Nevertheless, she was interested. And how many people over the years had ever been interested?

Still she hesitated. How much background should she give?

"Are you from around here?" asked Edna.

"Uh huh."

"But you haven't heard much about the missiles."

"Nope."

"Well, there are one hundred fifty of these monsters in a giant horseshoe around Minot. They were put there over sixty years ago to scare the Russians from attacking us, but we don't need them anymore because we have rockets on submarines and bombs in airplanes. And besides they're sitting ducks.

"I was standing there to bring attention to all this. And one more thing. They want to replace them all with new rockets costing about a hundred billion dollars. A lot of people don't know anything about them."

"Like me."

Edna nodded. Talking had helped her settle down. She was less frightened.

"My name's Edna. What's yours?"

"Dahlia."

"Nice to meet you Dahlia."

"Likewise."

They shook hands.

"They probably won't keep you long," said Dahlia. "You don't seem too dangerous."

"Neither do you."

"I'm more dangerous than I look. I pulled a knife on a guy, but he had it coming, the son-of-a-bitch. He hit me."

"Oh," was all Edna could think of to say.

"But they won't keep me for long."

"You've been here before?"

Dahlia frowned.

"A couple of times."

"I'm sorry."

"They don't do this in Amsterdam."

————

Dahlia had moved here from Fargo to be near the air base where she "dated" some of the men. They were mostly okay but occasionally there was a nasty one, but she could take care of herself, she explained.

They talked about the weather, about a trip to Disneyworld Dahlia had made when she was a girl, about the movies Dahlia had seen and liked.

"Did you ever see *Pretty Woman*?" she asked. Edna had not.

Later Edna had to use the toilet, a humiliating experience though the guards were women and Dahlia looked away.

———

Sheriff Andresen called Colonel Frank Nichols, commander of the 91st missile wing at Minot Air Force Base, with the odd story of a seventy-eight-year-old woman trespassing on a missile site.

"We've got her in a cell."

"What was she up to?" asked Nichols.

"Protesting against the missiles."

"She throw any cow's blood on the fence?"

"No. No blood. No signs either or anyone else."

"Is she a member of one of those nutty disarmament groups?

"No. Frankly, I think she's harmless."

"You never know but let's not give her any publicity."

"Let her go?" asked Andresen. "No charges?"

"Christ! Of course, you've got to charge her, just don't keep her in jail. Let her go to court."

———

In the late afternoon Johansen reappeared.

"Mrs. O'Hare, please come with me."

"Goodbye, Dahlia."

"Yea, take care."

On the way back to the changing room, Edna asked what was going on.

"Sheriff Andresen wants to talk with you and then you're being released."

In his office, on another hard chair, she waited for him to speak.

"I have half a mind to keep you overnight but… Never

mind. Just stay off those missile sites. You're still being charged with a crime. You'll get something in the mail. I suggest you not contest the charge."

She suppressed the urge to comment on his having half a mind, but her anxiety had turned to agitation and she couldn't repress her urge to speak.

"Bjorn, do you know how long it would take Russian rockets to hit these silos?"

"Frankly, Edna, I have other things to think about."

"Probably thirty minutes, if that. And that long for our rockets to hit their silos. One side will launch their rockets if they receive a warning that the other side has attacked. And they'll do this even if the warning is a mistake. And then billions of people will die. We need to get rid of them."

He had nothing to say.

———

Officer Johansen escorted her to the exit, where Amy Haugen was waiting.

"I've been here all day. I didn't think it would take that long. What happened?"

"They locked me up."

"Really?"

"Yes, they dressed me in orange like a pumpkin and locked me up. Dangerous little old me."

"Locking you up for misdemeanor trespassing seems over the top. I wonder what's going on. Do you need a ride back to your truck?"

As Amy drove, Edna began to relax.

"Did you take any pictures?" she asked.

"I did. Of the vehicle. Listen, Edna, I'd written up the

story from what you'd already told me. And when I was waiting for you I spoke with Wilburn about it. He wasn't interested."

"Wasn't interested? With the pictures and everything?"

"There are no pictures of you. Just of the vehicle. And anyway, he said no one wanted to read about a crazy old woman raving against a project that would make Minot a boom town all over again. Not even the farmers are grousing. He also asked if you were a peacenik."

"A peacenik? He knows James and I have wanted this rocket and its hydrogen bomb off our land forever and we were never called peaceniks. Most of the farmers, if they had their way, wouldn't have those monsters on their land either."

Amy Haugen shrugged her shoulders. A protest by a woman at a missile silo was clearly newsworthy, and Wilburn's rejection of it was censorship after all, but perhaps it was best that it had not appeared. Amy's husband would have called her out for helping a crackpot.

Edna experienced Amy's stillness, not as hostile or disinterested, but merely as pensive. And she was grateful for Amy's generosity with her time. She could have left Edna to her own devices.

"I swore to myself that I would do this... this campaign or crusade or whatever you want to call it, and I feel I'm letting James down and myself. It's a really bad feeling but I don't seem to have the get-up-and-go for it."

"Well, that's not so surprising. You're still in mourning."

Edna nodded but steered the conversation away from grief.

"You know, shortly after we moved here, James experienced for himself Minot's general disinterest in the ICBMs, which I'd warned him about."

"Yes," said Amy, "and it's still true. Out of sight, out of mind. They don't cause any problems. They are simply facts of life and finding someone who wants to talk critically about them is as likely as finding someone who wants to bad mouth the air force."

"Yes," agreed Edna. "James accepted reality and stopped trying to engage people on the issue. He understood his unique circumstances already made him foreign to these Midwesterners and he didn't want to seem even more foreign."

"Most everybody liked James, though," added Amy.

"Right, but when they announced that billions were to be spent on new missiles, he felt compelled to act.

"He was committed to bring this GBSD thing to national attention, as quixotic as that sounded. And here his unique background would enhance the newsworthiness of his efforts.

"But I disliked confrontation, still do, and was reluctant to say things that made people mad, specifically my brother-in-law Earnest Schmidt. The only real arguments James and I ever had were about this reticence and about my keeping my maiden name.

"James understood that I'd do what I could but that the burden would be on him but before he could do anything, the coronavirus put an end to his plans."

She choked up, not adding that he'd died in isolation in intensive care, and that she had been barred from an in-person visit.

"I'm sorry, Edna."

"You don't see anything wrong with these missiles, do you?"

"To tell you the truth, I've never given them much thought. But I understand what you're saying. I think I do."

She felt sorry for Edna, principally because she'd lost her husband of over fifty years, had no children, and lived alone, but also because she found sad the idea of a woman sworn singlehandedly to stop a juggernaut that might easily crush her. At the same time she admired the woman's spunk. Amy herself hadn't even tried arguing with Wilburn when he said no to her article.

———

A week later, returning from the supermarket to her pickup truck, a shopping bag hanging from each hand, Edna was shocked to see the word "Russian" and a five-pointed star sloppily spray painted in red on the driver's side of her truck.

The sun had warmed the sidewalk so much that the heat could be felt radiating back up from the concrete. Her black truck was hot, too, and when she gingerly touched the tip of her little finger to the red paint, a bit stuck. She rubbed it off on a tire.

She put the bags in the cab and, cursing under her breath, walked several blocks to a hardware store. A man in an apron bearing the label Strong's Hardware, It's Strong, asked if he could be of help.

"Yes, I need some black enamel spray paint. Glossy."

"I have just the thing."

Back at her truck she had the odd thought that she was fortunate to be dressed in black, now that she had to use the spray can, though she would not be as slap-dash a painter as the vandals who did this. Intently focused on the job, she covered the red paint with black.

As she got into the truck and sat behind the wheel, about to pull out into the light traffic, a wave of gooseflesh passed over her. She saw herself in the cross-hairs of a sniper's riffle. The red spray paint was blood. No. No. No. She told herself. That's as cuckoo as it gets.

Under the awning of an ice cream shop across the street, stood two beefy young men, boys really, in wine red football jerseys. Number 9's brown hair was cut in such a way that his head looked like an artillery shell. He stood arms akimbo, shaking his head slowly. Number 15's longish blond hair hung in his eyes. He carried a skateboard, which he moved from one hand to the other.

They were definitely staring at her and she had the eerie feeling that they were the vandals.

Her chest rose and fell rapidly now as she tried to come to a decision. It might be prudent to just leave. On the other hand maybe it wasn't prudence but simple cowardice. She got out of the truck walked the short distance to a corner where she could cross safely, and then approached the boys, stopping a few feet from them.

"Did you young men see anyone spray paint on my truck?"

"I don't know what you're talking about, lady," said number 9, tonelessly.

"That truck over there." She pointed. "That's mine. Somebody sprayed paint on it."

She couldn't believe she was doing this. Her heart pitter-pattered in her chest.

"We've got better things to do than look at your truck,"

said number 15, brushing hair from his forehead. "It's not much to look at, anyway."

"Sorry to have troubled you," she said.

———

On the drive home questions about that troubling encounter arose like bubbles from a swamp. Why were those boys so hostile? Was it possible that they themselves had done the dirty work? But if so, why? And how had she worked up the courage to face them?

She was still chewing over these questions at night. She couldn't sleep. Though she scolded herself and whispered to herself under her breath that it really was unnecessary, she got out of bed, padded downstairs into the kitchen, and poured herself an ounce of whiskey precisely measured in a jigger. She fell asleep.

———

Above the huge world map at the center of the North American Aerospace Command under Cheyenne Mountain a red number 4 begins to flash. Unidentified objects on the screen approach the United States. Now the red number 3 flashes. She swallows but her mouth is dry. Number 2 replaces number 3. At number 1 the computer generates a warning: 99.9% certainty of an attack on the United States. "Wait," she thinks. "Wait."

She waves her arms at the man in the control chair whose face she cannot see. She cups her hand to her mouth and screams, "Wait!" The man turns toward her, puzzled, shrugging his shoulders. He does not wait.

She sees and hears hundreds of missiles arise, roaring from their Great Plains silos. Hundreds more missiles arise, roaring from their Russia silos. Hydrogen bombs rain upon the earth.

Hundreds of firestorms from burning cities spew soot into the stratosphere. The earth is cast in darkness.

The flock of geese that triggered the alarm perishes in the doom.

CHAPTER THREE

The car's rear wheels spun as if they were in the final lap of the Indy 500, but the car just sat. Goddamn it! Will Larrabee felt a cursing binge coming on, but he clenched his jaw and the feeling passed.

Stuck in a summer thunderstorm at night in the middle of North Dakota. Nice. He turned the engine off. During the day the only feature of the landscape was a horizon-to-horizon yellow, green, or brown shag rug of one crop or another. He could only identify the sunflowers. Though the moon was out, they were now gray, except when a nearby bolt of lightning, splitting into jagged roots like an other-worldly tree, cast a ghostly light on them.

He'd have to spend the night in the car, not that he would be able to sleep.

Another flash and there it was, probably a house, as if it had just popped into existence like one of those virtual particles that nuclear physicists go ga-ga over.

Should he stay in the car and take his chances with the lightning or try to make it to the house not even knowing for sure if it was a house? Well, what the hell else could it be? A bright forking root of light pierced the ground not twenty yards away, making up his mind for him. You didn't have to be a naturalist to read nature's signs. The next thunderclap told him to get moving. He forgot all about the suitcase in the trunk. He pulled his broad-brimmed hat tightly down over his head and stepped out of the car.

He knew he would be soaked but what surprised him was the wind's frenzy and the rain stinging his face like hundreds of tiny whips. His feet sunk almost to his ankles in the mud as he slogged across the field to what now really did look like a house. It was completely dark.

He trudged up four wooden steps to the front porch, which wrapped around one side of the house. He knocked forcefully on the screen door. Five hits. Pause. Five hits. If there were nobody home he'd break the damn thing down. But he clenched his teeth again, telling himself he must wait. It was, after all, the middle of the night. Nevertheless knocking, waiting, knocking, waiting, took a great effort of will.

Almost simultaneously the inner door opened, the sky flashed again, and the porch light came on. An old woman in a white bathrobe stood there, a light on in the room behind her. He was in no condition to examine her with his usual thoroughness for signs of danger but saw that her hair was surprisingly red, that she was slender, and with her right hand over the grip, held a double-barreled break action shotgun cradled in the crook of her left arm.

He had the presence of mind to be aware how he must appear to her. A bedraggled young man with several days of dark scraggly beard and a scowl on his face. Hell, he could star in a slasher film.

"Sorry to wake you but I... My car is stuck in the mud. I wonder if...you might have a place for me to spend the night. I don't want to sleep in the car."

She stared at him as if concentrating on a particularly annoying crossword puzzle.

———

She'd gone to bed thinking of those two hostile boys and her vandalized car. Then had that dream and had to have a second shot of whiskey to get back to sleep.

And now this miserable but strong looking young man, a supplicant, polite, but what was he doing out here in the middle of the night? His appearance was not reassuring.

"Where are you going?" she asked.

"New York. To see my mother. She's sick."

"Where are you coming from?"

"Seattle."

The young man began to shiver.

"It's okay," he said. "I'll sleep in the car."

"Wait here," she said.

———

Wait here! He was going to crack a tooth if he had to keep clenching his teeth. He was glad that he hadn't kicked in the door though. Now that would have been a bummer. He could almost feel the buckshot in his chest. His shivering increased.

She returned holding the shotgun and dangling from her left hand a large blue plastic bucket, which she lay on the floor. She unlatched the screen door and stepped back and to the side.

"Better come in. You're shivering."

He opened the door and stepped inside, wordless.

"Now put your shoes and socks in there." She pointed at the bucket. When he finished she pointed to the stairs.

"Take the bucket and go up the stairs. There's a bathroom on the right."

So thoroughly was he soaked that the sleeves of his shirt and the legs of his pants made a sloshing sound as he ascended.

She followed behind him.

"The light switch is there." She pointed. He entered the bathroom.

"You can take your things off. I'll bring you something to put on."

He stood there, rivulets of water streaming from him, and began to strip. She returned, partially opened the door and, averting her eyes, handed him pajamas, a bath robe, and slippers. He left his soggy hat under the sink, where he'd spotted a hair dryer.

"This is really nice of you. I appreciate it. My name's Will Larrabee, by the way."

"Edna O'Hare. Give me your things. I'll hang them in the mud room."

Remarkably the slippers fit him as did the men's silk pajamas printed with green Japanese ideograms on a black background. The white terry cloth bathrobe, however, was a little small, probably for a woman, which reminded him of Katie Owens, a girl he'd been growing sweet on until it was clear, even to a thick skull like him, that she'd never go to bed with him, much less love him. She finally told him, after eating on his tab five times, that she wasn't totally comfortable dating a man almost twice her age—poor arithmetic on her part. She was nineteen, he twenty-four. Besides, she was a virgin she told him. Had he been an explosive device they would have been goners. As it was, he simply muffled a curse and excused himself from the table, returning when he'd gotten himself under control.

His temper, spring-loaded, got him into fights, almost got him a dishonorably discharged, but he fought the enemy even harder than he fought the MPs. He'd been reprimanded but he got his Purple Heart.

Dressed and slippered, he stepped into the hallway where Edna was waiting. He left his hat, its feathers drooping, in the bathroom.

"Downstairs, Mr. Larrabee." Again she pointed. He descended. She followed, still holding the shotgun.

His nervous system and adrenal glands had been revved up for months now, well before he'd taken off to see his mother while there was still time, as she had put it, and as he would tell anyone on the road who asked. His eye, intermittently, was keen as a fish hawk's. A moment later, in the rush of his own thoughts, he might be oblivious to the most obvious gesture. But when he was focused, the emotions behind people's expressions and postures were as evident to him as a fly in the soup.

Mrs. O'Hare appeared to be well past the age when most people's hair had turned gray or silver or white, yet hers, he noted again, was almost as red as a hazard flag. And with that shotgun she did present a potential hazard, but all it really meant was that he frightened her.

Eventually, after what seemed to him the time it would take to bury a jeep, they arrived in the kitchen, where he sat at the table while she made an herb tea, using only her left hand, the shotgun at the ready.

"Sorry. I'm harmless," he said. "Didn't mean to frighten you."

"I doubt very much that you are harmless, Mr. Larrabee. You look big and strong enough to me and men rarely are harmless. But we don't get many ax murderers around here and those that we do get don't knock on the door or follow directions. What's more, they have an ax with them, and they are wise enough to stay in the car in a thunderstorm, not that I'm implying you're stupid, you understand."

On the bright yellow table, she placed two mugs and a tea pot shaped like a cat on its haunches.

"Thank you for giving me the benefit of the doubt on the stupidity question. If lightning strikes, cars can sometimes protect you from getting zapped but if you touch anything metal, you'll regret it. A house is safer."

She poured a dark tea into the mugs.

"Try it," she said.

"I will not only try it. I will drink it all up." But after a few sips, he paused.

"What kind of tea is this?"

"It's an herb tea. No caffeine. You don't have to drink it if you don't want to."

Larrabee shook his head. "No. No. Of course I'm going to drink it. I was just curious. It's unusual."

He burst out laughing. The tingling in his chest that came with each breath reflected the relief he felt to be in this cozy kitchen, dry, and drinking tea before being hosted to a bed and possibly sleep. All this despite the gun, which no longer troubled him.

"I'm sure you have a funny story to tell Mr. Larrabee, but let's wait until tomorrow, shall we? I'm tired."

"Call me Will."

"And you may call me Edna."

———

He would be unable to sleep he was certain but remarkably his roller derby thoughts began to slow up and eventually he did sleep.

The next morning, while the washing machine sloshed his clothes back and forth, Edna in black pants and black blouse, served him a traditional breakfast of coffee, toast and jam, scrambled eggs, and bacon. Bacon! The secret of her longevity surely, he thought, chuckling.

She sat at the table, the shotgun across her lap.

He'd used the hair dryer on his hat and was wearing it now, feathers newly restored to their proud colorful selves.

Edna decided to ignore it.

"So you are in a rush to see your mother, but you decided to drive instead of fly?"

His mother had called, painting a dire picture of her situation, throwing in some legal jargon about involuntary commitment, to convince him that she was serious. The whole family was against her, she'd pleaded. He must do this for her. He must come immediately. It was an excuse to take to the road, even if impulsively. He disliked flying, being stuffed into those narrow seats with only enough legroom for a snake. Damn the greedy airlines.

Edna did not press him for more details, instead turning to a concern of her own.

"I wonder if you could do me a little favor."

He accepted hesitantly, sensing the possibility of entanglement, though he was grateful and believed in paying his debts. On the other hand, was he really that eager to get back on the road, that eager to see his mother?

"My brother-in-law is coming over this morning to talk with me about a little disagreement we have, and I'm concerned he may, how shall I put it, lose his temper. Not that he'd hit me or anything, but I'd like to have someone in the next room listening in. Just to comfort me, you see. Just to give me a psychological boost. I could stand up to him better. But you wouldn't have to do a thing. I just need to know there's someone there. Really, Earnest is harmless, but he scares me a teeny bit at times though he'd sooner smack his own behind with paddle than hurt anyone. Well, I think he would anyway. I don't expect him until around ten."

"Are you going to answer the door carrying that blunderbuss?" said Will.

"I'm sorry. Does it bother you?"

"You may not believe this, but it doesn't. You're a good Samaritan and if it makes you feel more secure that's fine with me. But I'd like to leave as soon as possible so I won't be here at ten.

A while later: knocketty knock. To Will's ears, a firm, but not desperate knocking.

"Just like him. Trying to catch me off guard by coming way too early. I'm putting you in the closet in the living room. Don't worry. This won't take long. Please get up."

"The closet?" he grumbled. "You said the next room."

"Shush," she demanded. "Please get up."

She had him walk ahead of her. She pointed to the closet. The knocking continued.

"Please do this for me."

27

He opened the door and walked in among overcoats and jackets. He turned to face her as she closed the door.

Thank goodness he didn't put up a stink. She could now keep track of him as she spoke with the visitor at the same time. No need to answer the door with a shotgun. She had to admit that the young man no longer made her quite so nervous.

———

Mistreated, his wishes discounted, his anger rose. But he was in the closet now. What if Earnest opened the closet door and had a heart attack or, just as bad, what if Earnest blasted him in the belly with a shotgun? Her shotgun. A flock of other what-if's were driven off by Edna's voice, which he heard fairly well. It must have been a cheap door.

"Good morning, Sheriff Andresen," she said formally.

"Morning, Edna. I'd like to speak with you. May I come in?"

A policeman! Under his breath Will produced a string of colorful expletives, some involving organs of excretion or hybrid blasphemous and scatological curses. He cursed like a marine.

Well, should he step out now and introduce himself, risking a tasering, or a bad case of lead acne or should he suffocate in silence until the goddamned cop left? When Will's nose began to tickle, he collapsed the nostrils between thumb and index finger.

———

Edna did not invite Sheriff Andresen in.

"What is this all about?"

The sheriff coughed, clearing his throat.

"Well, it's not about your trespassing on government property. You got off easy on that one. It's about your handing out leaflets in front of Earnest Schmidt's business office. In his capacity as a city alderman, he asked me to ask you not to do this. He said he'd spoken with you, but you ignored him. He says this is bad for his business. It associates him with the unpatriotic ideas you're peddling."

"The sidewalk is public," she said hesitantly. "I was walking down the street, and someone wanted a flyer. It just happened to be in front of his place."

"Back to that trespass matter," said Andresen. "I just hope you're not cooking up another hair-brained protest scheme."

"My name's O'Hare. So any scheme I cook up would have to be hair-brained." She was ashamed of her brazenness.

"Look, Edna we all know you're against the missiles, but they've been here for almost sixty years. Why the sudden interest?"

She was not about to tell him that she was having more frequent dreams about nuclear war, that she was frightened they actually meant something.

"My husband didn't want it on this land either. Now they're planning to replace these old monsters with new monsters and all the wires and pipes the new monster needs. They're going to tear up the fields with those ugly trucks and leave everyone in more danger than we're already in. I'm going to stop it this time." She paused. "Or try to."

"Edna," said the sheriff, exasperated, "believe it or not, I'm just trying to keep you out of trouble. And let's be honest, here. This is an ego trip. You can't ground the U. S. Air Force."

"Dear Sheriff Andresen, I don't want to be rude. I know you're just doing your job, but I have to say goodbye."

That Bjorn Andresen had driven all the way out here just to talk to her about handing out flyers, must have something to do with his reelection campaign. Edna's brother-in-law was not only an alderman, he was a long-time member of the chamber of commerce. Yes, Andresen was currying favor with Schmidt. There could be no doubt about it. It may even have been why he'd put her in that cell, if only for an afternoon. It made her mad, but it frightened her, too. How far would they go to shut her up?

"While you're busy enforcing the law, I think I should mention that someone sprayed the word "Russian" on my truck in red paint, but neither I nor the truck are Russian. Whatever can it mean, Sheriff?" she asked facetiously.

"When and where did this happened?" he asked, taking out his notebook.

———

There are yogis who can assume the most remarkable positions, walk over smoldering embers, or hold their breath for as long it would take to bake a cake. Will was not one of these. He could not even suppress a sneeze.

"What was that?" asked Andresen. "It came from the closet. Is there someone in there?"

Edna was silent.

"I'm coming in," said Andresen.

"You are not coming in. You need a search warrant to come in here. Go away. We're finished speaking."

"I have probable cause to think you are hiding contraband in that closet," he said absurdly. "I ask you to step aside."

After his second and third sneezes, Will came out of the closet.

"Couldn't find my damn coat. It must be in the bedroom," he said with a mixture of anger and amusement in finding himself playing a role in some screwball comedy. He tugged at the brim of his hat as if in greeting, hunched his shoulders, put a beats-me look on his face, swiveled around, walked up the stairs, and disappeared.

"Your contraband has gone," said Edna. "Now you be gone."

Andresen was nonplussed. Like everyone else in town, he knew that Edna O'Hare was a widow and lived alone.

As she was closing the front door, Andresen asked, "Who was that?"

"He's a complete stranger and that's the truth, I swear to God."

She shut and bolted the door.

With hands cupped around her mouth, she called up with a strong voice for an old woman, "Coast is clear, Mr. Larrabee. Will." But the confrontation had shaken her. She'd never spoken with anyone like that before.

———

Will came down the stairs, scowling at having been forced to play the fool.

"You said you wanted me in the other room, not in the closet."

"Well, it's more or less the same. You were nearby,

31

which is what I wanted. I'm so sorry I upset you. I really am."

He did not wish to appear a crybaby, so simply nodded.

"I can see that you are."

"And look. No shotgun."

"You trust me?"

"Well, I wouldn't go that far but I can't think of any good reason, except robbery, maybe, that you'd want to hurt me, and you've been a perfect gentleman."

It struck him as funny, which forced him to smile.

———

After putting his clothes in the dryer, she warmed up the eggs, and sat with him at the kitchen table.

"You should have seen the look on his face," said O'Hare.

"I did."

"You moved quickly. I wish I could do that."

Was it because of her awareness of Will's proximity that she'd risked being so cheeky with, even disrespectful of, Andresen? This wasn't like her at all. And now she found herself talking with ease—that is to say, with relative ease— to this young man to whom she'd recently been displaying her shotgun.

Edna finished her coffee, which had cooled off, and poured herself another cup. Will helped himself to another strip of bacon.

"Did you hear the conversation?"

"I did. It was about the missiles."

"I've been stewing about them forever but what could I do? The government had its little parcel, its access road, its silo, and its ICBM. That's short for intercontinental ballistic missile in case you didn't know. Oh, yes, and its hydrogen bomb. There's no shortage of hydrogen bombs in North Dakota."

"Yeah," said Will, "but that rocket's out there to stop the Russians from attacking us because if they did they'd be hit by the one in your back yard and probably a lot of others, too."

O'Hare began to put the dishes in the sink. Will rose to help her.

"*Probably* a lot of others," she laughed. "Minot Air Force Base has a hundred and fifty and so do the air force bases in Montana and Wyoming."

One basin of the kitchen sink was filled with hot soapy water, the other with clean water. As if they'd worked this job before, Edna washed and rinsed the dishes and Will dried, putting them into the cupboard. As he got more excited, he became less careful.

"So don't you care about the country?" He was gesturing and speaking faster now. "You know what the Russians are like." He made a face, showing his teeth.

She hummed a few bars of the Volga boat song.

"If the farmers around here all got rid of their rockets," he continued, "we'd be a whole lot less safe, like holding your shotgun overhead to show the wolf and then tossing it into the manure pile."

He went on like this for a while until he broke a coffee cup, knocking it off the edge of a shelf with the sleeve of his robe. He picked up the pieces immediately. Edna indicated the waste basket under the sink.

"My, you do have quaint similes, young man. The wolf indeed."

"The Russians have lots of land-based missiles, too," said Will, pumping himself up and down on his calves. "So nobody wants to start a fight."

"Maybe so," said O'Hare, ignoring his movement. "But what if there were a false alarm? What if we thought a flock of geese was a bunch of missiles? I'm not making this up, you know. If they hadn't found the mistake it would have been nuclear war."

"Or what if a terrorist exploded an A-bomb in Washington? Wouldn't the U.S. think it had been attacked?"

They faced each other at the sink.

"These devils are on hair trigger. And you can't call a missile back once it's launched."

Her cheeks had turned red. She'd spoken with rising forcefulness but, having come to an end, sat again at the table. He was unable to sit, instead leaning, hands on top of the back of the chair.

"Geese are still flying. So the false alarm threat is the same. Why are you protesting now?"

She stood, turned her chair so the back faced her, put her hands on it, and leaned toward him.

"I told you. The military aerospace industrial complex has decided to replace all the Minuteman missiles with new missiles at an estimated cost of between eighty-four and a hundred forty billion dollars and that's not counting maybe another hundred billion or so for upkeep. I needed a little kick in the behind to get started and that was it." The impetus of her husband's death she did not mention.

He didn't want to offend her, but the laughter just broke through, imagining her scolding a room full of scowling, beribboned generals and captains of industry.

"How are you going to stop them?"

She stood up straight. After the silo protest fiasco—specifically the failure to have the protest written about in the paper—she felt defeated but arguing with this young man had reinvigorated her.

"Well, first of all I'm going to hand out some more flyers."

CHAPTER FOUR

After Edna had gone off to town, Will dressed in his newly laundered clothes, and left the house, the latch clicking distinctly into place with apparent finality as he closed the door. Well, that's that, he thought. He walked to his car, which was parked on the side of the main road, about thirty yards from the house. At attention a thousand sunflowers faced him, annoying him in some ineffable way. Did their bright faces mock him?

"Go to hell," he spat.

The road had no shoulder. The spinning rear wheels had dug deep holes for themselves and now the rear bumper almost rested on the soggy ground. The situation did not look promising. He had no shovel and didn't know where to look for one; his cell phone was dead; and the nearest town was not even visible from here. He climbed into the car and started it, gingerly touching the gas pedal. The tires whirred. His mind whirred. Walk to town? Run to town? Wait here? His mother. Katie. The sunflowers…Afghanistan.

Yes, he'd been through worse.

———

Sitting atop an armored vehicle, he travelled with his comrades over a primitive desert road, making a short side-trip outside of Jowman to see if Taliban activity had taken place there the night before. But from his vantage point behind the machine gun he saw no people; no resources; no villages; and, of course, no water. And he saw nothing on the road. The sand, though, he could taste.

"Everything good up there, Willy, baby?" yelled a buddy from the driver's-side window.

The explosion occurred shortly thereafter, the vehicle bucking Will onto the sand where he lay dazed but feeling no pain, despite broken bones. Not immediately. The vehicle burned. He heard a scream. The helicopter landed sometime after. His buddies were dead. But he was not.

The experts couldn't agree whether the shock had caused his outbursts or whether he'd always been so obstreperous. As soon as he could walk, he wanted to leave, and to prove that he was ready, he did a somersault on the hard floor, splitting open some wounds. He cursed, and on one occasion sung all night, to the discomfort of patients and staff alike. A psychiatrist saw him but didn't think he was manic.

———

He cursed. He'd locked himself out of the damn house. He removed the jack handle from the trunk, hefting it, brandishing it at the sunflowers, and again told them to go to hell.

He snorted. He stomped up the front steps. He opened

the screen door. He wedged the tapered end of the jack handle between the doorjamb and the door lock, noted how much it looked like an ordinary crowbar, and was about to pry open the door, when he caught himself and removed the instrument. He turned the knob and walked in.

Country living, he thought. Not an ax murderer for miles. Why lock up?

In the living room he began his search for a telephone, figuring he'd systematically work through each room until he found it. The walls here were covered with vertically striped silver and white wallpaper, which had slightly peeled off near the ceiling in one corner and near another corner near the chestnut brown floor, which looked worn at the entrance. A long royal blue sofa, a short sofa and two matching armchairs were arranged around a coffee table.

He worried Edna would come home to find him snooping around. Though he had a good reason to be here: he was completely stranded, and she might be tied up for hours brewing up trouble or being burned at the stake.

Stop, he told himself. Stay focused.

But the framed pictures on the wall beckoned him. Here was an attractive young red-headed woman dressed as a witch beside an equally attractive young man dressed as a scarecrow, his right arm encircling her narrow waist. The picture next to it showed the two in the same pose, same costumes but in this photograph they were old.

There were pictures of two girls standing on the bed of a hay wagon. The youngest, or at least the shortest, was O'Hare. Next to these hung a tattered, old black and white photograph of a Japanese family: father, mother, son, and daughter.

On an adjacent wall hung a series of watercolors,

modestly initialed E., of pastoral scenes: fields of sunflow-ers, cows grazing, a girl on horseback.

Having covered the living room's perimeter, he moved into the kitchen, then into the five other rooms on the first floor. Where the hell did she have her phone? After briefly being troubled by the idea that she might not have a land line, he clomped up the stairs, to demonstrate to himself that he had not given up hope.

He checked the bedroom where the only thing of interest was a black book, lettered in red, *The Doomsday Machine: Confessions of a Nuclear War Planner,* lying on a bedside night table. He left it untouched and moved his search oper-ation to the bathroom next, where he allowed himself the time to urinate.

Of the six upstairs rooms only the master bedroom and bath appeared lived in. Sheets covered the furniture in the other rooms, one of which appeared to be an office, whose desk, cluttered with piles of books, and stacks of newspaper clippings, looked as if it had been in use, when, in a moment, it had been put into suspended animation.

It was highly unlikely that a telephone hid under one of those sheets. But like a dust devil he began pulling sheets off pieces of furniture, tossing them willy nilly all over the room. Then abruptly he stopped. It had felt good doing something but now he felt like a dumb cluck. Why would anyone hide a telephone in an unused room? Half-heartedly he covered the furniture again.

Down the stairs to the first floor and then, after a search behind various closet doors, he descended to the basement. No phone.

He would walk to town. Hell, he'd march to town.

CHAPTER FIVE

Edna returned to her truck after having handed out only a few flyers. It wasn't much in the way of physical work, but her discouragement was taking deeper root. People were simply uninterested. And making matters worse, someone had struck the driver's side window with a heavy object instantly producing an ominous spider web of cracks.

She tried calming herself. Yes, this was frightening but she didn't want it to paralyze her. She was not a coward. She'd let a stranger into her house in the middle of the night. But, on the other hand, she couldn't sit by her truck with a shotgun in hand.

On the way home, she saw Will a mile and a half away, though she didn't recognize him until he was closer. It looked as if he were marching, arms swinging rhythmically at his sides. She pulled to the side of the road and stopped. He came around to the driver's side to speak with her. She rolled down the window, the spider-webbed glass disappearing into the door.

"You don't have a goddamn phone in your whole goddamn house." Then he started his march again.

For a moment she was puzzled, then thought good riddance, but felt the bite of conscience almost simultaneously. The man was obviously disturbed. It was hot, very hot, and miles to town. Traffic was practically nonexistent on this stretch of country highway, though he might not have tried to hitchhike even had someone driven by. She made a U-turn, passed him and parked.

As he approached, she got out of the truck and called out to him.

"Please let me give you a ride."

He strode by the car.

"You're stubborn as a tree stump," she said. "By the time you get there everything will be closed. Then what?"

He turned to face her but was silent. He took his hat off, fanned himself with it for a second, walked to the car, and got in.

"I got overheated," he said. "I'm sorry about that but I need to get on the road and my car is dug in about as deep as it will go."

"Have you been rummaging around my house?"

"I was looking for your goddamn telephone."

"Now you listen here, Mr. Larrabee. If anyone's going to do the swearing around here it's me. Did you see my window? Someone bashed it, probably because they don't like me. I'm not swearing. You can swear without blaspheming, you know. Leave God out of it. He has the destruction of mankind to worry about."

"Just like you," said Will.

For a few minutes they were silent.

"Where do you want to go?"

"Someplace that can haul my car out of its pit."

"I can do that."

It would be better if she did it her way, she explained, because it would be quicker and cheaper. She made a U-turn, heading back home as soon as he accepted her offer.

After a few miles she asked about his mother, because she was interested, but in part to get her mind off her own problems.

Will's mother had called, begging him to come immediately. They were going to lock her up and electrocute her brain and his brother was all for it. Will was the only one she could trust. The only one who understood.

"Are you talking about electroconvulsive treatment for depression?"

"She's not depressed. Sometimes her judgment is a little off, that's all. She buys things at garage sales. Things she doesn't need. Or she doesn't buy them; she just takes them. Or she argues with people she should know better than to argue with. Or she makes big plans she can't carry out, but she doesn't need shock treatment. She's scared to death of it."

He removed his hat, straightening the feathers, then turned the hat around and around, using thumb and index finger on the brim.

They had wanted to put the old buzzer to his delicate skull, too, but the psychiatrist said he wasn't manic, just angry at life.

O'Hare had questions but kept them to herself.

"So what's with the window?" asked Will.

"Someone's unhappy with my flyers."

"I'm sorry. That's a bummer. Do you know who did it?"

"No idea. Must have been kids."

"Where's your telephone?"

"In my purse."

"No. Your home phone."

"In the kitchen cabinet along with the shotgun."

"Funny place for a phone and a shotgun."

———

She examined the tires and the deep holes they had burrowed, turned away, walked to the tractor shed, removed chains and hooks from their sturdy pegs, and placed them behind the tractor's cab. She gave him a shovel. He said nothing.

Grimly he dug ramps in front of each rear tire. She attached the tractor to the car and pulled it free.

He thanked her.

"All in a day's work," she said. "Wish I were that efficient with my campaign."

He removed some bills from his wallet.

"I'd like to give you something."

"Are you sincere?" she asked.

"Yes. I want to pay you back for your kindness."

She didn't wish to get him in any trouble, but she wasn't about to ask him to do anything illegal or dangerous.

She just needed to make an impression. Get people talking. She didn't need the money—at the moment anyway—she needed him to help her make a sign and bring it into town.

"I want you to pay me back a different way."

What she was proposing would be a delay in Will's departure. Well, she had sheltered and fed him, even clothed him after a fashion by washing and drying his clothes and then pulling out his car. A few days wouldn't make much difference, would it?

———

She needed a sign that was light enough to carry and a simpler, more stylish flyer with the basics about the Ground-Based Strategic Deterrent—that mouthful of a name for the missile scheduled to replace the Minuteman.

"Would you mind driving in your car? I'm a bit edgy at the moment about using my truck, which apparently is easily recognized."

Will drove them to the university bookstore in Minot to get what they needed.

The clerk, a perky young woman wearing a t-shirt with a large white M on a red background, pointed at Will's hat.

"What kind of feathers are those?"

"Horse," he said, straight-faced.

"That's what I thought," said the clerk, smiling at him.

———

The felt markers and the three-by-four-foot cardboard presentation boards lay on the dining room table. While Will unpacked his suitcase upstairs, O'Hare sat at the table, ruminating. She'd already given the problem some thought but finding the right thing to say, and the right way to say it, was tricky. Her first flyers were amateurish.

First of all, how many people knew what GBSD meant? Did she literally have to spell it out for them: GBSD stands for Ground-Based Strategic Deterrent? No. It would take up too much space.

. . .

The GBSD is unnecessary for deterrence.

The GBSD is a tremendous waste of your money.

The GBSD brings us a step closer to nuclear war.

Say no to the GBSD.

Tell your congressman and senators now.

––––––

If people didn't know what the GBSD was, they could ask. Anyway, she'd have flyers with her, laying out the arguments and citing the references. She attached a wood handle to the cardboard. If this sign didn't get people's attention, she'd make a different one. Clean shaven, Will Larrabee, came downstairs to look at the poster.

"What's GBSD stand for?"

"It stands for the new missile they want to put in. Ground-Based Strategic Deterrent. I asked myself what kind of muddle-headed committee came up with this moniker."

Without mirth, Will said, "How about The Bomb Bucket, or The Last Hammer or The Big Pisser or Up Yours or—"

"Do you want a cup of coffee?" she said, purposefully interrupting him.

"Thanks, that would be good. My phone should be fully charged in a couple of hours. I think I'll leave then."

"Would you take me downtown first?"

"You didn't like my names, did you? Bomb Basket."

O'Hare frowned. "The warheads the Minuteman missiles now carry are as powerful as three hundred forty thousand tons of TNT, about twenty-five times more powerful than the bomb that destroyed Hiroshima. So it isn't funny, not to me anyway. No offense. You're very creative."

No, there was nothing funny about it except maybe "the funny business" of getting congress to authorize so damn much money for something so expensive and unnecessary.

"When do you want to go?"

"It's a little late to go now. Would you be willing to spend another night here and take me in the morning?"

As soon as he agreed, she began thinking about a protest site, flip-flopping between Minot State University or Minot High School. On the one hand some of the university students were of, or close to, voting age. On the other hand high school students around the world were agitating for strong laws to fight climate change, but it was summer vacation. So it was the university.

She prepared dinner for the two of them and then insisted he watch some YouTube videos of Daniel Ellsberg giving talks about nuclear weapons.

"He is a former analyst who leaked a secret defense department report showing that the government had lied to the public about the extent of the war in Vietnam. His action was a key to the ending of the war. And now he's trying to prevent another—the last war. World War III."

———

Two muscular men each holding a handle on a wooden crate hanging heavily between them, walk from a truck into an alley, a quarter mile from the White House. They take a freight elevator to the tenth floor and leave their cargo in a hallway.

She cannot see their faces.

A ball of brilliant white light engulfs the capital. The White House disintegrates. WW III begins.

———

They had breakfast silently.

"What's wrong?" asked Will.

"Nothing."

"You look like the food's going bad in your mouth."

She sipped her coffee as if to wash away a bad taste. She smiled weakly.

"Bad dream," she said.

"What about?"

"A terrorist attack on Washington, leading to nuclear war."

"Oh."

———

At around nine Will drove her to the university. She would find a way home she reassured him. She'd lived in Minot all her life and had people who would drive her home. After they shook hands and wished each other well, Will turned to leave, then thought better of it, and simply stood to the side to observe. He would begin his road trip again, he told himself, in a minute or two.

Built in 1913, Old Main, the red-brick heart of the campus, was three stories tall in the center, flanked on either side by a two-story wing. A long set of stairs, red handrails up the center and along the sides, led to the entrance. Two columns on each side of the entrance dignified the building.

Only summer school classes were in session, so the

staircase was not thronged with people, but students in ones, twos, and threes entered and exited the building. At the foot of the stairs she put down her canvas shopping bag with her provisions, opened a folding chair, sat down, and raised her sign, which she put down from time to time when her arms got tired.

It was thirty minutes before anyone came to talk with her, though most gave her at least a glance. People often made her nervous, especially if they were hostile or dismissive so her very public protests caused considerable anxiety, now heightened by the thought of her vandalized truck.

———

Will was about to leave, when, finally, two teenage girls, each with a small backpack, approached. The taller, her blonde ponytail swinging, wore a pale blue summer dress. The shorter, her brown hair bobbed, wore skinny jeans and a tight t-shirt printed with the words "Frailty Thy Name is Woman. B. S."

"What's GBSD?" asked the blonde girl.

O'Hare explained that it was a missile being developed to replace the old Minuteman and told her what the initials stood for. The girls didn't make her too nervous.

"These sitting duck land-based missiles are easy targets. The Russians have the same kind. If one side gets a warning that it's being attacked it must decide within minutes if the warning is true. But once the missiles are launched, they can't be called back and it's doomsday. Do you know what nuclear winter is?"

The blonde girl shook her head, remaining where she

stood as the brown-haired girl took her elbow and gently tried pulling her away.

"After a nuclear war, fire storms will raise millions of tons of soot into the stratosphere, blocking out seventy percent of the sun's rays. With so little sunlight harvests will end and it will get very cold. Not many people will survive."

"We're not having a nuclear war. Come on, Karen, let's go," said her friend.

Will, initially a mute observer, now spoke up, surprising himself. That he spoke from a wish to be noticed by the girl in the blue dress only occurred to him later.

"Mrs. O'Hare knows what she's talking about," he said, rather more loudly than he wished. Indeed, there was an edge to his voice. O'Hare give him a questioning look.

The brunette ignored him, but the blonde girl looked him in the eye, before turning back to Edna who continued.

"There have been false alarms since the silos went in. Any one of them might have started a nuclear war. It's all here on this flyer."

The blonde girl shook her head vigorously,

"No," she said. "The point is to scare the Russians so they won't fire. We need those missiles."

Perhaps what was becoming a heated give and take moved the brunette to release her friend's elbow and speak up.

"Do you think North Dakota is going to give up all the business that installing those new rockets is going to bring in. No way. Our senators and congressman want those missiles and so do the people who live and work here. And so do I. They've protected us a long time."

Edna forced a smile. That should be enough for right now. She didn't want them to have a bad impression of her because that impression would taint the information she was providing. There was so much more she could say but it might come across as hostile. That, for example, it was not just North Dakota that was affected by this. Just because the GBSD was a boondoggle for North Dakota, Minot in particular, didn't make it a good thing.

"Well, I see your point," said Edna diplomatically. "Read the flyer and see what you think."

"No one wants nuclear war," continued the brunette, peeved, "but you want us to disarm. We need rockets."

"Of course, we do. Of course. But the twenty missiles launched from a single one of our atomic submarines can destroy an entire country. Each missile has five warheads. And then there're the airplane launched missiles and bombs. We have plenty of deterrent without those stuck underground."

"Come on, let's go," said the brunette and turning to Edna, "You're wasting your time. Her father's a sergeant at the air force base. It's like trying to take a peanut from an elephant. Oh, that didn't come out right. Sorry, Karen."

Edna and Will watched as the two girls walked away. The brunette took the flyer from her friend and her friend took it back again. Flyer now again firmly in hand, Karen Haugen looked back for a moment, shaking her head, as if to have the final unspoken word.

A while later two stocky boys in football jerseys came over. The same two she'd spoken with in front of the ice cream parlor: number 9 with the crew cut and number 15 with the skateboard.

"You still peddling that crap?" said number 15, the taller, a baby-faced boy whose nose had been broken. His friend unabashedly gave a middle finger salute. They walked off, laughing. She could not easily dismiss the feeling of being threatened.

Only a few more people came by, none of whom took a flyer, and at noon Edna was sweating and disheartened.

Unaccountably, Will had stood beside her the whole time, but it was time for him to go.

"You sure you can get home?" he asked.

"I'm sure. Thank you for your help."

"I didn't do anything. Thanks for getting my car out of the rut."

She took his hand and shook it. He left.

By 12:30 she'd eaten her sandwich and drunk her water. She was exhausted and depressed. Oh, why, oh, why hadn't she asked Will to drive her home? Now she'd have to spend money on an Uber or a Lyft.

CHAPTER SIX

Demoralized by the lack of any interest in her protest and more so by her apparent inability to stoke an interest, she also worried about hostility that might be more deep-seated than a little nastiness and red graffiti on her truck indicated. Now burdened with a bag, a sign, and a folding chair whose portage she had not planned for, she could have kicked herself for not thinking this through.

She was about to call for a ride when she wondered if she might be so bold as to call Amy Haugen, not necessarily for a ride, but just to talk. In her grief and preoccupation with her futile attempt to do anything effective, she'd lost contact with most of her friends. They had called, asked to see her, but she had demurred.

She and her sister were still in touch, but Fiona felt obligated to justify Earnest's worry that Grumman might take some of its business to Grand Forks, as little sense as this made.

Now in a bit of a bind, Edna reached out, her friendship with Amy's mother counting for something, she thought.

Diligent Amy Haugen, trim and fit at forty, had been working on a story from home today but was glad to have a break.

"Yes," she said. "I'll be there in ten minutes."

Edna O'Hare had not been far away. Minot stretched only five miles from north to south, three from east to west. Nor had Amy any objection to driving her home. Indeed, she herself suggested it.

————

They sat on opposite ends of Edna's blue sofa, the coffee table before them.

"I understand how you feel about it. How James felt," said Amy. "Everybody did, but no one I know agreed with him, and with his background he couldn't possibly be objective, now could he? So, you can't really expect anyone to agree with you. And frankly, I don't either. We're all proud of doing our part in the national defense."

"The reason no one, or hardly anyone, agrees with me," said O'Hare, "is that no one has heard me. I've probably reached only twenty or thirty people with my flyers."

They sipped coffee.

"You know what you need," said Amy. "You need a public relations firm. No, don't get me wrong. I don't think you'd convince anybody, but you'd reach a lot more people."

Edna put her cup down and smiled at her friend, for she must be a friend given her helpfulness.

"Are you saying," said Edna, "that although you disagree with me you wouldn't object if I got my message out to a lot more people."

"Why would I object?"

"Because you think I'm wrong." Before Amy could reply, Edna added, "If I did something dramatic, something newsworthy, would you write about it?"

"I tried writing about your protest at the missile site. Wilburn wasn't interested."

"But you'd still write if...if I...I don't know. Did something?"

CHAPTER SEVEN

Acoustic panels, punctuated by recessed lights, covered the ceiling of the conference room. A slice of lemon rested at the bottom of each of two carafes of ice water, at either end of the long narrow table. Each of six place settings was marked by a glass, a napkin, a pad of paper, and a pen.

North Dakota senator William Hennings, in royal blue suit and red tie, was so tall he could reach out and almost touch the paneled ceiling and occasionally did so for reasons of his own. No staff member dared to ask why. He did so again today as he entered the room ahead of retired Air Force General Sam Clayton, silver haired and distinguished looking, a former ICBM missile wing commander, retired, now working for Northrup Grumman, who subtly shook his head at Henning's little demonstration of who knows what. The two waited at the far end of the table as the rest of the entourage filed in, two more on either side of the table. The last person to enter, sixty-nine-year-old Defense Department physicist Zach Mann, closed the door.

Among the attendees were Henning's legislative

assistant, efficient as scissors, Sylvia Wong in rhinestone-framed designer eyeglasses; Grumman's GBSD public relations manager, vivacious Claudia Cummings, glossy black hair to her shoulders; and Vice President of the GBSD program at Grumman, serene Ellen Conklin.

"As you know some members of the House Armed Services Subcommittee on Strategic Forces have raised the possibility of reducing or cancelling the GBSD program," began Hennings. "I'm here as the chairman of the Senate ICBM coalition to host a little discussion about this so you won't be blind-sided by questions when you go out to Minot for your visit."

"These well-meaning but misguided individuals not only question the cost of the modernization but even its necessity for deterrence. Some argue that the very existence of four hundred and fifty land-based ICBMs is destabilizing. As untenable as these positions are, they are being seriously discussed. I'd like to hear your thoughts."

"As regards the need to replace the old Minuteman missiles, no one will deny that they're age is worrisome," said General Clayton. "We can't rely on rusty rockets."

"Indeed, we cannot," said Hennings.

Rusty rockets, sparks from sockets, popped involuntarily into Zach Mann's head. He had been struggling for some time with his conscience about the program, expressed silently by spontaneous silly rhymes. God forbid he say aloud anything that might be construed as an attempt at humor. He would be seen as a dotty old man.

"Counterforce strategy," continued Clayton, "the targeting of one's enemies' weapons, is common policy among nuclear armed states, usually with two warheads designated for each target. So, given ICBM silos spread across North Dakota, Montana, Wyoming, Colorado, and Nebraska, a force of nine hundred warheads would be used to destroy these targets. So, in addition to being a deterrent, our land-based ICBMs are sometimes referred to as a warhead sink or sponge, costing the Russians a lot of money to cover and utilizing many of their warheads. An additional justification."

Mann had to speak up.

"And what about the argument that because they are literally sitting targets they encourage a use-them-or-lose-them mentality risking the start of a nuclear war if they're launched on a false warning of a Russian first strike?"

"If the president is so eager to fire our land-based missiles before they are eliminated, that is, even risking a mistake," said Clayton, "then he must consider them crucial for us to reach our objectives. It makes no sense, then, to eliminate them if they're crucial."

Clayton's argument was a non sequitur but Mann still wondered how many people in this room believed, as most of the American public believed, that only the president could launch a nuclear attack. Were that the case and everyone in Washington died in a Russian decapitation, there would be no one left to counterattack. But of course, there would be. Around the country and even out at sea and in the air certain military commanders, under certain conditions, had authority to launch a nuclear attack. Mann thought of Brigadier General Jack D. Ripper from the movie *Dr. Strangelove* who triggered a nuclear war because he could not tolerate "...the international communist conspiracy to sap and impurify all of our precious bodily fluids." *Jesus H. Christ.*

"I don't think the public is going to be moved by sophisticated arguments," said Claudia Cummings. "We need to keep emphasizing that these land-based missiles along with the other two legs of the triad have protected us from a nuclear attack since the 1940s."

"Also, that neither the Chinese nor the North Koreans could ever hope to eliminate all our land-based missiles," said Clayton. "They just don't have enough warheads."

Mann again spoke, addressing Clayton.

"General, forgive me for not understanding," said Mann, "but if the president mistakenly thinks the Russians have launched a first strike, then the ICBMs are no longer a deterrent. Why then rush to fire them off to kill millions of innocent people.

"I think discussion of nuclear policy is important," said Hennings frowning, "but making sure we have public support is what we should be talking about here."

Mann nodded and was again still.

Claudia Cummings thought it important to talk about how much more dependable, flexible, and accurate the new missiles would be.

"The public needs to know that GBSD will completely overhaul the ICBM system," she said. "The missiles will be new. The launch control buildings will be new. And the logistical and communications infrastructure will be new. This will be expensive, but the public is getting its money's worth. The Minuteman III fleet still needs eight-inch floppy discs to work."

———

Hennings thanked the group. This delegation from Northrup Grumman would be visiting Minot to meet with business leaders and contractors about the GBSD replacement of the Minuteman. The chamber of commerce would be one of the biggest boosters of the program. Hennings would pass on the points of this discussion to the other member of the Senate ICBM coalition, the senators from states with interest in missiles: North Dakota, Wyoming, Montana, and Utah.

Perdition coalition thought Mann.

CHAPTER EIGHT

On his way to Grand Forks along US-2E, large swatches of green and brown farmland carpeted the ground to the horizon, the occasional trees clumped together as if, lonely, they'd sought each other out. Minuteman missiles, on the other hand, abhorring the proximity of others, were spaced widely apart over thousands of square miles in the upper Midwest.

Sparse traffic on the road, made his erratic driving—his speeding and then stomping the brake pedal when he frightened himself—less dangerous than it would have been had there been cars around him.

He was not a knight errant traveling the highways looking for adventure, but that would be nice, he thought. Instead he was again giving into his mother's demands that he help her extricate herself from a sticky web of her own weaving. Oh, no, he must not think of his mother as a spastic spider, but he resented being called again. Why didn't she call his brother? Why always him? He knew damn well why. Because his brother wouldn't do anything.

The speedometer read ninety-five. Oooh! His foot hit the brake pedal and withdrew in an inkling. He was thrown against the steering wheel, recovered quickly, and reduced his speed.

The funny thing was that he felt in no hurry. He was just keyed up, that was all. Keyed up like his mother. He put the thought out of his head.

Pleasant memories of her. He needed some. He sang the first verse of Brahms's Lullaby, as the car again accelerated.

Lullaby and good night, with roses bedight
With lilies o'er spread is baby's wee bed
Lay thee down now and rest, may thy slumber be blessed
Lay thee down now and rest, may thy slumber be blessed.

She would sing, and he would fall asleep. But then his parents' arguments woke him up. He'd pad into the living room. They'd reassure him that everything was alright—lies —and usually were quiet for the rest of the night. But still, she did sing him lullabies through toddlerhood. A definite plus.

What else? When the family went to the beach in the summer, she swam with him in the ocean. Another plus.

He remembered a time when he was sick that she read him stories from Mad Magazine, now defunct. Three pluses should earn her something.

He had only two memories of his father taking the kids anywhere: once to a park to play three flies up and once to a pier in Huntington Beach to fish.

He was jolted when a car passed him, the driver beeping wildly, as if encountering a kindergarten class that had wandered onto the highway. His speedometer read twenty-five. There had been plenty of room to pass. Some people are just idiots. He pushed down the gas pedal accelerating, overtaking his temporary nemesis, and passing her. He didn't beep. He just left the horn on continuously until he was several car lengths ahead of her and moving away rapidly. She reminded him of his mother. Domineering.

She had controlled her children, not by education, persuasion, reasoning, or even punishment. No. She used intimidation, with a scowl that would cow any rational person, biting her fist at the same time, a gesture that suggested she was at her limit. What were the offenses? Wandering away from her in the supermarket to look at the seductive cereal boxes up there on the shelf with their smiling tigers, Olympic champions, and dancing cartoon figures. They never touched the boxes nor did more than suggest she look at them.

Or if they dallied after school, coming home a little later than expected.

"You're to come straight home after school. I'm not joking," she said as if warning them away from an electrified fence.

Of course, she wasn't joking.

Friends were never allowed in the house. In her inimitable, silent fashion, she enforced this stricture as strictly as if their friends were crawling with bedbugs, tucked away in all the right places. Right places for bedbugs, that is. She would not have gone so far as to accuse them of purposefully bringing in bed bugs. Though, now that he thought about it, she believed that a dentist, on purpose, had poisoned her teeth, explaining her premature toothlessness.

She feared that their friends might see or hear something. Might observe her. Might tell their parents what they observed.

"Hey, Mom, Mrs. Larrabee's closets are filled with broken lamps and shoes and toasters and things."

Was that the sort of thing she would allow no children, other than hers, to see? Her children knew, that under penalty of her withering anger, that they must not discuss anything about the family with anyone else.

Her attitude toward the girl he had a crush on in high school also infuriated him, though that girl always had a boyfriend other than him.

"Will, you've been on the phone now for half an hour."

It was usually only a few minutes. She acted as if the girl were a magical slut somehow projecting her tits over the phone for her spellbound son to ogle. But his mother was an equal opportunity girlfriend hater. His brother had the same experience. Keeping her sons out of trouble might have been the way she would have explained her behavior, if at sixteen he'd had the wisdom, experience, and battle-readiness necessary to ask her about it.

And here he was again, heeding her call for help. Several times she had asked for money, which he didn't have on hand, but which she needed immediately. She wouldn't say why, nor did he waste time trying to pry it out of her for which he would have required a crowbar. However, it is disrespectful to use a crowbar on your mother. And he was nothing if not respectful. Sort of.

Or when she insisted he drop whatever he was doing —"Will, I'm your mother and I need help"—to rush to her side to explain that the new neighbor was not listening in on her phone calls. That came to nothing, of course. She just had to learn to watch what she said.

Or the time she was arrested for shoplifting something so inexpensive she could have bought a wheelbarrow full of them. He couldn't even remember what it was. Later he understood, of course, that the drama, excitement and especially the distraction of getting arrested, was her way of coping with the death of her daughter at age thirteen, when Will was sixteen. A death that she kept from her other children for a couple of months.

———

The siren screamed, "You're in trouble, bean brain." And the red and blue flashing lights swiveled in agreement, "Big trouble." He slowed down and pulled over.

In blue, short sleeve shirt, dark pants, and white helmet, the highway patrolman sauntered over to the car.

"Show me your hands."

They'd been resting on Will's lap.

"They're clean, officer."

"Wise guy, huh?"

Thank goodness I'm not black, he thought.

"I'm sorry, officer, I'm not myself. I'm going to see my mother who's dying and I'm thinking about my dead sister and... Never mind. I'll show you my driver's license."

"Do you know how fast you were going?"

"Probably around ninety, officer. I'm sorry. I wasn't paying attention."

Holding Will's driver's license, the patrolman walked a few paces away from the car and made a phone call. He returned to the car.

"What did your sister die from?"

"Leukemia. She was thirteen."

"What's your mother dying from?"

"I don't know."

The patrolman put his hands on his hips and extended his back as if it ached. He put his thumb under the front rim of the helmet, adjusting it. Will wished he knew something about North Dakota's football teams, so he could make small talk.

"You exceed the speed limit again and you're going to jail. We can do that. Do you understand?"

"Yes, sir, I do."

"I've never let anyone get away with driving like that. This is a first. I had a brother who died of brain cancer when he was six. You'd better watch it from here on out and, by the way, if I ever find out you lied to me. Well, let's just say you'll regret it."

He was back on the road again.

His mother wasn't dying, but his sister had. The mixed story, truth and fiction, just popped out of his jumping jack brain. He still thought of his sister from time to time.

CHAPTER NINE

Before arriving in Grand Forks, Will's phone rang, but he ignored it. He knew who it was and didn't feel up to answering it until he'd had something to eat and gone to the bathroom.

In town he sat on a red stool at the red lunch counter of a 1950s style diner, its floor a checkerboard of large white and black squares. When he agreed to a third cup of coffee, he knew he was dawdling because drinking too much coffee gives one's bladder more work than it needs, especially if you're on a road trip. It may not complain now, but it will later. All the kids nowadays were wrapped up with these comic book superheroes with special powers. After watching one of these movies they'd say things like, "My superpower is speed," or, "My superpower is strength". Well, if he could have a superpower it would be a bladder with the capacity of an oil tanker. On second thought, just a half gallon would do.

Next to Will sat a big-boned man with dark skin, black hair in a ponytail, in a short-sleeved olive uniform bearing the logo Silverhawk's Gas and Auto. He wore a beaded necklace.

Waiting for his sandwich, Will turned to the man and asked, "Enjoying the summer?"

Under the right conditions, Will might even strike up a conversation with a tree.

"Yeah, pretty much. How 'bout you?"

"Yes," he lied. Might as well avoid forced sympathy. "I'm driving to New York to see my mother."

"Driving all the way from North Dakota to see your mother. You must love her very much."

"I started in Seattle."

His eyes grew large.

"That's some trip. She must be a sweetheart."

A little later his telephone rang.

"Will, for heaven's sake, where are you?"

He held the phone away from his ear.

No preamble. No hello, how are you?

"I'm in Grand Forks."

"Rand orcs! What in God's name are you talking about?"

She spoke so loudly that the man next to him surely heard every word his *sweetheart* of a mother was yelling at him. Well, at least the man's presence would keep Will from flaming into sacrilege and profanity. Funny how he could curse his mother and still do what she asked of him.

Ignoring the question, he said, "I'm on my way."

"You're on your way?"

"Yes, Mom, I'm on my way."

"You're calling from the plane?"

"I'm driving, Mom. I don't like to fly."

The man next to him was engrossed in his coffee,

holding the cup in both hands and peering into it as if it were a portal to a parallel world much nicer than this one. A world, perhaps, where mothers and sons enjoyed talking with each other. Oh, yes, and in which there were no atomic bombs.

"Well, please hurry."

Lowering her voice, she added, "If you don't get here soon, they'll…"

Her voice faded to an inaudible whisper before she spoke again.

"Just step on the gas, Will. For your mother."

He resisted the impulse to ask her how he could be sure it was her. After all, this could be a telephone scam, a talented actress on the other end imitating his mother's voice perfectly and about to ask him for his credit card number. He wished it were.

"I will but I have to go now."

"Thank you, darling."

As Will was paying for his meal the man said, "Long trip. Your car holding up all right?"

Was this clairvoyance or business acumen? Indeed, for the last fifty miles or so Will thought, but was uncertain, that he'd heard his engine complaining, but so faintly as not to spoil anyone's good time by complaining too loudly. Not spoil anyone's good time at least until the engine blew up.

Will took the man's card, which in addition to the name, address, telephone and email numbers, showed a blue circle with eleven red teepees resting around its circumference. Will pointed to it.

"Symbol of the United Sioux Tribes," said the man.

Will recalled a protest against an oil pipeline and a

major oil spill on a wetlands area but thought better than to mention it.

"Thanks for the card, my car may need a little work."

———

It needed more than a little work. Will had to check into a motel. Shortly after unpacking, he plopped down on the bed and asked himself aloud, "Do you love your mother, Will? Come on speak up?"

He answered with a mock German accent, "Ve haf vays to make you talk, you know."

He caught himself about to produce a hackneyed little thespian interlude he didn't need.

After his car had undergone some needed upkeep, he was back on the road. The speedometer read eighty-two, seven miles per hour over the limit. He slowed down.

He was driving east, away from the sun, but he saw it from time to time in his rear-view mirror, this burning ball of plasma, smashing hydrogen nuclei together to make helium, just like the H-bomb does. Wasn't there a book *Brighter Than A Thousand Suns*? You'd go blind looking at one of these explosions.

———

Thoughts of the sun's perpetual brightness failed to drive out thoughts of his mother's periodic darkness. Did he love his mother? Did it matter? What would happen if he didn't show up, or showed up in a week? The more he thought about this, the angrier he got.

Didn't that old lady back in Minot need help as well? He

pictured her lugging around her pitiful protest sign. And an image of that blonde girl flickered in his thoughts.

He pulled to the side of the road and called his brother, asking him to tell their mother that he was having car trouble, that he was fine, but that he'd be late.

"Why don't you tell her yourself?" His tone was calm, reasonable. Working in the New York City Department of Finance, which among other things, dealt with taxes, he had practice sounding calm and reasonable.

"I sort of did," he fibbed.

"We're going to see if we can have her committed, maybe get ECT."

"Oh, don't do that."

"She needs help," said his brother.

"That's why I'm coming, Tom. I can calm her down. You know that."

"You can't even calm yourself down," he said, his tone still calm and reasonable. "Look, you can calm her down for a day or two, maybe a week, maybe a month. Oh, let's not get into it, okay?

They were already *into it* weren't they?

"Well, I'm still coming," he said. "Tell her I'm having car trouble."

"You already said that. I will. Take care of yourself, Will."

"You, too."

They used to have fun together until they started wrangling over how best to help their mother.

Why did he want her to know he was having car trouble? To explain being late? Why late? Did he plan to see the sights? The Flood Memorial Obelisk? With global warming and climate change, he'd better see it before it was under water. Not funny.

He turned the car around. He was going back to Minot. That woman needed help. Only once did he ask himself what the hell he was really doing. He didn't even believe in her crusade.

CHAPTER TEN

They were in their bedroom packing Lieutenant Joe Calderone's duffel bag, when Maria Calderone finally hinted at what was bothering her.

"What's she like?" she asked.

The drive to the missile alert facility, a small complex of buildings surrounded by a wire fence, would take six hours. He'd sleep there tonight, and tomorrow, in a freight elevator, he and Makenna Washington would descend eighty feet to the launch control facility where they'd spend the next twenty-four hours together in close quarters. In the winter, if a heavy snowfall delayed the arrival of the next missile combat crew, the two might be down there together for four or five days in a row.

For a month now, Maria's husband had already been dressing next to Washington, sleeping in the same bed she had slept in, noting her fragrance. Only a curtain separated the sleeping area from the workspace, though a door had been fitted to the tiny bathroom after women had been admitted to the missile launch crews. Conversation filled

long lulls in activity. Missileers had similar educations, back
grounds, aspirations and temperaments. That crew members
often became friends was not surprising. During the eight-
month tour of duty he'd get to know her better than he knew
anyone besides his wife.

A month ago, when Maria learned that her husband's
new crew partner was a woman, she'd asked to see a picture
of her.

"Cripes, Maria, what is she going to think?"

"Tell her your wife wants to see it."

He groaned.

"Well, it's the truth."

———

Maria had examined the photo of a fit, attractive, young
black woman, smiled weakly, handed back the smart phone,
and said, "She looks nice." The subject had remained
dormant, like a hibernating bat. Until today.

Calderone didn't want it fluttering around the room
causing mischief.

"What's she like? I don't know... Normal, I guess."

But had anyone else asked him the question he would
not have described Makenna as *normal* Not that she was
abnormal, of course. But she was in some ways exceptional.
She could make funny faces and speak in funny voices. Her
impersonations of some of the higher-ranking officers at the
base were immediately recognizable. But as regards her
duty as a launch control officer she was fittingly as serious
as expected of anyone charged with the oversight of ten
intercontinental ballistic missiles topped with thermonuclear
warheads and indeed would probably soon be a better

missileer than him. She'd already learned more codes from memory than was necessary and could find the relevant page in a code book or manual in seconds. She never scored less than one hundred per cent on the routinely administered proficiency tests that were uniformly disliked among the missile corps.

He was fond of her but that was all.

"What do you talk about?"

"Work mainly. The weather. Sports. I don't know. Most of the time we're busy taking tests, studying, going through drills. There's not that much time to talk."

Maria, Joe knew, could quickly develop a corroding acidic jealousy, threatening the bonds of affection unless it were quickly neutralized with a few basic facts gently presented or a humorous remark precisely timed. But now, with little time remaining before he left for duty, he wished simply to avoid discussion.

———

During his training prior to their move from Vandenberg Air Force Base to Minot Air Force Base, Maria saw her husband glance at the well-proportioned buttocks of a woman in a grocery store whose shorts were so short and clinging that they might as well have been absent. As they transferred groceries from the shopping cart to the trunk of the car, Maria asked, "Did you know that woman?"

"Which woman?"

Maria dropped a shopping bag into the trunk.

"The woman whose butt you were so taken with."

"That woman with the short-shorts? For crying out loud. I looked at her for maybe a millisecond. I look at a lot of people. I looked at the old lady with the pink cane. I looked at the woman with the baby. Come on. It doesn't mean anything."

On the ride home, Maria became increasingly caustic, accusing Joe of having a wandering eye and lust in his heart. When Maria admitted that she, too, had looked at the woman's behind, Joe theatrically groused that she'd never told him she was a lesbian. The brief silence was broken by Maria's laughter. That was the end of it, but Joe had not forgotten. He was grateful when Maria turned to a chest of drawers for the underclothes she had unnecessarily ironed for him.

———

And there was their disagreement about marijuana. Joe had been let in on a little secret. High quality marijuana was available on the base. By discretely asking around he learned that Airman Charlie Forster was the man. Calderone purchased some and brought it home, looking forward to using it as an aphrodisiac, the well-known effect of the evil weed, satisfaction guaranteed, but Maria was horrified.

"Marijuana! You must be out of your mind. Give me that."

He'd hesitated.

"But Maria—"

"No way are we going to have marijuana in this house. I'm surprised at you. Please give me that."

She emptied the contents of the plastic bag into the toilet and flushed.

He had been blindsided. They'd used marijuana together once, though he'd had to talk her into it, patiently repeating that occasional use was entirely harmless. She finally relented and the experience had been good but afterwards she told him she thought it had been a sin and she'd confessed it to her priest. He hadn't even considered that she might not have changed her mind. Maybe it having been a sin explained why it had been so damn good. He kept the thought to himself.

Given the tension in the home, Joe had been unable to study for the proficiency exam the way he'd planned. In truth his worry about the exam, and his plan about what to do about that worry, overshadowed his disappointment about the missed opportunity to make love to his wife under the influence.

He was in a bad mood when his ride arrived to pick him up.

"I love you and don't you forget it," he said, as he leaned forward to hug and kiss his wife goodbye. As soon as the door was closed he pictured the once promising brown leaves swirling in the toilet's whirlpool. And he thought of the exam.

CHAPTER ELEVEN

The one-story missile alert facility housed bedrooms, a lounge with TV, a washroom, bathroom, dining area, a kitchen, and a communication room. Bunkbeds filled one of the bedrooms. But since this building was a real home to no one, the walls were bare of pictures, the paint and carpeting a dull air-force-issued brown.

The kitchen was an exception with white walls, white wraparound cabinets, and white countertops shining brightly, daylight through large windows illuminating the deep steel sinks and the room beyond. Best of all was the chef, Airman First Class Ayesha Khoury, who had learned to cook at the side of her Lebanese grandmother and was the person most likely to keep morale high. When the schedule and weather allowed, Airman Khoury went on long runs through the countryside.

The panoramic view through large windows of hundreds of acres of farmland and the endless sky redeemed the building from utter blandness—a view suggesting peace, despite the four hundred fifty missiles distributed out there over thousands of square miles.

They sat at a dining room table eating breakfast. Chef Khoury had made an omelet with peppers and chives for Lieutenant Makenna Washington, pancakes with whip cream for Lieutenant Joe Calderone.

"How was your time off?" asked Washington.

"Okay. Had dinner with friends. Caught a movie. How about you?"

"Prepping for the exam."

He nodded, his expression neutral, fearful that inadvertently, by word or gesture, he might hint at his secret. He didn't know her well enough to say anything, so he joked.

"You're always at it, Makenna. You've got to learn to live a little."

She squinted at him.

"Do I know you?"

Joe shook his head. "I'm not sure, but I sure know you. Doesn't matter how many times you score a hundred. With that bad squint of yours, you'll never get promoted. I can't see your eyes. How're you going to read the codes? What if *the* order comes and you can't find your key?"

Washington laid her fork on her plate, clasped her hands, and hung her head in mock embarrassment.

"True, I won't be able to read the ultimate code when it comes, God forbid. But as long as you are crew commander, and I'm only deputy commander, there's not much I can do about this squint. I guess that'll be ten fewer missiles dropping in over Russ— Hmm. Not funny. Missiles dropping in on anywhere. Not funny. Nuclear war, on the whole, bad."

Joe mimicked her, putting his fork down and bowing his head.

"Confession time," he said, ignoring the nuclear war business. "I studied, too. Had my wife turn the TV down so low she probably couldn't even hear it."

"You told me you could have become a farmer if you'd wanted," said Joe, changing the subject. "Nice outdoor work. Instead you're stuck underground baby-sitting these brutes. Why'd you join?"

"It's true. I could have lived on a farm, even inherited it. Mine was one of the few black families that have owned land since the end of the civil war. My parents were proud of that. They wanted me to stay.

"But you know what, I was squeamish about killing chickens and that was a big part of the business. You put them in a cone with the wide end up. It holds them snuggly so, according to theory, they don't feel so stressed. Only a chicken's head and neck fit through the narrow end of the funnel. So, they are, upside down and helpless. Then you slit their throat and the blood runs out. No, man. I couldn't do it.

"I joined the air force to become a pilot, but it didn't work out that way. Still there's no work more important than stopping an enemy from destroying your country. And I like the people. Present company excepted, of course. Why'd you join?"

Joe smiled. "I wanted to be a pilot and my family didn't even have any chickens."

———

They took the industrial-size elevator eighty feet down. Lieutenant Tom Marshal had already opened the ten-ton blast door leading from the atrium into the control center. The door, huge, black, and slightly convex, reminded Washington of a whale. Should an adversary's nuclear warheads explode nearby, but not too nearby, the whale would shield them.

Was humor a plus or minus on this job? The crew of another control center had painted their blast door to look like a pizza box reading, "Worldwide delivery in thirty minutes or less. Or your next one is free." Was this funny? That might be a good question for a personality test, a battery of which they had all taken. The tests, however, only identified instability, anxiety, depression, fanaticism, and other undesirable traits. As far as she could tell, a sense of humor was not assessed.

In large red letters on the wall next to the blast door a decidedly unfunny sign read:

NO LONE ZONE
TWO PERSON CONCEPT MANDATORY

A steel room the size of a small school bus, the control center was surrounded by a wrap-around, four-foot thick rebar and concrete cocoon affixed to four shock absorbers.

Lieutenants Tom Marshal and Greg Kelly, looking forward to seeing natural daylight again, enthusiastically shook hands with the relief crew before sitting back down in their red chairs.

Pushing with their feet, they slid their chairs along a steel track, past row upon row of knobs, switches, and little red lights, to their respective work areas. They swiveled to face Joe and Makenna.

"Don't worry, Makenna," said Kelly. "We've removed the Playboy magazines."

She was accustomed to, if sometimes annoyed by, the

ribbing from a small minority of the men, but she'd never been passive in the face of adversity.

"You've been on duty all night," she said. "How'd you get them out? If you broke the no lone rule, I'll have to report you. Maybe I'll report you anyway. Sexual harassment."

The silence was heavy.

Kelly looked as if he'd been slapped. The other two men frowned.

After a moment Washington burst into laughter, stopped, caught her breath and said, "I'm sorry. I'm sorry. I couldn't help myself."

They all laughed now, fear of being involved in a me too moment having evaporated.

"You really got me, you know," said Kelly. "I won't mess with you again,"

"No. No. Please do. I like jokes."

"But only in good taste, right?"

"Well, that's preferable but a properly chosen dirty joke can go a long way. Did you hear one about the golden retriever that could count ducks?"

"If we're lucky we may also find a little time to give a report," said Marshall, interrupting the banter.

For the next forty minutes Marshall reviewed the status of each of their ten missiles and silos, equipment function, and messages.

Slowly, as if speaking to a small child or an idiot, Marshall now finished up his report.

"And we had a trespass at B-02 a while ago, or so we've been told. Happened before we came on duty."

Kelly nodded solemnly and then Marshall did.

"Well?" said Calderone.

"A team went out there," said Marshall. "They saw this old woman as soon as they entered the access road. She hadn't breached the fence. She was just standing there."

"Old woman?" said Washington.

"About as old as they come," said Kelly, "lives on a farm just outside of Minot. And she invited any airmen interested to come over for coffee and cake," said Marshall.

"Fat chance," said Joe.

Kelly and Marshall left. Washington closed the whale of a blast door. That woman sounded interesting.

CHAPTER TWELVE

At the dinner table, Karen Haugen told her father about the red-headed old woman she and Suzy had spoken with on the steps of Old Main. She did not mention the young man because her attraction to him made it a personal matter.

Given that her father was a sergeant at the air force base, she'd been embarrassed that she hadn't known what GBSD stood for, nor nuclear winter for that matter. Keeping her embarrassment to herself, she repeated some of the woman's arguments.

"That's the same woman our security team picked up," he said, ignoring the arguments. "The Russians have a lot of missiles aimed at us. They know better than to use them, though. Peaceniks always know better than the experts. And if there's a nuclear war, we're going to win it."

He lay his knife and fork on the plate.

"Are you upset about that lady, Daddy?" asked ten-year-old Lilly.

"Your father had a bad day at work. Let's just let him eat dinner in peace," said Amy Haugen.

"I wasn't bothering you, was I, Daddy?" said Lilly.

"No, you weren't bothering me." But he wasn't bantering with his children as he usually did, nor did he have any educational stories to tell. He didn't ask his wife how her day had been. Though a disciplinarian, he was usually not a sourpuss.

"Is it that lady?" asked Karen, repeating her sister's question.

"Of course not. Old ladies don't bother me. Neither do young ladies. Most of the time."

"Really, kids, let him be," said Amy, who managed her husband as if he were a domesticated lion.

"It's all right. I might as well talk about it," he said. "The tail gate of a Humvee opened while the vehicle was traveling and a box of grenades fell out, if you can believe that."

"Oh, no." said Karen. "They didn't explode, did they?"

"Apparently not. But they're still missing so if you find a heavy green metal box that says, 'Thirty-two grenades' on it, let me know."

"Are you worried a terrorist will get them?" asked Karen.

"Not so much. But I imagine some deranged weapons enthusiast, or bank robber, or, like you say, maybe even a terrorist, paying two or three hundred dollars for a grenade."

His frown alone probably kept his men under control and had somewhat the same effect on his family, when he used it. He was a martinet, insisting on a dress code, on seeing Lilly's homework assignment when she was in school, on quizzing them on the multiplication table at meals. But he was not generally glum. He barked or growled or hissed or made other animal noises when one of his children broke a rule but had never struck them. The only time Karen had been spanked was when, at three years of age, she'd dashed into the street. Her mother gave her a single swat on the behind.

"So, did she talk about mutually assured destruction?" asked her father.

"Yes," said Karen.

"That sounds really bad," said Lily.

"Actually, it's good," he said. He explained, at a precocious ten-year-old's level, that the country was safe because it had all these super powerful bombs atop super powerful missiles, including the sixty-foot-long, six-foot in diameter missiles around Minot Air Force Base, each protected by a steel and concrete silo.

"So, no one would attack us because if they did, we'd blow their whole country to smithereens."

"What if some crazy person, some terrorist or something, tried to blow up one of those missiles?" asked Lily.

"Even if they got through the fence, they'd have a heck of a time getting to the missiles. The cap on top of the silo weighs as much as three eighteen-wheelers"

"What are eighteen-wheelers?" asked Lily.

"Eighteen-wheelers are very large freight trucks," said Amy.

Karen imagined three long trucks lying across the silo, one on top to the other.

"Can I go and see one?" asked Karen.

"Don't even think about it. You can see everything you could possibly want or need to see on the internet."

"Daddy," said Karen, "I'd like to go to the movies this weekend with Jack. I don't think I can be home by eleven. The movie starts late."

She thought she might preempt her father's invoking the standard curfew.

"What are you going to see?"

"*Firestorm*. It's about fire fighters."

"What's its rating?"

"It's an R, Daddy, but I'm eighteen."

"Let it go, Roy," said Amy. Remarkably, he did.

———

Later that evening in the privacy of their room, their voices lowered, Amy sat at the dresser while Roy paced.

"It's the damndest thing. The team that lost the grenades is the same team that picked up the O'Hare woman at the silo. What the hell that means, if anything, I haven't the slightest idea.

"So, the long and short of it is that they've reprimanded the team chief and put my promotion—or demotion—on hold until the investigation is over."

"If you'll forgive me for saying so," she said, "that makes my job all the more important. If I lose it, making ends meet will be hard and if you're demoted *and* I lose my job we won't be able to pay the mortgage."

Roy Haugen continued his back and forth pacing, but now clasped his hands behind his back as if he'd been arrested and were being led off to a jail cell. They should have heard that low tailgate open, the shifting of the box, the thump as it hit the ground. The way they described it, the jiggling and rattling of the storage area's haphazardly packed contents made it hard to hear much of anything, explaining why they'd turned up the volume on that country and western song about a yellow dog to foghorn volume.

And to top this off, some asshole had failed to secure the tailgate.

"You're not listening to me, Roy."

"Sorry, go on."

"Rumor has it that old man Wilburn's going to lay off reporters. Every newspaper in the country is doing it as things go digital. I don't think he'll can me, but you never know. You censored me when I wanted to report that rumor about drug use on base."

"And it's a good thing, too. Nothing came out on that."

"Nothing came out of it because none of the higher-ups were interested in looking into it. Those missile launch officers must be bored out of their heads down there, bored and stressed alternately. I could understand their wanting to zone out on some Mary Jane from time to time."

"Don't even talk like that."

"Look, Roy, a scoop about missing grenades would be a feather in my bonnet."

He snorted but squelched the commanding bark. She was not a disobedient airman.

"That's a bad idea, Amy. I'm in trouble enough already. Don't do it."

"All right, but don't ask me to censor myself again. I swear I'm going to write what's necessary to write."

Had she already transgressed in trying to have that article about Edna O'Hare's protest published?

CHAPTER THIRTEEN

She could not sleep after this. Amy Haugen thought about cults. The media regularly reported stories about young people giving themselves completely over to dictatorial cult leaders, abandoning their belongings, their families, their identities. How could one understand these things?

She'd begun thinking about this herself after having written a story about a cult in Fargo, whose leader was, in this case, an out-of-place Indian guru who rented a sprawling farmhouse where his *family* lived. He represented the uniting of the divine and the work-a-day world; and a work-a-day world it was, keeping up the farmhouse, the barn heated, and following rules of behavior, strictly enforced. In return he would teach them the path to bliss on earth. Not unusual in such cults, the demigod encouraged sexual offerings to him as signs of faith and of the wish to achieve higher planes of consciousness, whatever that meant.

So why were some people attracted to cults like this? To leaders like this? Why did they accept being told when, where, and what to eat; when, where, and with whom to sleep; when to arise in the morning, what to wear, which chores to do, which thoughts to have and not to have. The list of strictures was long.

She thought of children whose parents laid down and enforced rules of behavior against which they may have chafed but, being children, had no recourse but to follow. Rules about when to be silent, table manners, being in bed at seven when it was impossible to sleep, and curfews.

Now grown, away from home, on their own, would people who'd had such parents—that is parents who parented—wish to be subjected to the whims of a dictatorial guru? Not on your life. Once was enough.

But what of people who as children ran wild, coming and going when they wanted, and doing whatever they wanted to do? Children whose clothing needed attention? Who had to scrounge for something to eat? How might they see a completely structured life with a figurehead who cared enough to set the rules? It was Amy's hypothesis that these people, once neglected children, were those who fell under the spell of the uber-parent, albeit often a kinky one.

Amy herself was a latchkey kid whose mother was intermittently depressed and hence intermittently absent. Their father had disappeared from their lives when they were little. Amy was often on the loose. She and her sister took money from their mother's purse and went shopping. They cleaned house and did laundry, including the sheets from the master bedroom. Amy recalled feeling sad when she arrived home with something interesting to tell, like the dissection of a frog or how the teacher read her essay in front of the English class, only to find her mother in a darkened room lying in bed still in pajamas.

"I have a headache dear, tell me later," she might say.

So, was Amy an exception to the rule? Cults never held any attraction for her, but she did end up marrying a military man who made and followed rules at work and at home. She had been comfortable with this, even a little cosseted, but the comfort was slowly wearing away as it rubbed against the man's hardness over the years.

CHAPTER FOURTEEN

Edna made a cup of tea, placed it on a small side table, then plopped into her favorite chair, which had been her father's favorite, later her husband's. She pictured James in it, feet resting on a footstool, his boots exchanged for slippers, a newspaper held before him. It was almost as if they were both sitting in it together. This fantasy comforted her, but she was still grieving. Her sadness was worse. Her anxiety was worse.

She allowed her mind to wander. If it hadn't been for her parents, she would never have met Jim. She was sixteen when her parents called her into this same room for "a little talk."

"Your sister says she's interested in farming, but she's never shown it," said her father. "You, on the other hand, couldn't wait to drive a tractor. So, we think you should inherit the farm."

"But that's not fair to Fiona and anyway I want to be a doctor, not a farmer. And you're not planning to die anytime soon, are you?"

They ignored this last remark.

"We're going to help her buy a house when she's ready," said her mother, "and that may be soon if she and Ernie Schmidt get married."

"Earnest won't like it," said Edna. "He's had his eye on this place. I know."

"We want to talk about your education," said her mother, "not what Earnest wants. You know we're going to be fair to your sister."

"She should be here for this discussion."

"Edna, please," said her mother.

"So, your father and I have decided you need to learn about the business in an up-to-date way. We've done a little research—"

"But I want to be a doctor."

"Fine," said her father. You can be a doctor after you get a degree in agricultural science."

"But that's not a pre-med major."

"You can do a post baccalaureate premed program."

She was going to fight it, if it took a hoe and pitchfork, until they told her she could go to the University of California at Davis. The thought of spending the winters in California immediately melted all resistance.

And that's where she met Jim. She'd known about Hiroshima, of course, but from him she learned a great deal more about the aftermath of the bombing which had killed an estimated 90,000 to 120,000 people, either instantaneously or over months from injuries or radiation sickness. And many more over the years as people developed leukemia and cancers of the stomach, lung, liver, and breast.

There was literally no one on campus who knew more

about the bombing of Japan than James. Yet he, like she, was majoring in agricultural and environmental sciences.

He'd worked summers on his uncle's strawberry farm in Southern California, unaccountably taking a liking to the work, or maybe it was just the strawberries.

———

Edna had waited about six months before speaking with Amy about a newspaper article. There was never a guarantee that it would be published. Well, she could do something more dramatic than just trespassing, although that whole drama had exhausted and frightened her. She was not strong like those civil rights workers who were undaunted by the thought of going to jail. That short time at the jail had intimidated her. And what did she expect from a visit to a small college in the summer? Her protests were incorporeal stones thrown into the water, which made no ripples. But she'd done so little. If she only had more umf. But wasn't it futile?

She really did think the world was in danger. She really did believe what the Union of Concerned Scientists were saying, that the doomsday clock was now set at 100 seconds to midnight, the closest time to nuclear annihilation since the cold war, and what was most likely to trigger it was a simple accident leading to the launch of ground-based missiles, which could not be recalled if a mistake had been made.

Before she could even sip the tea, a big sobbing cry burst out, her eyes flooded, her nose running. She got a box of tissues.

Eventually the sobbing stopped. She'd gotten some

relief, but still felt defeated. She arose from the chair, her tea now lukewarm.

It would have been nice if that Larrabee boy had stayed for a while longer.

———

They stand in a vast expanse of rubble, Minot's every building having been so thoroughly blasted apart that only hints of their prior existence, here and there, poke up through the debris. James extends his right arm and index finger, pointing at the annihilation before them.

Absurdly, but not less painfully because of that, his gesture feels like an accusation.

Edna O'Hare awoke with tears in her eyes, her heart beating rapidly. Placidly shining through her window, the moon took a few moments to reassure her that this was just another one of those damn dreams.

CHAPTER FIFTEEN

Karen Haugen, high school senior, and future pediatrician, along with her friend Suzy, was taking summer courses in biology and math at Minot State University.

Late one Saturday afternoon Suzy invited Karen over to watch a movie in her room, which was itself covered with movie posters. They sat on the bed, propped against the wall with pillows.

"I found it during my research for my paper. It's from 1964. Ancient. But it's sexy."

"Oh, my God. If my father finds out I watched this, my goose is like totally cooked."

"Just tell him it's a war movie if he asks. World War II. This English nurse's husband is killed and she's lonely, so she sleeps with this American Navy guy. It's called the *Americanization of Emily*. Anyway, he's probably never even seen it.

"I'm not going to mention it at all. Maybe I'll even say we didn't watch a movie, I mean, if he asks."

"Good for you. A little white lie in the service of some harmless racy fantasy."

During a scene, in which a towel-draped woman stood by an officer's bed, Suzy's mother peeked in to ask if the girls wanted a snack. Karen grabbed the remote to darken the picture, but she only froze the half-naked woman in place on the screen. Suzy thanked her mother, but said they were fine.

"You are jumpy," she said after her mother had left.

"You are too laid-back," said Karen. They laughed.

"World War Two was pretty awful," said Karen. "My father's working to prevent World War Three."

"Whoa! You're getting awfully serious there. That old woman got under your skin, didn't she?" asked Suzy.

"Well, didn't she get under yours? You were a bit ruffled. I could tell."

Instead of answering, Suzy pointed the remote at the screen and clicked. Temporarily lulled by the sweet romance, they remained silent until the end of the movie.

When it ended, Karen confessed that she'd looked up GBSD on the internet and that the old woman wasn't the only one questioning the need to replace the old rockets.

"I'll give you the websites," she said.

"Give me a break, Karen. I don't want to read about rockets, but now I can blackmail you. If you don't do exactly as I say, I'm going to tell your father you've becoming a doubting Thomas—I think that's the expression."

Karen's glum expression quelled Suzy's laughter.

"I'm just kidding."

Of course, she was just kidding, perhaps to change the topic from nuclear topped missiles to something lighter.

"That guy was kind of cute, wasn't he," said Suzy.

"Which guy?"

"Oh, don't play the dumb blonde with me because if anyone isn't dumb, it's you. The guy with the protest lady."

"Yeah, I guess."

"You guess?" said Suzy, teasing.

"I'm not thinking about him. I'm thinking about Jack. I need to ask you something, but it's hard."

"Go on."

"When you…when you first did it, did it hurt?"

"Did it? Oh, you mean *it*."

"Not so loud."

"You want to know if it hurt," said Suzy in a stage whisper. "A little, but it was barely a pinch and there was hardly any blood. Some women don't have any pain at all."

"Did it…feel good?"

"It did for me."

"You won't tell anyone about this, will you?"

"Well, except for you father and mother, I won't."

"Thank goodness for friendship."

CHAPTER SIXTEEN

Now that he was headed west, the sun was in his eyes from time to time. That yellow furnace had long since burned all the clouds from the pale blue velvet sky. It was a beach going day, though there was no beach to go to as far as Will could tell and certainly no ocean beach. And thank goodness for that. Had the ocean been nearby, the pull on him would have been so great he might have detoured completely away from his destination.

From Will's East Los Angeles childhood home, the ocean was only a thirty-five-minute drive away and essentially the only place they went to as a family and that only in the summer. Those trips ended in his junior year when his sister died. That was probably when the bolts began slipping out of his mother's hinges. Then his father abandoned the family.

At sixteen and unable to mourn, in large part because his mother disliked seeing her children cry, he occupied his mind with science fiction, reading one thick anthology after the other.

During his junior year in college, his mother purchased a Hummer, a high-end surveillance system, and new plumbing, wiping out his college money and ending his education. The Hummer, of course, was repossessed, the surveillance system disabled, and the replacement of old water pipes unfinished, but this was of no help to him.

He remained in Berkeley for a year, working in a supermarket and living in a rented house with five others. He lived for a year with his brother who was finishing graduate school, but they had a falling out over the proper approach to their mother and the house she still lived in.

Having no place to go and no money, he joined the marines, thinking it would be good for him in some ill-defined way. The IED blew up a year into his service.

In the hospital in Germany he fell in love with—or was it merely a routine concupiscent infatuation—a nurse, but although she laughed at his jokes and clearly liked him, she was unavailable, and probably too wise to get involved with this good-looking but rootless man. Back in the states he moved in with his mother for a while, then back to Berkeley. His mother sold the house and moved to New York to live with her mother.

In college he'd been majoring in chemistry, with vague plans to go to graduate school in biochemistry and then work for a pharmaceutical company.

He'd had a girlfriend Babette, but she decided to spend a year in France and the breakup was permanent. His couple of romantic relationships after that—flings?—were short because he couldn't commit to them. The girls weren't right.

Aimless as a windblown leaf, he went where the breeze carried him, settling on the ground only to be lifted by another breeze and whisked away again.

On the way back to Minot he engaged in truncated dialogues with himself, sometimes aloud, sometimes silently.

"I'm going to help that old woman and then turn right around and go to New York," said his self-confident side.

"Oh, yeah? What are you going to do? Make more signs? She can only carry one at a time," said his doubting side, a side possibly inherited from his mother.

This parry shut him up for a few minutes, while he examined each cow in a field of cows as closely as he could without losing control of the car. There was no traffic.

Then he thought of that blonde girl in the blue dress.

CHAPTER SEVENTEEN

Makenna and twenty-nine other missile launch officers hunched over their monthly proficiency test. Promotion without consistently high performance was considered impossible and failing to achieve ninety percent on a test meant a talking-too at first, a scolding at second, and a who-knows-what at third. She put these thoughts out of her head and read question number 23.

―――――

23. An electromechanical maintenance team has penetrated silos B-09 and B-11 to adjust malfunctioning sump pumps after a freak summer thunderstorm. The team last authenticated with you twenty minutes ago. You now receive a seismic alarm at B-10. What will you do?

1. Declare Security Situation?
2. Have flight security controller obtain two authentications from B-09?

3. Contact B-11 to obtain two authentications from the electromechanical maintenance team?
4. Contact missile maintenance mission control?

The seismic alarm indicated vibration at the B-10 site, suggesting the possibility that someone may be seeking illicit access to the warhead. Typical, thought Makenna, all that stuff about the maintenance team that had nothing to do with the situation. The correct answer was 4.

After answering three more question, she stretched her spine and shifted positions on her chair. Joe Calderone sat to her right. She noticed that, for the third time, he tapped the watch on his left wrist with his right index finger.

Despite continuing to read the exam questions, she was prepared to look at his watch face, should he tap it again.

When he did, a column of numbers, next to a column of letters appeared. Damn. They were the test questions and answers.

Calderone was still intermittently tapping his watch. Had anyone else noticed? But it was probably only the location of her seating that made for furtive observation. Stop this, she thought. Get back to work.

———

Charlie Forster had been on that security patrol out to B-02. Makenna found him and asked about the encounter.

"If you want some entertainment, she'll give you free coffee and likely cookies and some antinuclear guff for good measure."

"Are you going?" she asked.

"You must be joking. Fraternizing with the enemy. I'd shut her up, if I could."

"I though the Russians were the enemy. What's her name?"

"Edna O'Hare."

Some of these anti-war protesters were a little cuckoo, but, as she reluctantly admitted to herself, she was bored. Imagine that. Sitting in front of that console, she could, with the mere flick of her wrist, hurl ten missiles across the world to cause ungodly death and destruction, the end of civilization, yet she was bored. Unvarying checklist routines, coupled with extreme vigilance, and nothing to do stifled creativity and joie de vivre. This old woman sounded amusing.

———

It was easy to get her address. Edna O'Hare was well known in town. One day, during a break in the routine, Washington exchanged her military uniform for slacks and a blouse. Characteristically thinking ahead, she'd purchased flowers the day before: a bouquet of red carnations, yellow daisies, and purple monte casinos.

O'Hare's two-story white farmhouse needed touching up but was not in visible need of repair. Four gables under the pitched red roof faced in four different directions, like sentinels.

The screen door was closed, but the heavy oak door to the house was wide open. Climbing the front porch steps, Washington realized that she was nervous. She prepared herself for a frosty reception like those past frosty receptions from certain elderly white women.

Through the screen door, holding the bouquet in her left hand, Washington watched as O'Hare approached. Washington liked her looks: erect, slender but not gaunt, dressed in jeans and a short-sleeved blouse, her red hair in a bun, a quizzical look on her face.

"Good afternoon, Mrs. O'Hare. My name is Makenna Washington. I heard that you invited airmen from the base to have coffee with you, so I thought I'd drop by. Sorry I didn't call first. I couldn't find your number. If this is an inconvenient time, please tell me."

O'Hare smiled and opened the screen door.

"I really didn't expect anyone to come." She welcomed Washington, took the flowers, thanked her for them, led her to the kitchen, and invited her to sit at the table. After putting the flowers in a vase with water and admiring them, she asked, "Would you prefer tea or coffee?"

"Coffee, please."

"Regular or decaf?"

"Oh, definitely regular. I don't know how I'd survive without caffeine."

O'Hare alternately addressed Washington or the coffee machine she was readying.

"I'm the same way. This old motor won't start in the morning without a little jolt. Did you know that the most frequently asked question in this country is 'Coffee?' I read that in a book."

O'Hare took a place at the table to wait for the water to percolate through to the glass coffee pot below.

"A book about American customs?" asked Washington.

"Oh, no. It was called *A Girl Named Cricket* about a mother, father, and daughter hiding in a small Mojave

Desert town because they were undocumented aliens—aliens from another planet."

"A play on words. Was it funny?" said Washington.

"Yes, it was. But a lot of science fiction is just sort of like wild west stories except they're in space. There's no humor in them at all." After a pause, she continued. "Well, now just listen to me talk. Like I was an expert or something. And I'm not. I don't even like science fiction."

Edna brought saucers, cups, spoons, napkins, sugar, cream, and a plate of cookies to the table, and then poured the coffee. Picking up the cream pitcher, she asked if her guest would like some.

"No thank you. I take mine black."

Washington smiled. Edna smiled back.

They nibbled cinnamon stars and macaroons, and sipped their coffee, occasionally peaking over the rims of the cups to examine each other.

They discovered some of the things they had in common: they grew up on farms; they had chickens, never truly getting used to their slaughter, though able to wear a mask of indifference when called for; and their parents loved them—the most important commonality.

Both had gone to college, Makenna to study computer science and aviation, Edna agronomy. Each knew little about the other's major, though Edna had a computer and used it.

Unselfconsciously, Edna talked about her husband and their long marriage. They'd never had children. She did not mention her husband's worry about the future for children born in the atomic age.

Washington left a boyfriend behind. He'd worked summers on her parents' farm. She cared about him but was rankled by his seeming lack of ambition. Yet they still wrote to each other.

Edna, as Makenna now thought of her, asked what she liked about him.

"Tyrone's honest, hardworking, gentle, and cute, of course. Well, we'd better change the subject, or I'll start missing him. By the way—and I don't mean to be rude—but we've been talking for well over an hour and you haven't said a word about the missiles. I was expecting a lecture about them, I must admit. They detained you at one of the silos, didn't they? You were arrested. You must have very strong feelings about this. Are you sparing me for some reason?

Edna laughed.

"The truth of the matter is maybe I was. I don't know. I was enjoying the conversation and didn't want to spoil our visit. But, yes, I did invite you airmen out to talk about land-based missiles. In part to find out what you thought about them, if you gave them any thought at all. Frightening what we can get used to, what becomes ordinary, hum-drum, like humanity getting ready to destroy itself. So, tell me about your job on the base."

When she heard that Makenna was a missile launch officer, Edna got up for the coffee pot, refilled their cups for the third time, sat down again, and pulled her chair a little closer to the table.

"I thought you wanted to talk about the missiles, to tell us how bad they are," said Makenna. "Do you really want to hear about my job?"

"Hmm. I guess what I want to hear is how you feel about your job. I mean about the prospect of us blowing ourselves up, and radiating a bunch more to death, and starving the rest. And please keep in mind, I don't feel you're in any way guilty of...of anything."

"Edna, may I call you Edna?"

"Yes, and I'll call you Makenna."

Makenna stood, put her hands on her hips, and extended her back.

"One thing about work; I do a lot of sitting when I'm on duty. Could we go for a walk?"

———

They strolled along a path through a sunflower field.

"I don't think anybody thinks about starting a nuclear war," said Makenna. "We think about preventing one. To think too much about the apocalypse is one big bummer. It doesn't do any good. Do you think about that much?"

"Naturally. I've got a Minuteman on my land not a mile from here. And they're spread out like poison mushrooms from here to the horizon. Well, you've got me started, though you know all this already.

"When the alarm is given that we're being attacked, the person or persons responsible only have a short time to decide whether or not to fire. It's a use-them-or-lose-them situation. Since they're sitting ducks, they're on hair trigger alert. Launch-on-warning. And that goes for a false alarm that isn't detected in time."

Makenna was shaking her head.

"It's not persons. It's the president who makes the decision."

"Oh, now, Makenna, are you sure?"

Makenna stopped walking, perhaps for emphasis,

perhaps so she could better observe her new friend, look into her face and see her reaction.

Makenna said that it was an absolute certainty that only the president had authority to launch the rockets. She talked about the briefcase, the so-called nuclear football, that the president always had with him, with its top-secret codes of targets on credit-card-thin discs, themselves wrapped in plastic.

O'Hare listened attentively. Makenna thought Edna understood and accepted what she'd just been told. She even read into that wrinkled face an admission of error. Once more she repeated that only the president was authorized to launch the missiles. Edna nodded.

They returned to the house without talking and sat again at the kitchen table. Washington refused another cup of coffee, asking instead for a glass of water. O'Hare put the cups and saucers in the sink but left the cookie platter on the table.

"Forgive me, but I think you are a little naïve," said Edna evenly, picking up the conversation without a hint of combativeness, "If the capital is gone, someone else must have authority to fire, don't you think? And if that person is out of commission, a third person must have authority. And down the line it goes. I don't know; there might be dozens of people who could start a nuclear war."

Makenna sipped her water before speaking. She could think of nothing to say, except to deny the premise.

"The capital couldn't be destroyed by surprise because so very many sophisticated systems would warn of incoming missiles."

"There are other ways to deliver bombs to their target," said O'Hare. "What about a very-low-flying cruise missile from a submarine? Or from that atomic-powered cruise missile the Russians are working on that can stay in the air for months? What about an atomic bomb brought into the city by truck? Or by boat? Now don't you think someone besides the president, or vice president, or speaker of the house, or anyone in Washington, must have authority to launch our missiles if the capital is gone?

Washington was nonplussed. When had any of her instructors talked about these scenarios? That only the president had such authority was a creed everyone believed in. But what this woman said made sense. Only one of these formulations could be true. Only the president or not only the president. To give herself some time, Washington picked up a cookie, finished it off, sipped her water, and reached for another cookie, which she held up between thumb and index finger like a tiny shield.

"Well, that's all too theoretical for me," she said before biting into the cookie.

"I hope I haven't upset you," said O'Hare.

"No, of course not. I think it's stimulating. You've really made a study of this, haven't you?"

"Oh, I've done some reading."

They talked a little about the weather—once upon a time a safe subject—before Washington departed, having accepted Edna's invitation to return and to bring some friends. They exchanged telephone numbers.

———

On the road back to her small apartment in Minot, Makenna reviewed her visit. She'd enjoyed it and she liked Edna, but she still felt uneasy about it. She recalled reminding Charlie

Forster that it was the Russians who were the adversary, not an old woman with unpopular ideas, but now she had second thoughts. Edna was an adversary, albeit a powerless one.

Unless planting an unorthodox idea in a person's brain was a kind of power: people other than the president launching nuclear tipped missiles. She disliked that idea. It increased chances of error and with nuclear war making capacity there must be zero chance of error. But that was impossible no matter what the truth was.

She regretted not having probed Edna's mind. What did she know about North Dakota's missiles? What did she know about the launch crews? Did she plan to protest further? How?

Was it impossible to bring a bomb into an American city on a truck or a boat? Difficult, yes, but impossible? And wouldn't such an attack, by a terrorist for example, be interpreted as an attack by Russia? And lead to nuclear war?

She had expected an amusing afternoon and the effortless rebuttal of any antinuclear argument with the word "deterrence." But O'Hare wasn't talking about nuclear disarmament per se.

And the whole time she was with Edna, Makenna had suppressed the image of Joe Calderone cheating on the exam. What was she going to do about that?

CHAPTER EIGHTEEN

Edna met Will at the front door.

"Will! You're back. I thought you were going to New York. Has something happened? Is your mother all right?"

"I'm going to go but I first wanted to see if…if maybe you could use my help for a while."

He looked tired and worried. She invited him in, offering the ubiquitous cup of coffee.

"I've been thinking—thinking about the red paint on your truck and the window…about your being hassled. And about the logistics of carrying a sign, a chair, and everything."

She would be happy to have his help but disliked the idea that she'd be keeping him from his sick mother. He reassured her that his mother would "keep" as he put it, rather disrespectfully she thought.

"So, can I help?" he asked.

"I can't pay you—"

"Pay me!" he interrupted, offended. "I'm not asking for money."

"Please calm down. I'm sorry. It's just that you don't even believe what I'm telling people, so your wanting to help me is... I don't know. Umm."

"Never mind," blurted Will. "I see I made a mistake. Sorry to have bothered you." He pushed the coffee cup away, scooted his chair from the table, and stood.

"Will you please calm down, for crying out loud," demanded Edna angrily.

His departure arrested, Will, looked at his coffee cup, and sat down. He pulled it back across the table toward him.

"I don't like admitting it, but I could use the help. A bodyguard and a pack horse in one, actually, if I may be so crude. On the other hand, I'd feel guilty if I don't pay you in some way. I didn't mean to offend you. You are a delicate flower, I see."

"Who you calling a delicate flower" said Will, reestablishing balance and smiling weakly.

"You'd be of most help if you stayed here. How would that be?"

————

It was too late to make a sign for Will so Edna made dinner, after which they sat on the sofa together while she showed him some websites, including one called Nuke Map, a clinically cold, grisly website. One picked a city and dropped a bomb on it to see the extent of the damage.

"Let's do Minot," she said. The map on the screen now showed Minot and surrounds. "You can pick the bomb size."

"I don't know anything about this stuff," said Will. "I don't even know what the numbers mean."

Matter-of-factly O'Hare reviewed the basics. The W78

U.S. warhead, for example, released the explosive force of three hundred forty thousand tons of TNT, about twenty times more powerful than the bomb that fell on Hiroshima.

"The Russians have similar bombs. Let's use the W78. We'll do an airburst. You want to push the button?"

"Strange," said Will. "This is kind of like a game but it's spooky. Worse than spooky—ghoulish."

"I'm glad you think so. Here goes."

Concentric shaded rings appeared around the city.

The nuclear fireball, with a radius of two fifths of a mile, vaporized everything. The five-pounds-per-square-inch air blast, with a radius of three miles, collapsed most residential buildings. The thermal radiation radius, causing third degree burns, was five miles and beyond that windows as far as eight and a half miles from the center of the blast would shatter.

"I'm not going to be protesting the H-bomb. I just thought you might be interested in this."

"I don't suppose you have any whisky?" said Will.

"It is gruesome, I know. I'll get you some."

After two shots, Will was ready for bed and for the next day's work.

———

Smelling bacon the next morning, Will came downstairs, still in Edna's deceased husband's pajamas. After putting food on the table and coffee in the cup, she began the discussion of how best to get the town's attention.

"They ignored me by and large at the college. I should probably carry the sign somewhere else. But no matter where I picket, I'm still a little old lady and little old ladies aren't that exciting, are they."

"What about witches?" said Will. "They're so exciting that they burned them at the stake in Salem."

"They hanged them," corrected Edna. "That's all I need. People already think I'm nuts. The ridicule would rub off on my message. 'There goes that nut cake, the Russian Air Force's best friend.'"

"Christ, Edna! Haven't you ever heard 'there's no such thing as bad publicity.'"

"No more using the Lord's name in vain, please."

"If someone writes a book about Mexicans fleeing gang violence and someone criticizes the author for 'cultural' appropriation because they're not Mexican and were born into privilege, you think that hurts sales? Or criticism of a Sioux indian point of view story by an Englishman? Even an accusation of plagiarism will help sales. There is no such thing as bad publicity, at least not if you're trying to sell a story. True, bad publicity could hurt baby food sales, but you're selling an idea."

"You've made your point and I agree, but you don't have to talk so loud. I'm old but I can still hear. I've got a pointed hat. Kept it all these years. Nobody around here gives a damn that humanity may burn itself at the stake, but they may be interested in a witch carrying a sign, after all."

They made a list of places they might picket: the college, city hall, a downtown mall, the air force base, the Ward County branch offices of the at-large congressman and the state's senators.

When Earnest Schmidt knocked on the door, Will followed Edna into the living room and sat on the sofa. He was not about to get into that closet again, nor did she ask him to.

Edna and her brother-in-law had never taken to each other. Whenever she saw him, she was reminded of the time, seeing no harm in a little rough-housing, he'd thrown her into a lake during a family picnic. She'd fought him all the way to the water's edge and torn her favorite summer dress. And he remained bitter that Fiona, Edna's sister, and his wife, had not inherited the farm.

Finding a young man in the house, a young man in pajamas no less, Schmidt did not conceal his surprise.

O'Hare made introductions and invited Schmidt to have a seat.

"No. No. I... I'd like to speak to you privately," said Schmidt.

She addressed Will. "Are you finished with breakfast?"

On cue he said he was.

"I'm going upstairs to take a shower," he said, figuring he might take a long one to give them time to discuss their private matter.

———

"Getting arrested for trespassing on air force property wasn't enough. Now you're running around town trying to rile up college kids with your half-baked ideas. And with Grumman coming to Minot on top of it. What are they going to think of us?"

"You mean what are they going to think of you," said Edna.

"Minot's business climate may not be any of your concern," said Schmidt, "but it is most people's and it is mine. So, I decided to come over here personally to ask you to stop acting like a batty old woman. You've made your point. You don't like the missiles. Fine. Everyone knows it now."

"Is that all, Earnest?"

"It's not all, but it's enough." He sighed and turned to go.

"Who is this Mr. Larrabee?" he asked frowning as he stood at the door.

"A friend," she answered. "A dear friend."

"Where'd you meet him?"

Remaining civil was harder than she thought.

"On a dating site," she said, unable to control herself.

"What the hell!" he blurted.

"Joke, Earnest. Joke."

"Well, it wasn't a very funny joke."

———

They drove to the university where, at the foot of the steps to Old Main, they set up a card table and a folding chair. A bronze mask of her father weighed down the flyers. Will picked up his sign.

Edna had not worn her tall, conical black hat in the car. After they arranged the table and chair, she sat down and put it on, resting it toward the back of her head so her hair framed her face. With black pants and black blouse the picture was complete.

They'd discussed making an outfit for Will, as a scarecrow perhaps but in the end she just gave him an old white cowboy shirt of her husband's. It wasn't a costume exactly, but it was mildly theatrical with a fringe over shoulders and chest.

Will picked up the sign.

The GBSD is unnecessary for deterrence.
The GBSD is a tremendous waste of your money.
The GBSD brings us a step closer to nuclear war.
Say no to the GBSD.
Tell your congressman and senators now.

More people climbed and descended the stairs to and from Old Main today than on the first time she was here. No sooner had they set up than a tall young woman at the bottom of the steps stopped to look at them, hesitated, and then came over. Minot and the number four were printed on her loose-fitting jersey.

"Are you supposed to be a witch?" asked the young woman unsmiling.

"Well, of course," said Edna, "Who else would wear a hat like this?"

"Are you a good witch or a bad witch?" asked the woman.

"Have you ever seen *The Wizard of Oz*?" asked O'Hare.

The woman nodded.

"What color hair did the good witch of the North have? Do you remember?" said Edna.

"No, I don't."

"It was red, though not as red as mine. Good witches have red hair. I'm a good witch."

Will resting the handle of his sign on his shoulder, thought the interchange bewitching, smiling at his own joke.

He wanted to join in, but good judgment, which he exercised now and then, was against it.

The woman in the number 4 jersey smiled.

"That's good to know. So, what is the GBSD?"

Will raised his sign and walked in a tight circle next to the table.

As Edna talked about the missile that was to replace the Minuteman and how ground-based missiles were dangerous and superfluous, other students trickled by, most staying for only a minute or so, but some asking questions or disagreeing with her, by and large politely, though one middle-aged man angrily challenged her, after looking at the flyer.

"Do you think the air force would spend so much money if it were wasteful? He must have realized what he'd said, given stories of $10,000 toilet seat covers. He walked off without waiting for an answer. Waste money? Oh, no, the military would never do that.

The woman in the number 4 jersey introduced herself as Betty Carlson and took a flyer. "I'll read it. I might even write an article for the *Red and Green*. I mean if I believe what you're saying after I read this."

In all, seven people took flyers before Edna and Will left for their next destination.

———

City Hall, a pale brown, two-story building, with a protuberant boxy entrance and two wings, looked out on a long U-shaped driveway, which looped around an expanse of grass. A sidewalk bordered the driveway. Since there was no one to be seen, they decided not to set up their table, but simply walk back and forth in front of the building.

Will carried the sign. From time to time Edna waved at the six large windows on the right wing, and then, after they'd walked to the other side of the building, at the six large windows on the left wing.

Before long they missed having an audience and walked back to the car. But they'd had an audience.

CHAPTER NINETEEN

To his embarrassment, ordinarily punctual Dr. Andrew Rasmussen, an alderman, and the newest member of Working Group A, had missed the meeting with the mayor, the city council president, the president of the chamber of commerce and the members of Grumman's Ground-Based Strategic Deterrent team.

A patriot, he'd suffered from a guilty conscience because he'd been unable to join the armed forces due to an old knee injury from his rugby days. His father had served in the army and Andrew had been the prototypical army brat. When asked recently to join Working Group A, dedicated to supporting Minot's Air Force Base and its mission, he was happy to do so. His failure to get to the meeting was due both to his limp and an unexpected minor emergency with one of his patients.

Fortunately, rotund, jovial Mathew Jackson, president of the chamber of commerce, was his friend and had a good relationship with Ellen Conklin, Vice President of Grumman's Ground-Based Strategic Deterrent team. Arranging another meeting had been easy. This time Rasmussen was early.

Rasmussen set the pace as he and Jackson walked down City Hall's brightly lit hallway toward the meeting room.

"You didn't have to make up for it by arriving forty minutes early for this meeting," said Jackson. "What are we going to do? Play cards?"

"No. No cards. You're going to bring me up to date so I won't look like a total idiot when they get here."

As they sat at the round conference table waiting for the Grumman team to arrive, Rasmussen asked, and Jackson answered questions.

"…and Boeing has long since dropped out of the competition because of problems with their new airplane," continued Jackson. Grumman had three years to make a proposal—phase one."

"What did the air force pay Grumman for the phase one proposal?" asked Rasmussen.

"Two hundred forty-nine million."

"A billion here and a billion there," said Rasmussen. "Pretty soon you're talking real money. Some senator said that. I don't want to sound critical by asking about costs in the meeting."

"You can ask about money," said Jackson. "In fact, Grumman is proud that it could do phase one for less money than Boeing had proposed, before it dropped out of the competition. It makes them look good."

Jackson went on to summarize the previous meeting while they waited.

———

Rasmussen met the members of Grumman's Ground-Based Strategic Deterrent team as they entered the City Hall conference room.

Ellen Conklin, Vice President of GBSD development at Grumman, stepped forward, shaking Rasmussen's hand firmly.

"Nice meeting you, Dr. Rasmussen. This is General Clayton, formerly an ICBM missile wing commander."

"A pleasure," said Clayton, a dignified man with silver hair, in suit and tie.

"And Claudia Cummings, Grumman's public relations manager for space systems."

Cummings, thought Rasmussen, looked more like a dressed down fashion model, in red jacket, pink blouse and dark skirt. Unlike Conklin's rather severe pageboy, Cummings's lustrous black hair reached to just above her shoulders. Her handshake, however, was as firm as Conklin's.

Rasmussen and quarrelsome Earnest Schmidt, also an alderman, already knew each other.

When everyone was seated, Jackson thanked the group for its generosity. They already had a busy schedule, after all.

"Working Group A has been so supportive of the base, its planes, and its ICBM's over the years," said Conklin, "that we didn't want to miss out on meeting even a single member of the group."

"Thank you. I appreciate it," said Rasmussen.

"Let me catch you up a little," continued Conklin, who was clearly in charge.

"The air force will replace the Minuteman missiles one-for-one with the GBSD between 2028 and 2035. It wants the next generation ICBM system to be adaptable to changing threats over time so we've made it modular. You can update one part of the system without rebuilding other parts. The entire system, missiles and infrastructure, should be good until at least 2075.

"Sounds expensive," said Rasmussen.

"The cost is estimated to be between $85 and $140 billion and another $150 billion to maintain and operate over fifty years," said Ms. Conklin.

"But it's worth every penny to deter nuclear war," interjected Jackson, "and Minot is proud to do its part."

"Technology maturation and risk reduction was phase one, which has been completed," continued Conklin. "Phase two is engineering, manufacturing and the initial installation of some missiles. Phase three is full production and installation."

"I've read that some people have spoken against replacing the ICBMs," said Rasmussen, "Even against maintaining them. What can you tell us about that?"

General Clayton inhaled deeply and exhaled. "Yes," he said, mildly annoyed. "There are a few of these anti-ICBM people around but they're small in number and have no traction in Washington and certainly not at the Pentagon." He crossed his arms across his chest and shook his head. "Nothing to worry about."

"I agree with General Clayton," said Claudia Cummings, "but it's still very important that we—everyone involved with the GBSD program—bring the modernization story to the public. We want as much support from ordinary people—"

"Taxpayers," interjected General Clayton.

"—as possible," concluded Ms. Cummings.

"I am in full agreement with Ms. Cummings," said Clayton. "Even a little bit of negative publicity is a bad thing."

"I don't think that will be a problem," said Jackson. "Last time anyone protested the missiles was ten years ago when a loony scaled the fence of one of our silos wearing a feathered headdress and a neckless of crystals around his neck. I don't think he changed too many minds. Certainly not mine." He laughed. The others smiled.

"They all have razor wire up there now, I hope," said Clayton.

"Forgive me for saying so," said Rasmussen, "but not everyone opposed to the ICBMs is a loony. Chuck Hagel considered eliminating some of them and he was secretary of defense."

"And you may remember what happened,' said Clayton. "The Defense Department planned a study of the environmental impact of eliminating the ICBM silos. Your senators and the rest of the Senate ICBM coalition put a stop to it. There is no significant organized opposition to the GBSD program, nor would we allow anyone to put our nation at risk by amputating one leg of the nuclear triad."

Jackson's secretary knocked at the door and then peeked in. "I think you should look out the window," she said smiling. "I think it's Professor McGonagall."

————

They stood at the window in two rows. Clayton, Cummings, and Conklin in front, Jackson, Rasmussen and Schmidt behind them. "GBSD" was visible on the sign.

"Does anyone know them?" said Clayton.

"No one else in town has hair like that," said Jackson. "That's Edna O'Hare."

"Oh, crap," said Schmidt, "she's my sister-in-law."

"I wonder why she's dressed like a witch?" said Cummings.

"A gimmick to get attention," said Clayton. "Who's Professor McGonagall?"

"She's a witch from the Harry Potter books," said Rasmussen, wondering how it was possible that Clayton, who had children, did not know.

After the meeting Cummings got Earnest Schmidt's telephone number.

———

"Is she a member of an organized group?" asked Cummings.

"No," said Schmidt, "She's had this bee in her bonnet for a while now but is totally inept. Everyone thinks she's a little cuckoo. You really shouldn't be wasting your time thinking about her."

"Thank you. I was just curious, that's all."

Schmidt had maintained a nonchalant tone on the phone, but cursed O'Hare's name after they hung up. He wondered if there was anything to do to silence her.

CHAPTER TWENTY

In the launch control room again, Makenna briefly wondered why their chairs were on rails. Was it to prevent them from being knocked over, to make movement quicker, to keep the two launch officers on their side of the console?

It was like this down here. Her mind tended to wander when the work had been done. She picked up her book, a sui generis supernatural crime novel about the Devil coming to earth to revenge himself on God. *Lucifer's Revenge* was quirky, but suspenseful. It kept her interest though she didn't believe in the Devil and, even occasionally, questioned her faith in God, but not usually for long.

Nor did she believe in witches. She had recently seen Edna O'Hare in downtown Minot dressed as a witch. The woman had seemed perfectly normal when they'd had coffee and cookies together. Well except for her misguided ideas about ICBMs.

But lurking below these thoughts was another from which she wished to free herself. Joe Calderone had appeared to be reading test questions and answers from his watch. To ask him about it, though, seemed impossible. Even to mention the rumor that some airmen cheated on the proficiency test was taboo.

So she changed the subject in her own mind.

"Joe, has anyone ever complained to you about the GBSD?"

"What? Are you kidding?"

"You've heard about that woman, Mrs. O'Hare. Well, I paid her a visit and I have to say it was very nice. She has some offbeat ideas though, like we don't need our missiles, the ones in silos, at least."

"Oh, I'll bet there are lots of so-called peace groups that say the same things. And hell, who wouldn't like to get rid of all the nukes, but you have to be realistic."

"She mentioned that land-based missiles would have to be fired even with an ambiguous warning because otherwise they risked being destroyed. We've talked about this in class but never got much of an answer, just reassurance that we're constantly improving our surveillance systems."

Joe Calderone swiveled himself twice around in his chair.

"This stuff makes me dizzy," he said. "And I think it makes you dizzy, too. Best not to think too much about it, if you ask me. Think about something else."

"Like the exams," said Washington. It had come out after all.

"Sure, like the exams."

"Joe, I saw you looking at your watch during the exam." She'd stepped onto a fast-moving escalator now and couldn't get off until it reached the top—or the bottom.

"Huh? Don't you check your watch?"

"I saw a list of numbers and letters." She paused for a

response before continuing. "They were the questions and answers."

Was Calderone's expression one of indignation? Anguish? He punched his left palm a few times.

"Yeah," he sighed finally, "it was a one-time thing. I got panicky because I hadn't done so well on the last exam. What are you going to do about it?"

"You could have been caught if someone else had seen you looking at that damn watch. Amazingly stupid. Why didn't you just memorize the answers? How did you get the answers? Man, oh man. I'm buffaloed."

Joe said he'd only done this once because his last two grades had been too low, and he panicked. He had some trouble at home and had been unable to study enough.

"What are you going to do?" he asked.

"I know what I should do."

"If you're thinking of reporting me, think again. Even the brass doesn't like a snitch, and you'll hurt some of us pretty bad. Keep it to yourself and I'll pass the word that someone knows about it and it's got to stop."

She clasped her hands, her fingers interlocking, like a thoughtful judge, sitting at the bench, and pushed her chair a couple of feet away from Calderone, more perplexed.

CHAPTER TWENTY-ONE

It was unusual for commissioned officers to strike up friendships with noncoms but when Calderone heard the rumor that Charlie Forster was some kind of drug kingpin, he approached him to talk, and soon he, Caulfield, and Forster were smoking weed together when they could arrange it. Maria Calderone had forbidden smoking at home. He'd kept her ignorant of these occasional get togethers.

They rented a cottage on the outskirts of Minot, a safe house where they could smoke marijuana. The three of them held the secret of their meeting place as tightly as they could, but many on the base knew that Charlie Forster could discretely supply marijuana.

Early one afternoon Charlie Forster, Jake Caulfield, and Joe Calderone gathered to try a freshly acquired sample of LSD, the first LSD any of them had ever tried. The house was well suited for this experiment because the closest neighbor was a quarter mile away, so if someone needed fresh air, he could, without fear of being observed, be dazzled by the cloud formations during the day or by the stars during the night.

They sat, circling a small round coffee table on which lay a sheet of LSD, divided into thirty-six ¼ inch squares, each square stamped with a whimsical image of the Mad Hatter from *Alice in Wonderland,* not a copy of Tenniel's original drawing.

Forster did the honors, cutting out three squares with a scissors, not daring to trust the perforations to do their job. Before handing out the tabs like communion wafers, he crossed himself, a bit of sacrilege that did not sit well with Calderone.

"There's some beer in the fridge," said Forster, "some chips, dip, and eggs if we really get hungry, but nobody gets the munchies on this stuff."

"You always have a supply of something," said Calderone. "Where do you get it?"

"Sorry. Can't reveal my sources, but I'll say this, if you ever need acid or Mary Jane, I just got a big load from my suppliers." He laughed, pleased with himself. "And I didn't even pay cash this time. Okay, I'm talking too much. Let's get down to business."

———

Forster thought about his stroke of genius. When the loss of the box of grenades was discovered, he'd wasted no time borrowing a car and heading back to retrace the route they'd taken out to a silo over a hundred miles from the base.

He remembered a short stretch of uneven, bumpy dirt road that they'd mistakenly taken thinking it was a short cut. After they'd turned around, the song lyrics on the radio had seemed clearer to him but he quickly realized that was because the rattling in the back of the Humvee had diminished. So that's where the tailgate had opened and the grenade box had slipped out.

He parked and walked for hours before finding the box in a rut at the side of the road. He put it in the trunk and returned to the base. The official hunting party didn't begin until the day after he'd found the box.

He didn't need a whole box. One or two should be enough.

———

They sucked on and eventually chewed and swallowed their bits of blotter paper, each tab presumably containing about a hundred micrograms of lysergic acid diethylamide. Joe noticed the effects in about forty minutes, the rug's floral patterns now kaleidoscopic pinwheeling eddies of iridescent color. A half hour later he dared not look at his colleague's transmogrified purple alligator-like faces.

He went for a walk.

Bloated clouds silently mouthed words through puffy, parted lips. He wondered what they were trying to say until distracted by thousands of brightly smiling round yellow faces, which swelled and shrunk rhythmically.

Did anyone go permanently crazy from this stuff? He walked a little faster as if to put the unhealthy thought behind him. And it worked for a while.

Approaching a lone elm, he was dazzled by the light's reflection from its leaves. He stroked the trunk's elephantine bark and thought he felt the tree sway in response, frightening him. He continued his walk. The hallucinations were more vivid now. With its empty window frames growing larger and smaller, an abandoned shack appeared to be chewing on something.

Now with each step he took, he felt the road push back.

He passed the edge of the sunflower fields into an expanse of a brown crop cut uniformly flat at two feet. The image of the earth as a disembodied head with brown hair in a crew cut came to mind, but it was not amusing. And then the hair was gone, and the fields were brown oceans on either side of the road, rolling toward him in waves. But he felt his chest swell, ready to resist. If the waves reached him, he would be swept into a parallel universe. He was flushed with excitement, but a moment later he was fearful, his hands having transformed into shimmering purple, webbed claws.

He approached a farmhouse, itself phantasmagorical, every window moving, the entire façade awash with changing colors and grotesque shapes.

It was better than looking at his hands so he just stood there gaping.

An old woman came out of the house, appearing angelic at a distance, surrounded by a rainbow aura, but as she came closer, she appeared demonic, though the aura remained. It was hard looking at her scaly red face with its elongated nose and protruding eyes.

She looked him in the face, then at his fidgeting hands, which he put behind his back when he saw her. Then, thinking they really weren't claws, tried to let them hang at his side, but now that he was no longer walking he could not do so for long, so he clasped them together and pressed them to his chest.

"Is something wrong? You look worried."

"I do?"

"Would you like a glass of water? Why don't you come in for a minute? It's hot out here."

Maybe getting out of the sun would help. He was frightened just standing here, the thought of insanity, of permanent brain damage, hard to escape.

————

She had him sit at the bright yellow kitchen table, like an egg yolk lake, its surface undulating. All he wanted was water. He grasped the glass with a claw, the colors still remarkably bright, though he was indoors. He had a few gulps, put the glass down, then put his hands under the table. He averted his eyes from her.

"You're not well, are you?"

"Doctor gave me a new medicine for my…blood pressure. He said it might make me dizzy."

"You're just dizzy? That's all? Are you having trouble with your car?"

"Why do you ask?"

He hadn't meant to be brusque. He was worrying about what he might say or do in front of her.

"Well," she said, "there's nothing out here but farms. I doubt you walked from town so you must have driven. But here you are on foot. So I thought your engine must have died or something."

After a pause she added, "You're not out here to visit me, are you? I know I invited people from the base, and you're welcome to stay for a while, but I don't get the feeling that you're here for a visit."

Metal pots, their rims wavy, hung on hooks over the

kitchen sink. The pots looked okay, friendly enough, simple to understand. He gazed at them as O'Hare gazed at him.

"How'd you know I'm from the base?"

"You're a young man, with short hair and a certain shade of Khaki pants. It was just a guess. Are you a pilot?"

He finished his water. His soul was expanding from within his chest, growing larger than the house, larger than the sky, melding into the background of existence. He would be absorbed, and all worry would vanish. He was flushed with euphoria. The woman's face had become angelic. He no longer had to keep his eyes on the dangling pots.

"Better than a pilot. I'm a missile launch officer."

He took his hands from under the table and examined them, moving his fingers as if he were playing a piano whose keyboard was a foot above the table. They were no longer webbed claws, their changing colors beautiful now.

"Are you sure you're all right?"

Later, when his mind was clear, he would wonder what sort of impression she'd gotten of him. Would she deduce the truth? She couldn't see him having hallucinations and his speech was unaffected. He didn't say anything outlandish. Had he looked at those pots for five minutes? Why didn't she speak?

"I have never felt better." And to show it, he arose from the table and bowed.

"Thank you for the water."

"You're very welcome. Come again when your blood pressure isn't so low."

He headed back to the rental house. The hallucinations strong as ever but his fear gone, feeling that his essence had expanded to fill the universe and made him one with it. He was at peace and enlightened.

A half hour away from his destination, he turned away from the friendly sunflower faces and thought of Makenna Washington. What was she going to do?

When he arrived, he found Forster sitting in a chair in the back yard drinking a beer with two empty bottles on the ground.

"Where's Caulfield?"

"Went for a walk," said Forster.

Unlike marijuana, LSD apparently did not draw people together, but Joe was now euphoric having conquered his fear, and so was Forster. He got his own chair and bottle of beer.

"Washington found us out," said Joe without prelude.

"What do you mean?"

"About the tests."

"Damn it. What's she going to do?"

Calderone shrugged, for once not particularly concerned.

————

That young man must have been on drugs, thought Edna. His speech was well enunciated. He wasn't drunk. He wouldn't look at her. Maybe he didn't want her to see his pupils, which seemed large to her. He was fascinated with his hands and waved his fingers in the air. It was probably marijuana. And he could launch missiles. She shuddered.

CHAPTER TWENTY-TWO

In order to come to a decision, Makenna knew she needed to talk this out but to her surprise, decided to discuss the matter with Edna O'Hare, of all people. She did not wish to talk to another airman because it was unlikely that another airman would be objective. Oh, and she might, without even knowing it, talk to someone who was involved.

———

Edna welcomed her by taking Makenna's right hand and holding it for a moment with both of hers before inviting her in.

They sat in the living room, Edna on the long sofa, Washington in a lounge chair facing her. A coffee pot, cups, saucers, spoons, sugar and salt rested on a serving tray on the coffee table between them.

"So what's on your mind, dear?" asked O'Hare after they were seated.

"Forgive me for mentioning it," said Washington, "but I

wouldn't want you discussing this with anyone."

"This thing you want to discuss, it doesn't concern me, does it?"

"No. Not at all," said Washington.

"This I won't discuss with anyone."

"Some of the missile control officers, are cheating on the monthly proficiency exam. It's a multiple choice test and they have the answers. How in the world they're getting them, I don't know. I don't know what to do. If I report this, I'll be asked how I learned about it and who is involved. If I say that I saw someone using a smart watch crib sheet, they'll ask who it was.

"If I tell the whole truth one of my colleagues will lose his security clearance, be taken off missile duty, and... I don't know. He'll be punished more than that, maybe even dishonorably discharged. And so will the rest of them."

"So," said Edna, "you don't know if you should report the cheating or not."

"I should report it, but my colleague said he'd talk to everyone and that they'd stop it, the launch officers, I mean. Shouldn't that be enough? These aren't bad people. It's the pressure. There's no chance of advancement without top grades. Some people have fallen behind, I guess."

"How would you know if they've stopped?" asked Edna.

Makenna leaned over to take her coffee cup in hand. Until now it had been untouched. She took a few sips and set it down again.

"I'd have to depend on my colleague to tell me."

Edna pursed her lips and nodded weakly, but the meaning of the gesture was unclear.

"What would happen to you if you reported the cheating but were vague about how you'd learned about it. What if you said it was scuttlebutt, if that's the word? You know, a rumor."

"I'd feel a lot of heat."

O'Hare now took her coffee cup in hand. The two drank silently for a short time, understanding that this was a pause so they could think.

Makenna pointed at the wall of pictures.

"Do you mind?" she asked.

"Be my guest."

Makenna placed her cup on the table and went over to the pictures. One of them showed an unmistakable O'Hare sitting in a chair, holding a baby on her shoulder.

"Your child?" asked Washington.

"No, my sister's. He died shortly after that picture was taken. Meningitis."

"I'm so sorry," said Makenna.

"She never had another child, but she managed. My brother-in-law—" She almost named her brother-in-law, who'd suffered even more, losing an heir to his business.

Makenna returned to her chair.

Edna asked, "What happens if the cheating is discovered, and they find out you knew about it and said nothing?"

"Bad news for me."

———

Makenna returned home, her conscience weighing on her even more heavily than before because, with Edna's help, she'd clearly laid out the alternatives and could no longer tell herself that action was delayed because she needed to think.

But she was still undecided.

CHAPTER TWENTY-THREE

Makenna rowed as intensely as if struggling against a receding tide in the Bay of Fundy, her strokes on the machine, quick and powerful. She glistened. Her regular workout in the base's well-equipped gym also included weightlifting. She could press sixty pounds overhead.

Watching this powerful woman from the room's entrance, Charlie Forster reconsidered what his tone of voice should be when speaking with her. Fortunately she was entirely focused on her work out and did not see him watching her, which, if she had, might have unnerved him. Or made him angrier than he already was.

Airman Forster grew up in a poor Kentucky coal mining family, but then how many rich Kentucky coal mining families had he known? The air force had allowed him to escape poverty, while serving his country. His father, who'd died years ago from a particularly severe case of black lung, would have been proud of him. And now his career was being threatened by this woman because he'd provided, for what he considered a fair price, the answers to missile launch officers' proficiency exam questions.

He'd just been lucky enough to have had a friend at Warren Air Force Base whose proficiency exam was routinely administered two days before it was administered at Minot. An investigation would reveal him at the center of this mischief, and he would be discharged. Would speaking with her make her more or less likely to spill the beans?

Or was there another way to discourage her from speaking about this with anyone? Good judgement prevailed. Forster left the room brooding.

CHAPTER TWENTY-FOUR

Karen, having re-read Edna's flyer several times, each time more carefully than the last, and having used the internet to easily identify experts who agreed with the flyer's arguments—the woman's arguments—was now herself convinced that land-based missiles were not merely unnecessary but threatening in the extreme. It would be more than just lax to do nothing, it would be immoral. This line of thinking made a visit to Mrs. O'Hare a necessity.

She asked her mother for O'Hare's phone number.

"I suppose it's none of my business," said Amy, "but do you mind my asking why?"

Without revealing her brand new and surprising opposition to land-based missiles, she said that she had some questions about them and wanted to speak with "the lady." That she wanted to speak with "the lady" face-to-face she neglected to mention.

Will Larrabee opened the door.

"Oh," said Karen Haugen, surprised. "I came to see Mrs. O'Hare."

"I know. She said you were coming. Come in."

They introduced themselves to each other and Will offered her a seat. Karen tried wishing away a not-unpleasant lightness in her chest.

"She's upstairs. I'll get her."

This was the boy—the man—who'd intrigued her when she'd first seen him standing by Mrs. O'Hare at the bottom of the steps to Old Main. And here he was again with that smile and oddball hat. Or maybe it was only odd that he was wearing the hat indoors in the summer. What was that all about?

Two minutes later Edna, with Will behind her, slowly descended the stairs.

"Oh, Karen, so nice of you to visit," she said, extending her hand formally.

"Can I get you kids something to drink? Kids. Forgive me. I know you're not kids. I'm a little old-fashioned in some areas."

"But not in others," said Will.

———

Edna carried in a tray of three glasses of fresh lemonade and placed it on the low table before them, then joined Karen on the sofa. Will took his glass in hand and stood.

"I'll give you two some privacy. Thanks for the lemon-ade, Edna."

"Oh, no," said Karen. "That's not necessary. It's about the rockets."

"You sure?" said Will.

"Yes. Please join us," said Karen.

She had read the flyer and searched the internet. She'd become convinced that Mrs. O'Hare's assessment of the danger was correct, which frightened her. She spoke of her fear's tangled strands: fear of the missiles themselves, fear of how her conviction would affect her, and fear of how her father would react when he learned of her conviction.

"I am no Greta Thunberg," she said, feeling foolish as soon as she made the non-comparison, "but I can't just twiddle my thumbs when the weapons right here in my backyard threaten the whole world just like global warming does."

She hoped she didn't sound self-congratulatory, sound like the brave little engine that could, but no matter, it felt good to speak up. Ordinarily she might have talked to her mother about her feelings, but it seemed this would be like asking her mother to hold her end of a rope in a tug of war between her and her father.

"Oh, dear," said Edna. "I've sidetracked Will, who was on his way to see his troubled mother and who knows what kind of trouble you'll be in if you join our little...what shall I call it? Protest? Demonstration? Resistance movement? No, that last one is a bit too grandiose. So you'd like to do something?"

"Yes," said Karen.

"All right. Listen to this."

CHAPTER TWENTY-FIVE

The Northrop Grumman Ground-Based Strategic Deterrent delegation was holding what it called industry day at the Grand Hotel on Saturday. Sam Clayton, a former commander of a missile wing, and now member of the Northrop Grumman GBSD team, would lead an open meeting. Later that day the Northrop Grumman representatives would meet with various Minot businesses that might supply services and materials when the new missiles were installed along with new infrastructure.

As Karen had explained, it frightened her to think of what the aftermath would be once her father learned of what she'd done, but doing the right thing was a moral imperative. And now, thank goodness, she was not going to do it alone.

The conspirators spent several hours discussing and then making the poster they would use to make their case graphic, lucid, incontrovertible. This was added to the picket sign and flyers.

———

The Grand Hotel was surrounded by a parking lot, the lobby entrance marked by six white columns. Business and town people would be coming and going all day, but the main presentation and the panel discussion began at 9 a.m. The three decided that inside at the meeting was not the venue in which to publicly challenge the need for land-based missiles. Instead, at 8 a.m., to the side of the lobby entrance so as not to impede traffic, they set up their three-by-four-foot poster on a makeshift scaffold that Will and Karen had made in Edna's workshop.

They'd discussed how the poster should be headed. Will, happy at his newly established friendship with Karen, offered, "Silos for silage? Take the bullseye off Minot? Time's up for the Minuteman?"

Karen allowed herself to be entertained, for she had no doubt about Will's seriousness, nor about his anxiety, as he reduced his own tension through humor. Amusement in no way reduced her seriousness either.

Edna had decided on a two-part heading: No to Land-Based Missiles: Submarines and Airplanes are Deterrent Enough.

The poster was divided into three parts, the first about atomic submarines and their ballistic missiles; the second about airplanes and their capacity to hit targets with nuclear weapons; and the third about how superfluous and dangerous land-based missiles were. They had also made cards with a website reference to the arguments against the GBSD.

Most people entering the hotel that morning merely ignored them and their poster. It appeared that there would be no drama, maybe not even discussion. Perhaps we should have parked our poster "smack dab" in the middle of the lobby, said Edna, knowing of course, that they would then have immediately been escorted off the premises.

At 8:35, dressed in a dark business suit, Amy Haugen, in her capacity as reporter for the local daily newspaper, walked from her car to the hotel entrance.

On seeing her mother, Karen briefly considered hiding behind a parked car, but by then Amy had spotted not only her, but Edna O'Hare wearing a black outfit and a tall black conical hat, and a young man wearing a cowboy hat.

"Good morning, Edna, Karen," said Amy, perplexed. "What are you doing here?"

"Morning, Mom," said Karen.

"Hello, Amy. This is Will Larrabee," said Edna.

"Good morning, Mrs. Haugen," said Will.

"Hello," said Amy Haugen before turning to the poster.

"Oh, my goodness. What do you...?" She fell silent, then resumed.

"How long will you be here?"

"All day," said Edna.

Amy said, "There's a morning talk scheduled, which I can't miss. I'll talk with you later."

After her mother entered the hotel, Karen, face flushed, said, "I should have thought of that. She's reporting for the paper. At least she didn't tell me to go home."

A few people stopped to look at the poster but had no questions. A heavyset man in pressed khaki pants and long-sleeved red plaid shirt read the poster and then matter-of-factly said, "Do you know what would happen to Minot if they cancelled the replacement program?" He didn't wait for an answer. "No, you don't."

Amy Haugen appeared again at around 9:45.

"I just heard General Clayton give a talk about the GBSD project. I know how Edna feels about this, but do you kids think you know more about this than he does?"

In this very public space she spoke in a professional, measured cadence as if interviewing someone for a story. She seemed more surprised by their presence than angry.

"Not everyone agrees with him, Mom."

"Well, everyone in this town does. Everyone I know does."

The three of us disagree with him, thought Karen.

"Are you going to write about us, Amy?" asked Edna.

"I have to go back in."

As Amy Haugen walked away the three turned to gaze at a passenger plane in the eastern sky approaching the airport. For a second, Karen imagined it being a missile.

Several people, presumably taking a break, exited the lobby. A handsome, fit-looking, white-haired man, immaculately dressed in a hound's tooth suit, and an ebullient young woman in a red jacket and dark skirt approached.

"Don't talk with her," said Claudia Cummings. "You'll be giving her a spotlight."

"I'm curious and they're harmless," said the general. "Let's hear what they have to say."

Amy, who was about to leave, stood aside.

Clayton smiled, said good morning, and read the poster and then began reading the flyer. He was nothing if not thorough. You can't be responsible for hundreds of hydrogen bombs if you were not thorough.

Claudia Cummings looked at the protesters. Her appraisals of people unusually shrewd, she was gauging their earnestness and energy.

The young man wearing a hat intrigued her. He appeared to have trouble standing still, raising himself on his toes from time to time or walking a few paces and returning to the same spot. Plenty of energy and nice looking, though perhaps a little cuckoo. Was that his girlfriend? Cummings doubted that there was anything to their protest other than what was there for all to see. No conspiracy. No hidden motives. No moneyed backer. No political—in the sense of elections and electioneering—motives. No large following.

It might be fun though to perform, if that was the word, a little espionage, Mata Hari-like. She smiled at the young man and he smiled back.

Will examined Cummings in return. That she was good looking he put out of his mind by looking at Karen and then at the general when he had finished reading and began to speak.

"It's good having people interested in current affairs, but I'm afraid this information is incorrect. We would be a lot less secure without the new missiles and the ones we have now have prevented war—nuclear war—for over half a century."

Karen and Will looked to Edna.

"This is a complex matter, but the experts all agree we need these weapons," continued Clayton.

"With all due respect," said Edna nervously, "the experts don't all agree. William Perry, former Secretary of Defense, one of the experts I'm sure you'll agree, said it was safe to scrap our land-based ICBMs. He said they were dangerous and wasteful, and that the US submarine force alone was deterrent enough and he wrote a letter to the president saying so."

The sight of a general arguing with an old woman

dressed like a witch, began to draw people to O'Hare's table. By this time Amy Haugen had returned and was taking pictures with her cell phone. Will and Karen stood next to each other, smiling and excited. Will squeezed her hand and let it go.

Clayton was now explaining that missiles around air force bases in Wyoming, Montana, and North Dakota would act as a missile sponge since two Russian rockets would likely be aimed at each of the silos and this would deplete the Russian stock of warheads by nine hundred.

"And what's the Midwest going to look like after nine hundred hydrogen bombs explode overhead?" And how about the states getting the fallout?"

Before Clayton could prepare an answer for that question, Edna continued, her voice shaky, but louder.

"And after the sponge does its work the Russians will still have seven hundred fifty warheads to destroy the rest of the United States."

A man in the crowd called out, "Where do you get your numbers?"

"They're in the new START treaty. You can find it on the internet but if you're going to read something, read Daniel Ellsberg's book *The Doomsday Machine* because that's what we have now."

When people began directing questions at the general, Claudia Cummings whispered in his ear. They made their way out of the crowd and back into the hotel.

Will and Karen began handing out flyers and reprints of a policy paper from the Arms Control Association.

Amy inhaled and exhaled deeply several times, as if she'd been holding her breath.

"That was General Clayton."

"You should write a story about this," said Karen. "Really, you should."

"Oh, Karen," said Amy. "Just don't mention this at dinner tonight. Okay? Maybe in a few days. Let me think about it. I've got to go now."

Will proffered her a flyer and article. She took them and left.

———

Half an hour later, Jack and two friends from the football team appeared. Karen knew Baxter and Wayne, disliking them both since seeing them push wobbly, blinking Eddie Driscoll off his cafeteria chair. Edna recognized them as the boys she'd spoken with about her truck, Baxter, the brown-haired boy with the severe crew cut, in jersey number nine and Wayne, the blond boy in jersey number fifteen, still carrying his skateboard.

Baxter lifted the paperweight, the bronze mask of Edna's father, from the stack of pamphlets, and took a sheet in hand.

After a cursory examination Baxter said, "This is crap."

"Please put that down," said Edna, pointing at the mask.

Baxter held the three-pound brass piece over the card table and let it fall, making a thud.

Wayne put the skateboard under his arm and crumpled up a flyer and tossed it to Jack who caught it.

Will stepped forward, placing his sign on the table.

"That's enough. Why don't you boys go home?"

Baxter laughed.

"I'd like to see you make us."

The small group of people who'd been reading the signs moved back a few steps.

"Jack, please," said Karen. "Take your friends and go. Mrs. O'Hare doesn't want any trouble."

Baxter and Wayne looked at Jack, who, still holding the wadded-up flyer which he'd caught, shrugged.

Wayne and Baxter each picked up a flyer, crushed them into balls, and threw them at Will, who batted them away.

The two football players approached Will, who stood his ground. Karen stepped between them.

"Please Wayne," she said. "Baxter. Please."

They pushed past her and then bumped against Will, one on either side.

"You won't get off so easy next time," said Baxter to Will.

"And, lady," added Wayne. "You should stop handing out that garbage."

The three protestors spent the rest of the day outside the entrance, except for bathroom and water breaks, answering questions and talking with people who came by out of curiosity, having heard the rumor of an argument between a witch and a general.

O'Hare judged their protest at the Grand Hotel an overall success, marred only by the nastiness of those boys. Karen was apologetic. Jack, after all, was her boyfriend, or had been until he'd stood passively by as the bullies harassed Edna and Will. Jack could have—he should have—said something. That would have been enough. She wouldn't have wanted him to fight with his friends. The sort of potential violence she'd just witnessed appalled her. Will's steadfastness had impressed her. She and Edna thanked him for stepping in.

"I'm all wound up after that," said Karen. "It feels like there'd been a fight." But, she explained, her father's icy stare would cool her off. He would react as if her personal antimissile stance threatened world peace. It certainly threatened domestic peace.

Edna, pleased but exhausted, commiserated and excused herself.

"I'm going home. Will, are you coming?"

"I'd like to stay in town, maybe get a cup of coffee."

Edna looked at Karen and back at Will.

"How will you get home?"

He was now her house guest and she had driven him to town. He had no means of transportation as his car was at her place.

He was stumped.

"Uh, I'll...um. Maybe I'd better go with you after all."

"I can drive you back," said Karen, surprising all three of them.

They sat in a booth in a cafe that Saturday afternoon and ordered sandwiches.

"So tell me about it," said Will.

"I did. He's now the abominable snowman and our house is the north pole or maybe the south pole. In any case, it's cold."

"How does it make you feel?"

"Are you going to psychoanalyze me?" she said, smiling weakly.

"Sorry. You shouldn't talk about it if you don't want to. Come to think of it, I don't talk much about my problematic mother, though heat is more the problem than cold. We can talk about the weather."

Will examined Karen's pretty, oval face, flawless except

for a mole near the corner of her mouth, and a slight gap between her front teeth, which actually was winsome. As usual she was prim in a summer dress, but not so prim that her figure was hidden.

"It's just hard, that's all. I love my father. Okay, now it's your turn. Do you love your mother? And if not, why not? Start at age three and work your way up by decades."

They laughed together. He told her about his mother's derangement, fits of rage, hyperactivity, shop lifting, imperiousness and that he was on the way to New York to help her out of some sort of legal difficulty he did not understand.

"You must love her then," said Karen. "A man who loves his mother. A good sign."

"But not too much," said Will.

"Oedipus rex," said Karen.

"You're quick on the uptake."

"No, you're just obvious."

"Uh oh," said Will.

"Why uh oh?"

They joked with each other, moving easily from association to association, real cads to movie villains; movie villains to movie stars.

Karen mentioned the weekly Saturday night folk dance at the university and asked Will if he'd like to go with her. After he'd agreed, she called to tell her parents that she was going dancing and would be a little late going home. Fortunately it was her mother who picked up the phone. She had no objection.

———

Forty-two people stood in a circle in the university's large basketball court, surrounding a casually dressed couple, a man and woman in their fifties, who announced the name of a Macedonian dance—it sounded like hopskip to Will—and demonstrated the step. The dancers held hands, arms at their sides, Will and Karen both pleased with the opportunity to make physical contact without potential awkwardness.

Skopski Sa Sa was a relatively simple walking dance that Will had no trouble with, but as time passed the dances grew more difficult, with complex steps and rhythms. Will now stood behind the line of dancers, trying to copy their steps. Karen remained with the group of experienced dancers. When she danced the Hambo with an older man, he felt a twinge of jealousy.

She joined him behind the line of experienced dancers, taking his hand and following the dancers who'd mastered the most difficult dances. At 9:30 they stopped dancing and sat on the bleachers.

"Are you having fun?" she asked.

"I am. You're a good dancer."

"Thanks. I've been dancing for a while."

Will wanted to leave so he could be alone with her but was hesitant to ask, concerned that he'd be spoiling her evening, as the dancing was not yet over. He was also thinking ahead. She'd be driving him home.

"Would you like to go for a walk?" he asked finally.

"Sure."

Situated in a residential district, the university had no particularly desirable destination within walking distance so they simply wandered through the neighborhood. Will told her stories of his childhood escapades. Once, after school, when he was about eight or nine, the boy his mother had hired to walk him to and from school took Will to a raft, boarded with him, and shoved off onto a small lake. Will remembered seeing his mother rushing over the bridge, gesticulating wildly that he go to shore. She was as angry, yes, but also frightened as he'd never before seen her. He could not swim.

"Oh, my. How did she punish you?"

"I don't think she did. I don't remember being punished. She kept us under control by frightening us into thinking we'd be punished. She was probably so relieved I got safely to shore that punishment didn't enter her mind."

"When I was fifteen," said Karen, "I climbed out the window to join my friends. We weren't drinking or anything. It was dark. No lights on in the houses. On a dare —not by me, mind you—we took off our clothes, clutched them in our arms, and streaked down the street. We laughed our heads off as we got dressed. I got home, climbed back through the window, and was so wound up, it took an hour to get to sleep. Now who would think a thing like that would ever be discussed with a parent. Well, of course it wasn't, not by any of us, but one of the girls told a friend who told her mother, who called our mothers in a fit. When my mother and father questioned me about that night, I told the truth but stupid me, I told the whole truth, including the part about taking our clothes off. Big mistake. All that our anonymous little tattletaler had revealed was the climbing out of windows. She hadn't told whoever that we got stripped.

"My father bellowed at me but had the self-control to leave the room before he hit me—which by the way he's never done—and let my mother give me a lecture, grounded me for a month, forbid me to watch television or to use the computer unless I was doing homework, to go to bed at eight every night and do chores on the weekends. I don't climb out windows anymore and I only run around in my birthday suit at the many nudist colonies we belong to."

Will laughed and said nothing embarrassing or suggestive, yet Karen now wondered what she could possibly have been thinking to put the picture in his head of her running around like a burlesque queen. And that ill-considered joke about her birthday suit and the nudist colonies. This was so unlike her.

He took her hand.

"You were a thrill seeker. I was just an innocent soul lead astray by a boy with a raft. I had less common sense than a toaster, which at least knows when to pop out the toast."

They walked for an hour and a half before Karen said she'd better take him home otherwise she herself would be late.

———

"That boy, Jack, is he a friend of yours?"

Karen kept her eyes on the road, the steering wheel held firmly.

"Well, to tell you the truth, he used to be my boyfriend. We've known each other for a long time. In fact..." She stopped herself. She'd almost said, "he's the only boyfriend I've ever had" but that suggested she had some obvious defect, like the gap between her front teeth but more likely a personality defect. Maybe constant irritability, or contrariness, or weakness in the sex drive department. She laughed at herself.

"You had a funny thought. What was it?" asked Will.

"Oh, it was nothing. Now don't ask me otherwise I'll have to make something up and it's unlikely I'll be able to think of something clever on the spot."

She pulled into Edna's driveway. Though she wanted to stay and talk she also wanted to get home on time so her father wouldn't be angry with her. That thought made her angry with him, but she still needed to go so she left the motor running to signal this.

Will put a hand on her shoulder.

"You're a lot of fun."

"You are, too."

He leaned forward, kissing her on the cheek.

They said their goodnights and she left.

On the way home her anger at her father flared up as did her self-doubt. Would Will have showed more interest if she'd stayed longer? He hadn't even kissed her on the lips. Sure, he said she was fun. A roller coaster is fun but you wouldn't want to snuggle up with one. Is that what she wanted? Or did she just want to be freed of her damn virginity?

Ironic that Jack had brought her to this understanding of her sexual side and then given her cause to abandon him. She couldn't feel the sort of affection that led to love-making with a boy who lacked character. She still thought Jack good-looking but so what. He really should have stopped his friends from harassing them at the hotel.

———

Karen could not decide whether to tell her father what she'd done or just wait until someone else told him. She discussed this with her mother who finally said it would, after all, be best if Karen spoke with him, otherwise it would appear as if she were hiding something from him. And Amy would have to do the same.

She asked to speak with him alone in the den, having decided she didn't want her mother defending her or being overprotective.

She'd become convinced that the missiles must not be replaced, but instead be removed, that they were actually bad for Minot.

Almost as soon as she started speaking, Roy Haugen pressed his lips together to prevent himself from speaking. His eyes never strayed from hers, but he lowered his eyebrows as if concentrating hard to see something indistinct.

When she'd finished she fell silent and waited.

"Your father is a career missile wing sergeant, and you go public to poo-poo the whole enterprise. Don't get me wrong. I'm not just thinking about myself, but what are people going to think when my own daughter, in effect, says I'm wasting my time? Jesus! Did you give that any thought? It may well just be a tempest in a teapot, but that's the end of it. You hear?"

"Dad?"

"Go ahead."

"Are you going to have trouble at work?"

"If my superiors ask what's going on with my daughter, I'm just going to say…that you got a little mixed up, but we've talked about it and everything's okay. Is everything okay?"

Her anxiety had lessened to a degree though she still half-expected him to curse a few times and some form of punishment. Yet the more she made the argument against the missiles the more confident she was of the truth of it. She must not let this scolding session end without her asking one more question, though on formulating it before speaking, she tensed up.

"Don't you believe that submarines are harder to find and destroy than missiles that are stuck in one place?"

"Look, Karen, I know I'm not going to change your mind about this. I just don't want you making a fool of yourself and of me in the process. Understand? No more posters. No more ridiculous ban-the-bomb stuff."

Sadness seeped in, displacing anxiety. Had he even tried to understand her?

"Did you tell your mother about this?"

"Yes. And she was there."

———

Amy Haugen had come to the hotel to write an article on Grumman's industry day, which she expected would be much like her articles about the team's previous visits to Minot. Newspaper reports—even on major national events —often began with human interest stories meant to entice the reader to finish the entire article, so, for example, she might have begun with an interview of the owner of the Great Plains Construction Company about the GBSD program boon to new construction.

But here now was a real human interest story: a woman dressed as a witch protesting the Minuteman replacement program, a program that almost everyone in Minot supported, a program that, as part of the nuclear triad, promised the whole country protection from a nuclear attack for the next fifty years.

This story was real, even surprising news, but it was also unwelcome news, which would displease everyone in town, and "displease" might, in some cases, be euphemistic. Mathew Jackson from the Chamber of Commerce had seen the exhibit and was visibly annoyed. General Clayton and Grumman's public relations person didn't like it either, of course.

She would not include her daughter's name and she didn't know the name of the nice-looking man with the feathered hat.

How much attention should she devote to the actual content of their protest? To the tit-for-tat between O'Hare and the general? And should she read the references they'd provided her? Fact check?

That evening she did read the white paper by a visiting research fellow at the Arms Control Association entitled *The Future of the ICBM Force: Should the Least Valuable Leg of the Triad Be Replaced?*

Should she cite at least some of its conclusions? That "the deterrent value of the ICBM force is small and diminishing;" that "…the current absence of any foreseeable threat to the U.S. strategic submarines assures that no adversary can preempt massive retaliation by the U. S." And that "the enhanced capabilities for the GBSD are either unnecessary or may adversely affect strategic stability."

The paper was not excessively technical, but it made her head spin anyway. She'd been unaware of any serious opposition to the GBSD program, other than Edna's, of course. All right, she said to herself finally, Edna's protest was real news and some of her arguments had to be included in an honest article. She permitted herself to omit Karen's name from the article. She condensed some of the objections to the GBSD program, tightened up the wording, and submitted her article, *Local Woman Protests the GBSD*.

Brad Wilburn called her the next day.

"What's the idea, Amy? You trying to have that woman ridden out of town on a rail?"

"Brad!"

"Okay, sorry, I got carried away. I suppose we have to publish the damn thing. I've already gotten a few calls asking if I'd heard the news."

———

Because he was preoccupied with the search for the missing grenades, Roy did not confront Amy until a few days after the incidents at the Grand Hotel.

"You didn't mention the kid's little poster session."

"I thought it best that she tell you herself."

This gave him pause.

"I guess you're right about that, but what if she hadn't?"

"I don't know, but now it's my turn to make a confession. I wrote a story about their little escapade."

She took a copy of the article from a drawer in the bedside table and gave it to him. He stared at the photo.

"She supposed to be a witch? And who's the guy with the hat?"

When Amy didn't respond, he read the article.

"Edna argued with General Clayton. Unbelievable. He *led* a missile wing. Who knows more about these things than him? And now everyone will think my daughter is a peacenik."

"Her name's not in the article."

Before that talk with Karen, he'd signaled that he was in the mood, but now he rolled away from his wife and turned off the light on his night table. He was more upset than Amy had imagined. When had he ever reneged on the promise of conjugal pleasure? But what she'd reported was news, real news, and if she hadn't written it someone else would have. She wanted to touch his shoulder, but thought better of it, and didn't.

CHAPTER TWENTY-SIX

She hovers high about the remains of Minot. Miles from the hypocenter, people, hideously burned, stagger aimlessly about. Near the hypocenter the shadow of a child has been etched into what remains of a concrete wall. She is unable to take her eyes off it.

Gripped with horror she awakens.

And there is the moon outside her window having kept silent watch the whole time. It's message, though delivered coolly, is always a comfort, always the same: it was only a dream.

But how little would be required for the dream to become real. Once the button was pushed mankind's annihilation would be run by the doomsday machine, inexorably cranking out immediate and prolonged death. The worst thing that could happen would be to survive the blast to die slowly over the following weeks as you watched others die and the world go dark.

How the devil was she supposed to get back to sleep

thinking these thoughts? If only she could inject her dreams into the general's sleep and the sleep of those Grumman people. Into the dreams of the citizens of Minot, of North Dakota, of the country, of the world. If she could do that, she might not have them herself. If she could do that, she'd be able to go to the gravesite.

CHAPTER TWENTY-SEVEN

As a member of Working Group A, the Chamber of Commerce committee supporting the GBSD program, Rasmussen was dutifully present that Saturday to hear General Clayton, Ellen Conklin, Claudia Cumming and others make their presentations. The truth be told, he was unhappy he'd joined Group A because participating took too much time from his busy practice and he hated burdening his partners with the extra work of covering for him.

During a morning break he stepped out of the Grand Hotel and saw the small gathering—it could not be called a crowd—around Edna O'Hare, who sat behind a card table handing out leaflets. He saw Karen Haugen, one of his patients, among the group. Was she holding up a sign?

As he approached, he heard Edna mention submarines and then watched as Clayton departed with Claudia Cummings. She reminded him of a newspaper photo he'd once seen of Christian Barnard, the first physician to perform a human heart transplant, walking with his entourage amidst photographers, their flashbulbs popping around him. A few steps behind Barnard walked a stunning blonde woman in a form-fitting suit. He had wondered what their relationship was, his thoughts prurient. And now, on seeing Clayton and Cummings together, that question recurred. Prurient thoughts occurred to him more frequently these days.

He took a flyer, folded it in quarters, tucked it into a back pocket, and returned to the presentations. Once, during another break, he read it.

The man who'd been sitting next to him asked, "Hey, Doc, what do you think of that?"

"The Minuteman is over fifty years old," said Rasmussen, automatically mouthing a GBSD booster's talking point and dodging the question. "It needs to be replaced."

Holding up the flyer he asked, "Have you read it?"

"Nah. I just read their signs. There's a saying in German, 'Jeder jeck ist anders'. Every kook is different. They've got a right to talk baloney and I've got a right to ignore it."

"I think that's the right attitude," said Rasmussen. "They're not hurting anyone."

———

His wife had slowly become distant over the years because his long hours at work left him little family time. She remained civil, though she did occasionally comment on the hold his work had taken of him.

"It's really unnecessary," she would say. "They'll still worship you if you take care of yourself."

And when he told her he'd been invited to join working

group A, she said, "Is that really necessary? Do they really need you?"

"Well, Darlene, it's the civic thing to do and I think it would be good to have a doctor in the group."

"Why?"

"Uh... For balance."

"That doesn't make any sense."

She was right. His answer hadn't made any sense. He didn't respond.

He even worked on Saturdays, though he'd taken a few hours this Saturday to attend part of the Grumman presentation. He returned to the office to see patients. He was preparing to leave when a mother and her eleven-year-old son arrived by cab. The boy had torn the flesh of his forearm when, taking a shortcut home, he'd climbed a chain-link fence, the jagged fence top snagging his forearm as he jumped off.

Fortunately his arteries were untouched and because he had the presence of mind to keep the arm elevated, bleeding was not excessive.

Rasmussen injected lidocaine along the side of the wound and then sewed it up. The boy did not speak but winced with each stitch.

When Rasmussen had finished, he gently asked, "Mrs. Olsen, why didn't you go to the emergency room?"

"But Dr. Rasmussen, you're our doctor and you're wonderful."

What could he say to that?

"That didn't hurt too bad," said Joey Olsen. "Thank you."

"No more fence climbing. Doctor's orders," said Rasmussen.

"Yes, sir."

———

When she saw him in the kitchen, Darlene Rasmussen came in from the garden, staring at her watch as if she'd just missed a flight. Rasmussen hesitated before approaching to give her the customary kiss on the cheek. Over the years, their marriage had grown staid if not starchy. Indeed, it was as if they were only actors, playing husband and wife. The high tides of his libido were minimally higher than the low tides. He approached her every ten days or so, but she smiled weakly and said something that always meant the same thing: not tonight. When he approached her on Sunday afternoons, she would have other plans and, he admitted to himself, he didn't truly assert himself, nor even express frustration. The marriage was not loveless—or maybe it was —but it certainly was sexless. He understood that his work was a large part of the problem, but that was out of his control he thought.

"Sorry I'm late," he said.

"Robert called. They gave him a desk."

"Oh, that's good."

"I'll miss him at Christmas," she said. "I miss him already."

"It's a Catholic country. I'm sure someone will make him welcome at Christmas."

"I'm not talking about him missing me. I'm talking about me missing him."

"I was just trying to make you feel better," he said, immediately regretting his choice of words, regretting even having spoken. She didn't want to be *made* to do anything.

He would have handled a grieving parent better than he was doing now. Silence was called for.

Should he leave the room, to return in a few minutes? Or should he, with feigned nonchalance, look to see what the refrigerator might contain of interest.

Though when he had looked into it in the past, it was often empty, at least to his eyes. And then, with the ingredients from the same empty fridge, his wife would prepare a tasty meal.

If he left the room too quickly it would look like what it was. Escape. If he looked into the fridge too quickly it would look like what it was. Escape. So he stood still.

He put his arms around her as soon as the first teardrop straggled down her cheek. Finally he could do something more comforting than speak, though his timing had to be right and this time it was.

Relieved, she made him a chicken-and-rice dish accompanied by a glass of white wine. He told her about Joey Olsen's arm and then about the odd confrontation between Edna O'Hare and a general. He didn't speak of the leaflet's troubling arguments, which he had yet to find fault with.

In the living room after dinner, she sewed one-inch squares of cloth, each with a unique pattern and color scheme, into their individual little windows in a cathedral window quilt already consisting of almost a thousand framed pieces. By any standard it was a masterpiece.

Rasmussen sat across from her, computer on his lap, verifying the flyer's facts and figures. Damn if they didn't match with the reliable sources he'd examined. The submarines, for example, could indeed fire twenty ballistic missiles, each missile able to carry five thermonuclear warheads. A single submarine should be deterrent enough.

"Jesus!"

"What's wrong?"

"Oh, something I read surprised me."

"Well, are you going to tell me or is it a secret?"

He took the flyer from his pocket and read it aloud. Darlene put the quilt aside. He put the flyer back into his pocket.

"So if we have ten submarines at sea at any one time they could hit Russia with as many hydrogen bombs as there are windows on that quilt."

Darlene picked another square of cloth, then examined the quilt's border for an area in which the piece would be harmonious.

"And what if they destroy the submarines?"

"There've been studies. There's no plausible way of destroying them all and the submarines that are going to replace the ones we have will be even quieter. Locating, tracking, getting into range of and then destroying a submarine out at sea is almost impossible."

"So what do you think about the stuff you just read me? I mean, you're supposed to be a rocket booster—no pun intended—aren't you?"

"I don't know what I think."

"Well," said Darlene, "if all that's true, then we shouldn't waste a lot of money on new missiles, should we?"

"That's the logical conclusion. Yes."

"But how come this is only being talked about now? And anyway I can't see you putting in—" She was about to say, "a lot of extra time." He had no "extra time." If he had any time at all outside of work, it should have been family time. She stopped talking, but he didn't seem to notice.

———

Rasmussen spent the next forty minutes reading *The Future of the ICBM Force: Should the Least Valuable Leg of the Triad Be Replaced?* an article on the internet by a nuclear arms control expert.

That night, after lying in bed for thirty-five minutes, sheep counting having failed him, he arose to get a shot of rum. His wife was awake when he returned to bed.

"Is it bothering you that much?"

They said their good-nights. She rolled away from him, almost to the edge of the bed. He remained sitting up in the dark, sipping his rum.

Having put the horror of thermonuclear war out of his mind, he explored the implications for him personally believing what he now believed: that the Minuteman must not be replaced by a modern and extravagantly expensive new weapon, indeed, that the Minuteman itself should be removed. How was it possible that his mind was so easily changed? Or had he never had faith in the Minuteman in the first place? When had the topic of missiles ever come up in conversation at the office, at home, at a party, at a soccer game, anywhere that he could remember? They were literally out of sight, out of mind.

He finished his rum, put the glass on the night table, lay down, and gave thanks for the warm bed, for his good life, and for domestic tranquility if not—" Well, nothing was perfect.

The alarm awoke him at five the next morning as usual. He took a good look at himself in the mirror, asking if he were still sure he really believed what he thought he'd believed the night before.

At the office there was no such thing as free time. Even at lunch, when he had lunch, he talked about patients, office finances, diagnoses, or related matters. Today, however, Rasmussen spoke for a minute with his partners Rich Kovacs and Ben Mazurski, handing them copies he'd made of O'Hare's flyer.

"I'm curious what you guys think of this."

They took the flyers and got back to work.

CHAPTER TWENTY-EIGHT

Claudia Cummings was born in Las Vegas, not a hundred miles from the family's home in the little Mojave Desert community of Prickly Pear, California. Though she enjoyed and was good at her job writing for her high school newspaper, her parents urged her to become a doctor. Prickly Pear was doctorless, a common problem throughout rural America.

The last thing she should be was a reporter. They were only a little less disappointed that her college major was public relations than they would have been had it been journalism.

But she found a job at the prestigious New York public relations firm of Jinks, Nixon, Brinkwater, and Spitz only a few years after college graduation and, because she was spunky, ambitious and—it must be noted, attractive—was soon given important responsibilities, the most important of which was temporarily filling in for Grumman's staff public relations person who was out on prolonged sick leave.

Cummings main responsibility was assuring, as far as she could in her position, public support for the GBSD project.

Paid well and seeing no reason to marry, she had an active and varied sex life and was amused by the thought that some people might have referred to her as a slut puppy, slut no longer quite the pejorative it once had been, and puppy never having been one. She reveled in the impropriety of the description, which contrasted with her public presentation of serious professionalism. With two personas she felt special. Work and play, though, were separated by a steel fence. She cooled noticeably when any man at work showed that kind of interest in her.

She had been intrigued by the young man who'd stood by O'Hare's side. With those feathers in his hat and a witch as a companion, was he supposed to have been a wizard? Well, he'd cast a little spell on her. Whether it will come to anything, who knows, she thought, noting the unintentional pun. What a dirty mind you have, Claudia. Sweet and dirty.

She drew the curtain closed on erotic mental images. She had work to do.

Sitting on the bed in her hotel room she picked up the phone and called.

"Mr. Schmidt, hello, this is Claudia Cummings. Do you have a few minutes?"

Her message was simple. Neither the general nor the vice president of the GBSD team was pleased, to put it mildly, with that little protest, though it wouldn't—couldn't—make any difference in the long run. Nevertheless, prudence demanded that it be discouraged, and if that was not feasible, to find out who was behind it. Whose manure pile did that weed spring from? It was hard to believe that it sprang from the old lady's herself. Schmidt couldn't have been more willing to comply than if she'd asked him to keep breathing.

Next she called Mathew Johnson.

"Well, you know the chamber of commerce is totally supportive," he said. "We'll do whatever you think would be helpful, but frankly people in Minot are simply going to think she's a crank and ignore her."

"The GBSD team is grateful for your support and you may well be right, but we would appreciate it if you would find out what you can about this protest. Speak individually with those three, not with them in a group. Just say you're interested, or better, that you're fascinated by what they have to say. Don't be critical or they won't speak up. Oh, and get me the names of the two young people who were with her."

CHAPTER TWENTY-NINE

Grumman Missile Team Visits Minot dominated the first page of the *Minot Daily News*, followed, three pages later, by General Argues with Witch over Rockets, which either mildly amused or mildly annoyed readers. A few, though, were outraged. Why would anyone from this area wish to question Grumman's outreach to the community, which promised contracts, jobs, and all-around support for the city and the air force base?

They'd be installing the new rockets and removing the old ones for years, teams of people staying at Minot's hotels, eating at Minot's restaurants, going to Minot' shops, renting Minot's, tools, tractors, and trucks. The list went on.

———

LETTERS TO THE EDITOR
RE: General Argues with Witch over Rockets.

Not ironically this protestor dresses as an evil person trying to rid the air force base of a good thing. Some people are just plain ignorant.

Pete Gunderson, Minot

RE: General Argues with Witch Over Rockets

The Grumman team comes here to form a partnership so they can be ready on the first day to work with our businesses to everyone's advantage. This woman has obviously been infected with some vile pro-Russian disarmament propaganda. It makes me sick. These missiles have kept us safe for over fifty years.

Ralph Peterson

———

Of the readers of Amy Haugen's article, a scant number were moved to doubt the value of the Minuteman missiles or the need to replace them with new missiles. How could doubt be seeded if there was no seed, that is if there were no details of O'Hare's argument in the report?

Amy Haugen had considered putting the details into her article but in the end removed them. As it was, the piece would irk her husband. Repeating Edna's arguments would have made Amy seem sympathetic to them. Indeed, she thought Edna had gotten the better of the general.

CHAPTER THIRTY

Rows of seats in a semi-circle faced the dais. Draped behind the chairman's seat hung the United States flag. Steven Jones, Chairman of the House Armed Services Committee called the meeting to order and welcomed the outside experts who would present their perspectives on nuclear deterrence policy. He made introductory remarks.

"We'll go ahead and get started if everyone will grab their seats. Thank you, all, and I want to welcome our witnesses. We are here today to discuss the Nuclear Posture Review and future nuclear policy.

"I think this is an incredibly important topic to discuss. Two things I want to make clear at the start. I completely support a strong and robust nuclear deterrent. We need nuclear weapons in the world that we live in today in order to deter our adversaries and meet our national security objectives as a country. Personally I don't think that's debatable. We have certainly Russia with its nuclear weapons, China as well, rising threats from North Korea and Iran. And the best and most straightforward way to deter people from using nuclear weapons is if you are in a position to assure that they will be destroyed if they do. So having a nuclear deterrent is incredibly important.

"Second our nuclear weapons have been around for a long time and I have no doubt that we need to upgrade and update those weapons, look at what is working, what isn't working. We need to recapitalize our nuclear structure. What I question is whether we need to do it to the tune of 1.2 trillion dollars, as both the 2010 and 2018 nuclear posture reviews called into question. And this hearing, I hope, will help us answer that question. Do we have to have everything we had before plus what the administration is talking about adding?

"The congressional budget office just recently went through and analyzed all that is in the Nuclear Posture Review and gave some options in terms of 'we could not do that and here's how much money we would save.' Those are questions that need to be asked for several reasons. First of all, we have a twenty-two trillion-dollar debt that is going up by about a trillion dollars. In fact, it increased dramatically in the first quarter of this year over the first quarter of last year. We also have a large number of needs.

"We also have a large number of needs within the national security environment. Forget for the moment everything else that the federal government does.

"We've heard the secretary of the air force say she needs twenty-five percent more aircraft. Our missile defense program said we need a dramatic increase. The Navy still says it needs a three hundred fifty-five-ship navy, which is significantly more than we have now. The Army would like to build toward an in strength, which is substantially larger than it is right now. That math doesn't work. We are not going to have enough money to do all of that.

"So we have to think, in part, what can we not do. Where can we save money? And within the nuclear weapons area I believe that a credible deterrent can be presented for less than is called for in the nuclear posture review.

"Now I understand that a bipartisan group of people disagree with me on that, but a bipartisan group of people agree with me so we're here to have that discussion and that debate. So number one is can we save money here and still meet our national security objectives. Still deter our adversaries because, if we can, it's something we should talk about. And these are things people have contemplated.

"Former Secretary of Defense, Jim Mattis, when asked if the triad was necessary said he wasn't sure and talked about well if we had a dyad and didn't have the ICBMs then we would have a much smaller risk of miscalculation based on a false alarm.

"A number of former defense officials, including former Chairman of the Armed Services Committee, Sam Nunn, former Secretary William Perry, former Secretary George Schultz have said that we are stumbling toward a nuclear catastrophe because we have not rebooted any arms control discussion or any sort of discussion with the Russians since the end of the Cold War on how we prevent an accidental nuclear war.

"We are about to kick off another nuclear arms race."

CHAPTER THIRTY-ONE

Sylvia Wong, Senator Hennings's girl Friday was assertive, if not aggressive, even at times disagreeing with him over one policy stance or another. Ordinarily polite but never submissive, she could curse as well as any soldier on the battlefield, but refrained from cursing in meetings with the senator. She was no fool. Her mother had taught her prudence; her father, cursing.

She'd heard some troubling news and asked to speak with him. He sat across from her, not at his boat-sized desk, with the room's extra large window behind him, but, like her, in a stuffed chair in the cozy sitting area.

"How's your day going?" asked Hennings.

"Oh, fine, sir, except for that little situation I mentioned."

He gestured for her to go on.

"As you know the chairman of the armed services committee is inclined to deny funding for the GBSD, though the composition of the house may change in the next election. But for the time being we have a political fight on our hands. Now, support in Minot for the replacement—I was going to say, 'couldn't be stronger', but that's not precisely correct. A tiny contingent of activists is campaigning not only against the GBSD but against the Minuteman itself. I don't like it."

"They will have absolutely no effect on the town's support," said Hennings.

"You are probably correct about that, sir. But I'm not thinking about the town. I'm thinking of all the senators and congressman who do not have missile wings in their states. The ICBM coalition is going to have a fight on its hands to get funding."

"We've already contracted for the study," said Hennings. "The ball is rolling. Our interest—I mean the coalition's interest—is great enough that we're willing to do some horse trading even if we're at a disadvantage given that the other side knows how important this is to us."

Sylvia Wong leaned slightly forward putting her hands, which had been resting on her lap, on her knees. The senator had granted her this private time and she was worried he might see her concerns as unrealistic or trivial.

"The protest has been written about in the Minot Daily News. These people are publicity savvy. One of them dresses like a witch and there's this handsome young couple to draw in the youth set. If this goes on it may reach other state newspapers."

Senator Hennings looked skeptical.

"The whole state wants the replacement, not just Minot."

Was he really blind to the danger or was he just testing or teasing her?

"North Dakota has ten daily newspapers, eighty-two weeklies, and four alternatives. It has thirty-one TV channels. You can guess as well as I how many Facebook or Twitter users there are. If, like that virus, this protest jumps from the local paper to regional papers and then to national news, we'll have an epidemic on our hands. Some people inevitably will question the need for this critical weapon system. If the general public is against it no horse trading will be possible."

Hennings fleetingly touched his forehead with a knuckle as if to wake it up.

"You're always giving me trouble, Sylvia. What do you propose doing about it?"

"I'd get in touch with the chamber of commerce and the newspaper. Explain that this sort of reporting is clearly not in the national interest. With a little oomph in the explanation."

"Perhaps," said Jennings, almost as if it were his idea, "you might speak to someone in the Chamber of Commerce, just to get the lay of the land, but don't speak with anyone on the paper. I don't think that's kosher. And don't forget that time the secretary of state cursed out a radio journalist after the interview and damn if she didn't go describe the whole encounter on her next broadcast. Millions of people heard about his temper and his fondness for the f-word. No. No. Let's leave the press out of this. Besides, it's wrong, like I said, it's wrong."

———

It was not the president of the chamber of commerce she reached when she called, but instead a particularly avid member with no official position in the chamber, who, when he wasn't in his office filling orders for building supplies, was hobnobbing with the town's bigwigs, or hanging around the chamber office. On this day, the president was out so the secretary had the long-time member take the call in the president's office, noting that the man she was about to speak with was an alderman.

"Chamber of Commerce. Earnest Schmidt here."

Ms. Wong introduced herself and then asked about the old woman and the two kids who were getting into the news. Who were they? How much influence did they wield? Were people paying attention to them? What did people think of them? Were they associated with any organized groups? Who were these groups?

Chagrined that Edna O'Hare was his sister-in-law, Earnest Schmidt did not mention it. He answered as best he could, reassuring her that no one was paying attention and that he wouldn't be surprised if the paper ignored her from now on. She seemed pleased by this reassurance and shortly thereafter the conversation ended.

Unbelievable! Senator Hennings was making inquiries about Edna's shenanigans. His pique at the old fool increased. She was going to make him look like a fool by association. He could hear their voices. "Do something about her."

Discrediting her would be nice. What if she really thought she was a witch? Or just as good or better, what if everyone else thought she thought she was a witch. What if everyone thought she was crazy? Maybe he could even have her declared incompetent to handle her own affairs, so that Fiona could take charge of the farm. He knew, however, that he was as likely to get what was rightfully his as he was to grow wings and a halo.

He had to do something before people in the Chamber of

Commerce or in the town council began associating her anti-GBSD stance with him.

He'd once watched a TV program in which family members angry at the patriarch tried to declare him insane. They said he claimed to be Odin, that he talked to the moon, that he'd started brewing mead, which was unpalatable, and could have been deadly if anyone had drunk any. Of course, this went nowhere. But there was an idea in it.

––––––

Schmidt was acquainted with a psychotherapist in town, Ted Swensen, a man who had no framed credentials on the wall of his office, and about whom rumors once circulated that he hypnotized clients and examined them to discover any tense muscles or underactive erogenous zones that might be contributing to their distress. Apparently only women benefited from these hands-on explorations. Eventually the rumors ended.

On entering the office Schmidt noted the flat leather sofa on which some people lay during their sessions. It would facilitate Swenson's palpations of his clients, though like the rumors, the examinations likely had ended. After minimal small talk Schmidt made his proposal.

"That's not the thing I ordinarily do, Ernie," said Swenson, "Not that I couldn't do it, you understand. It's just that I'd have to work on it. And there's no guarantee they'd print it."

Writing an op-ed piece is usually something one does out of conviction; for example because the writer believes a certain candidate is unsuitable for public office; or that one must frequently wash one's hands to reduce the chances of getting sick; or that the nearest extra solar planet is too far away for aliens to be buzzing us in flying saucers.

Some people write op-ed pieces to promote themselves, their cause, book, movie or play. It is not difficult to imagine, that some might write a piece because a hidden party has paid them for reasons of their own.

Ted Swenson had never written an op-ed article but couldn't turn down Schmidt's offer of a little hard cash.

"I'll give you some key points," said Schmidt, "but you'll have to do the bulk of it."

"There's no guarantee they'll publish it."

"Let me worry about that."

Swenson got to work. Writing this was harder than he thought it would be.

———

What do I know about witches? And why am I writing about them now? Heaven knows, I have had only a few women in my counseling practice over the years who identified themselves as witches or at least as practicing witchcraft, including sexual magic. But to understand and treat these few women, I have had to understand something of witchcraft myself so I did the research. I even obtained for myself some magical instruments: a boline, a wand, a pentacle, and a chalice. So, what do I know about witches? Some.

But why am I writing about witches at this time? Readers of the daily news making an educated guess will probably be correct. It is because we here in Minot again have a witch, or wannabe witch in our midst. Without identifying my former "witches," I must say this, none of them professed an aversion to self-defense, indeed, their feelings of vulnerability led them to take up witchcraft in the first place. As for these clients' mental problems, I won't get into it.

Which brings us to the to the main topic. What's wrong with our current public "witch?" For one thing—probably the main thing—she's casting aspersions, if not spells, on the collection of rockets that has kept us safe for many years. She wants to get rid of them just like that. And to turn the town against replacing them.

Generally speaking, a psychological councilor should not make diagnoses of patients he or she hasn't met, and I won't except to say there's something seriously wrong with this woman. I have no proof, but she may even be dangerous.

A simple argument: if a wicked person is adamantly against something, that something is probably good.

These are my own personal thoughts.

———

When Earnest Schmidt read what he considered a sorry excuse for an op-ed piece, he just laughed and handed it back to Swenson.

"I don't know exactly what I had in mind, Ted, but there's no way the paper is going to publish this. And what's this stuff about sexual magic? Sounds a bit kooky to me."

"I can take that part out."

"Forget the whole thing."

Indeed, Schmidt did not know what he had in mind when he asked Swenson to write this. All he knew was that it should be damning, should raise the possibility of a series of named psychiatric disorders, and should sound like a considered expert opinion.

"Hey," said Swenson, "I spent valuable time writing this and it wasn't easy. You owe me that money."

"I said I'd pay you for the essay, but I'm not accepting it, so I don't owe you anything.

"How did you ever become an alderman?"

"How did you ever become a counselor?"

They parted in a bipartite huff.

CHAPTER THIRTY-TWO

Makenna Washington's small on-base apartment was not quite like home, indeed, very little like home, where her mother's bucolic watercolors still hung in her old bedroom surrounding the big brass bed that dominated the room. She'd insisted she wanted one for her sixteenth birthday. Fortunately, her father found one in a secondhand store and it still cost a pretty penny, which she only discovered later. He'd also found a makeup table with an ornately framed mirror in carved oak. It doubled as a writing table.

She now sat on her plain bed, surrounded by bare walls of a nondescript tan, and called home, picturing her old room.

Her father answered, delighted to hear from her as he always was.

"How's my rocket girl?" he asked in what had become a customary greeting. She wished it could have been "How's my pilot girl?" but that's not how things had worked out. He was still proud of her.

"Okay, Papa, but I have a little problem I'd like your opinion about."

"Fire away. I have opinions to spare."

She recounted her discovery of cheating on the proficiency exam. She had talked to someone who was a good listener, but she still didn't know what to do.

"Sounds like you got to tell somebody. These launch people got control of all those bombs. We got to be able to trust them. If they cheating it means they don't know their stuff. That's bad. You don't have to name your friend. Make up a story of how you found out."

This was exactly what she knew he would say. The value of asking him what she should do, she realized, was just hearing herself talk about the dilemma. Telling him the details of the situation would be no more valuable than describing the missiles themselves.

"Thanks, Papa. I'll think about it some more. How's everything going out there? I miss you."

"I miss you, too, sugar. We all do. Just a minute. I'll get Mama."

Tyrone was still working for them. He hadn't been dating anyone and was brooding about her, hurt at her decision to join the air force instead of going to college not far from the farm. He had never been interested in college. He enjoyed being outdoors, working on machines, and watching things grow. But he'd begun talking about a trade or technical school. He always asked how Makenna was doing when he heard she'd called them.

"Why don't you write him?" asked her mother.

"I am writing." But she always procrastinated before answering his letters because she didn't want to keep his hopes up, but that was stupid, wasn't it? And what would it be like when she returned home for a vacation? Life was complicated.

Makenna also told her mother about her dilemma, and for the same reason, to hear herself thinking aloud about it.

"Those are atomic bombs we're talking about," she said. "You want people in charge of those things to know what they're doing. This is scary stuff, Makenna. You're so smart. You'll find a way to fix things up."

CHAPTER THIRTY-THREE

Edna began to get a trickle of phone calls. How people got her number she wasn't sure. Most of the callers were upset with her and felt the need to voice their opinions, chief among them the necessity of replacing the Minuteman. She always tried to understand how the replacement would affect the caller personally. None of those with businesses sounded embarrassed when she noted that their laundry, restaurant, hotel, construction company or machine rental business—among others—would benefit by an influx of air force missile installers. Those who did not stand to profit personally, nevertheless mentioned others who would.

The same caller might remind her two or three times during the conversation, as if she were demented and needed reminding, that "This affects the whole town."

Those that convinced themselves that she did not under-stand the situation might express pity or at the extreme, say something nasty and hang up.

She got a few anonymous calls from people who thought

she was right but were fearful lest the townspeople learn of their doubts.

Still, the number of calls was less than twenty. And she stopped answering calls whose number she didn't recognize. They were a further burden.

———

At a coffee break at work, Rich Kovacs told Rasmussen that he'd read the flyer and that it made sense but that trying to stop the construction and placement of new missiles with flyers was a David-and-Goliath thing.

"Hey, Andy, I guess that O'Hare woman is David. Are you planning to be her second?"

"I just wanted your opinion and you said it makes sense."

"It does make sense but there's a whole other side to the argument that I haven't studied."

CHAPTER THIRTY-FOUR

Rasmussen's office partner, Rich Kovacs, had examined the arguments for the land-based missiles but they seemed less convincing than the arguments against them.

"I did the research," said Kovacs, "and I think you're right. We're less likely to have a nuclear war if we get rid of them."

"You sound annoyed," said Rasmussen.

"Yeah, maybe a little. What am I supposed to do, now that I think what I think? I'm a physician."

"I'll tell you what I'm going to do," said Rasmussen.

———

The president, the vice president, the mayor, and four aldermen sat behind what looked like a long judge's bench facing those attending. The venue resembled a courtroom. A lectern stood facing the councilors.

Ordinarily these bimonthly city council meetings were sparsely attended, usually by people who had some specific concerns they wished to present to the council. Today, was no different except for the presence of a woman in black, wearing a tall conical hat.

Following the roll call, pledge of allegiance, approval of minutes, and the adoption of several resolutions came the personal appearances.

Edna O'Hare was the first at the lectern.

"Your honor, members of the council, thank you for giving me this opportunity to speak. My name is Edna O'Hare. I'm here to talk about the Ground-Based Nuclear Deterrent, generally known as the GBSD."

In her allotted five minutes she gave reasons that the GBSD must not replace the Minuteman and the Minuteman itself should be scrapped.

Except for Rasmussen, the council members, looked grave, not having been fully prepared for this. When she'd finished and it appeared his fellow councilors had no questions for her, indeed wishing they had never given her this platform, which included a YouTube video of the meeting, Rasmussen spoke.

"I would like to add that I agree with Ms. O'Hare. As a physician I feel obligated to share my concern about these land-based missiles which make nuclear war by mistake more likely than it would be without them. I look at this as a public health issue. If I were aware that a certain food was tainted, say lettuce harboring E. coli, I would warn people against it."

The council was stunned, and alderman Earnest Schmidt was incensed, but the mayor, in order to minimize the added attention O'Hare would get if aldermen began vociferously objecting, prudently moved on to the next agenda item without comment.

When the meeting was over, Mayor Gustafson asked that the aldermen remain for a closed door session. After the visitors and the videographer had left the room, the mayor said, "What in blazes was that all about Andy? Why didn't you warn us?"

At the last minute, before anyone but the mayor knew about the change but was ignorant of the topic, Rasmussen had put Edna on the agenda. Had Schmidt or some of the others known, they might have let her talk but would not have allowed her to be videoed for YouTube.

No one thought quickly enough to stop the video from being made.

"I'm not sure. Maybe I thought… I don't know." Two little white lies. He felt bad about it, but what was there to do.

"This is like stabbing Minot in the back," said Schmidt. "You should be ashamed of yourself. Or to put it another way, you gave Minot a black eye. There are some more choice words I could use but I won't."

"We had to say what we said," said Rasmussen, "but you know as well as I, this isn't going to stop the GBSD program so why get so riled up about it?"

"I told you why. It makes Minot look bad to Grumman. They'll be less likely to contract with our businesses now."

"That's ridiculous. Where else are they going to go for supplies? Grand Forks? They're working on the Minot Air Force Base, remember. And Minot happens to be right next to it."

"I take it you're quitting Working Group A," said Gustafson.

Earnest Schmidt said, "I'm disappointed in you, Andy. People look up to you. They respect you. What good does it do to put doubts into their minds if it's not going to stop progress. And you know what else, some people are going to be scared, scared that the missiles make it unsafe to live here."

"People are scared of rattlesnakes and that's a good thing," said Rasmussen.

Schmidt couldn't contain himself. He stood, wagged an index figure at the turncoat, and stormed out of the room, only to bump into Edna O'Hare, who stood on the other side of the heavy wood doors, knocking her against the wall. They glared at each other silently. Before Edna regained her relative composure, Schmidt was gone.

CHAPTER THIRTY-FIVE

Well, she'd set up a table at Grumman's industry day, argued with a general, handed out leaflets, and spoken at Minot's town council. She planned to have a parade. She was campaigning, so why was she still unable to visit his gravesite? It was not as if she never spoke with him.

"James," she might say, "I'm working on it." Something simple like that. Of course, she rarely spoke aloud, or even whispered. So maybe she was just talking to him in her mind. Nothing wrong with that, was there?

When the question occurred to her she put off any prolonged effort to answer it as she might put off unpacking a box into which an unwieldy object with sharp edges had been crammed. Of course, she knew she was avoiding bad feelings but that was as far as she went.

CHAPTER THIRTY-SIX

Rasmussen's partners left at around six, but hardworking, dependable, and obsessive Margaret Axelson, R.N., was at her desk completing unfinished notes, reviewing the next day's schedule, and simply waiting for Rasmussen to call it a day before she would be comfortable also calling it a day. It was seven thirty.

"Go home, Margaret," called Rasmussen for the third time from his office.

"I'm working on it."

When the phone rang, instead of letting the answering machine do its job, she answered it. She explained to the caller that the office was closed but after some back and forth, she muted the phone and went to Rasmussen's office.

"There's a woman on the phone who thinks she has breast cancer and insists on seeing you. I told her the office was closed but she seemed to know you were still here. She has no lesions, bleeding, infection. She was vague about a lump. Nothing she said sounded urgent, but she was very upset. She's not one of our patients. I checked."

"What's her name?"

"Claudia Cummings."

"Holy smoke!"

"You know her?"

"She's with the Grumman group meeting with the city's officials and business people. Tell her to come in."

He looked at his watch.

"I hate to ask you to stay a little longer, but would you?"

"Of course."

"Thank you. You're a peach."

———

She wore dark slacks and a blue cotton blouse that matched the color of her eyes. Her glistening jet black hair was loose. She smelled faintly of apples.

In his office she explained that for some time now she'd been worrying that she had breast cancer and today she awoke convinced of it. She was growing more panicky as the day went on.

"I know I sound crazy. My mother died of breast cancer on this date."

She knew he didn't consider this an emergency and thanked him contritely for seeing her. Her last mammogram was over two years ago. She dabbed her eyes with a hand-kerchief.

He led her to a room, had her sit on the examining table; took her blood pressure and pulse; looked at her eyes, ears, nose and throat; and palpated her neck.

"Aren't you going to examine me?"

"I am examining you. I'm not finished yet."

He put his stethoscope on her back and asked her to cough a few times as he repositioned it.

"Okay. Now I'm going to step out for a minute. Please take off your blouse and bra, cover your chest completely with this cloth and lay on the table. I'll be back in a minute."

———

Rasmussen knocked on the door and opened it. He stepped in followed by Nurse Axelson.

"Margaret's here as chaperone."

"Oh," she said softly. Did she sound disappointed?

Standing at the examination table, Rasmussen exposed Cummings' perfect creamy white left breast, the size of a small cantaloupe, with a pert pink nipple on a quarter-sized areola. Starting at the top edge of the breast furthest from him, Rasmussen, with fingers flat, gently pressed as he moved them spiraling inward.

She looked him in the eye the entire time, all indications of anxiety gone. She appeared entirely relaxed.

Until he covered the left breast and exposed the right, he'd maintained his ordinary medical objectivity, or so he thought, but on seeing a single black hair emerging from the edge of her areola, a disturbing but not unpleasant image, flashed through his mind: a dark mons pubis below. He was almost certain that his face revealed nothing but was still glad Margaret was behind him. He imagined that Cummings was reading, or trying to read, his mind, but there was nothing he could do about that. Her expression though, had not changed even as he became aroused. After glancing at her flat abdomen, he concluded the examination by palpating her axillae, which to his amazement he'd almost forgotten to do.

"It tickles."

"I'm sorry," he said.

Back in the office, safely and discretely behind his desk, he recalled the sight and feel of her breasts.

"There's nothing wrong, Ms. Cummings, but I can certainly understand your anxiety. How long are you going to be in town? We could schedule a mammogram."

"Oh, no. I feel so much better, Doctor Rasmussen. Thank you so very much. If I can ever do you a favor, please let me know."

———

The next day he recalled a dream. He stood on a ledge high above a small pool of cool, dark surprisingly inviting water. He wanted to dive in, but large rocks surrounded the pool. He stood there undecided. If he missed the pool he'd be dashed upon the rocks. It didn't take long to interpret that dream. Too bad there was no one he could tell it to.

CHAPTER THIRTY-SEVEN

Moody at times, especially after talking with his mother or brother, and ambivalent about his decision to stay and help out, Will still energized Edna. Indeed, she wondered how she'd managed before without his encouragement.

One day she thought of going to the mall. She probably wouldn't be allowed to set up there, but what about just sitting on the octagonal wood bench surrounding the large clock standing tall in the mall's center? The witch, her picket sign and flyers beside her, would smile at the curious shoppers. She might even do a little shopping herself. She could think of no legal objection to her just sitting there minding her own business.

"I think I'll go to the mall."

"They won't let you carry your sign around in there," said Will.

"I know."

"I'd better go with you. You might get in trouble."

She did not tell him how happy she was to hear this, but her smile gave her away. Nor did she mention having invited Karen, who was unsure she wanted more public exposure.

———

The Dakota Square mall housed the usual assortment of stores and shops and, in addition, army, air force, and marine recruiting offices. Edna sat on the bench facing a jewelry store across the spacious courtyard, having placed her flyers to her right, her sign to her left. Will sat next to the flyers.

This Saturday morning business was brisk, and not only for the mall. They'd only been here for half an hour and already five people had taken flyers and others had stopped to talk and ask questions:

"Why are you dressed as a witch?"

"Are you the lady who made that fuss at the Grumman show?"

"You know, this is just what the Russians want. Unilateral disarmament."

"I don't think this is a good idea."

"You are a brave woman. That's all I can say."

"I'll take one of those."

"Well, bless your heart."

A man got overheated, but he posed no physical threat as had the football players. He kept saying that the experts had decided we needed these rockets, and she was no expert.

"If you mean I'm not a rocket scientist, that is correct. But you don't have to be a rocket scientist to see that these things are sitting ducks. They put us—the whole world actually—in danger."

"You are wrong, madam. You are wrong."

When, to Edna's and Will's delight, Karen Haugen arrived, Edna said she'd like a cup of coffee.

"I'll bring some back. What would you two like?"

Neither wanted any coffee yet.

When Edna returned she found Will still seated, but Karen engaged with two middle-aged women, one, frowning, in yellow Bermuda shorts and t-shirt, looking as if she needed a vacation, and one in a skirt and blouse, looking puzzled. Edna took a seat and listened as Karen calmly went through the arguments for cancelling the GBSD project.

At around noon, Edna dispatched Will and Karen to bring back some food. They returned with an enchilada for Edna; a bento lunch with rice, asparagus, and sashimi for Karen; and a hamburger for Will. Edna shared her water.

Will and Karen went for a window-shopping walk around the mall, comparing their tastes in jewelry, camping equipment, video games, etc. As they passed a Victoria's Secret window display of models in skimpy panties and bras, Will kept his eyes straight ahead, but Karen stopped to look.

"What do you think?" she asked.

"Trying to answer that question might be walking into quicksand so let me just say, I do like lingerie, but I am against the commodification of women."

"So pick an outfit," she teased.

One of the mannequins had a gap between her teeth. He picked her and her outfit.

"Hmm," said Haugen.

They returned to find an air force recruiter arguing with Edna. The insignia, three stripes on each wing, indicated a rank of e4, senior airman. He was from the base and Karen had met him at a party once.

"You've got no right to come in here and upset people," he said.

"This stuff is upsetting," said Edna softly, "but I do have a right to be here. I didn't ask you to come over and talk with me. I'm not asking anyone to come over. I'm just sitting here minding my own business. They come over to ask me if I'm a witch."

"I wouldn't be surprised if you were."

"Watch it," said Will.

The airman turned to Will.

"Airmen are returning wounded or worse and she's here putting down the air force. And with a base right here. That really stinks."

Will came toward him. "That's your opinion. I fought in Afghanistan; how about you?"

Instead of answering the question, the airman turned to Karen.

"Does your father know you're here?"

"Yes, Danny," said Karen, though it was a lie.

"It's not right," he said. He marched back to his office.

"My goose is probably cooked," said Karen, "though my dad would have found out one way or another."

———

Since her husband died, Edna had not come to town much because her grief or depression, or the even more potent combination of the two, weighed her down. But now in the mall she saw several old friends and acquaintances, all of whom remained friendly even after reading the flyer. They wanted to keep in touch and exchanged telephone numbers and in two cases email addresses.

"This is a very serious matter," said Vera Jansen. "and you know how often I've thought about it? Never. Do you have a website?"

"No, but now that you mention it, I will get one."

Edna turned to Will.

"Right?"

"Yes, ma'am."

———

Early that evening, before Will left for his date with Karen Haugen, they established a website called The Missiles of Minot, which made the case that land-based missiles were completely unnecessary, exorbitantly expensive, and extremely dangerous. The site provided links to sites documenting the arguments. Comments could be left on the site. The day had been productive. Edna was tired and went to bed early but as usual, fearful of dreaming, had trouble falling asleep.

———

They'd made arrangements earlier in the day. Will didn't see why he shouldn't be able to pick her up but she said her parents would then want to meet him.

"So what? Am I an outlaw?"

"No. More like the wolf that my father fears will lead his little girl astray, into the woods, so to speak. You are older and presumably worldlier. He won't like that. He was even suspicious of Jack who is my age."

Will put his hands in his front pockets. He rocked sideways back and forth.

"Aw, shucks, Sergeant Haugen. I ain't never even…uh… I" He sighed. "Okay, Karen, if you don't want me to come over I won't."

An uncomfortable heat rose within her. Why should she allow her father to control her so? She loved him, yes, but he wasn't faultless. She could withstand his disapproval, but what rationale could he have for disliking Will without even knowing him.

"Can you pick me up at six?"

In the Haugen living room that night, Sergeant Roy Haugen, having earlier been asked to be "nice" to Will, did his best to question Karen's date as amiably as he could, given that Will was much older than his daughter and worse, that he was just passing through. What father wouldn't have his misgivings? Only his wife knew the story of how Haugen's sister Maya had disappeared one day after striking up an acquaintance with an older man no one in town knew. Yes, that man was much older than this one, but the parallel was the same.

He'd decided, after painful deliberation, not to tell his daughters the story. He and Maya had been close. Indeed, at times, she had been more a mother to him than their mother had been to either of them. Perhaps she ran away from home and changed her name, escaping the oppressive atmosphere that surrounded them. Didn't he do the same thing by joining the air force? The dark alternative explanation of her disappearance was unbearable to think about. He pictured himself crying in front of his children if he told the tale. Unacceptable.

———

"So what brings you to these parts?" asked Haugen, after Karen had made the introductions.

Will had been coached. He was to be vague, to mention the GBSD, only if he wished to have her and her father turn frosty. He understood what she felt was at stake: a good relationship with him and with her father.

"I was on my way to see my mother but found a job on a farm nearby."

"How long do you plan to stay?"

"Oh, I don't know. For a while. It could be a long time. There's lot of work to do."

"So you're a hired hand."

"Yes, I guess I am."

Something about that answer irked Sergeant Haugen. A frown displaced his forced smile. The guy was working on a farm. Why did it only now occur to him that he was a hired hand? He was a vagabond for sure.

"You guess?"

"We should get going, Dad," said Karen.

"Just a minute," he said gruffly. "What did you do before you decided to see your mother? What kind of work?"

Roy Haugen thought he now saw dishonesty in the man's face and would shortly be fed some bullshit.

"I haven't had a regular job since I was discharged from the marines."

It was as if the curtain had been drawn on the second act of a play that had appeared, in act one, to be a gloomy family drama, but had now revealed itself to be a light-hearted comedy.

"The marines?" said Roy Haugen.

"Yes, I was in Afghanistan."

"He has a Purple Heart," said Karen.

"Karen!" said Will.

"No. No," said Roy Haugen. "I'm glad to hear it. Not that you were wounded. I mean, a couple of my friends were marines." He laughed at the inanity of what he'd said.

Karen took Will by the arm.

"We have to go."

"Have a good time," said Amy.

"Nice meeting you, Sergeant Haugen, Mrs. Haugen."

"Likewise," said Roy Haugen, slightly off balance.

CHAPTER THIRTY-EIGHT

They went to an early showing of a sci fi movie. A small family of extraterrestrials had left their dying planet (shades of global warming) to settle in a little Mojave Desert community where they were in constant fear of being discovered. Karen identified with the heroine, a sixteen-year-old extraterrestrial girl angry at her parents for having tricked her into leaving home. When the movie ended they emerged from darkness into twilight.

They had no plans. Karen suggested they go for a walk on a trail through the woods by the Souris River. In twelve minutes they were there, parking the car on the side of the road. Will took a small blanket from the trunk of the car.

"To sit on," he said.

"Do you always have a blanket with you?"

"Only on special occasions."

He had foreseen the possibility of some exploration of hills and valleys. He was even prepared for a comprehensive expedition, though he was not hopeful.

The moon was almost full, the woods dark. Holding

hands they slowly made their way to the river, walked a short distance, and then, once at the bank, sat on the blanket.

"Do you come here often?" asked Will.

"That's a pickup line, isn't it?"

"Not an original one. I once read a book where a demon picked up a girl in a bar by telling her he had a tail, which he really did have."

"I've never been here before but a girlfriend of mine told me about this place."

Will put his arm around her, kissing her on the lips, a lingering kiss. They lay down next to each other, she supine, he prone and up on elbows. The next kiss invited her tongue to tango with his and it did. He put his hand on a breast. She stiffened.

"You're supposed to ask permission to do that," she said.

"May I touch your breasts?" he whispered.

She sighed. He rolled over on his back so he wouldn't be tempted to ignore her wishes.

"Yes, but only that," she said finally.

He unbuttoned her blouse.

"May I take off your bra?"

He saw her nod in the moonlight.

She had to roll a bit to the side for him to reach the clasp.

When he began to kiss her nipples without asking permission, she didn't protest.

He put his hand under her skirt waist and stroked her abdomen in circles, again without asking.

"May I touch you?"

A long pause.

"I guess, but nothing else."

She wanted very much for him to touch her, but her

excitement made it hard for her to think. What if she'd say "yes" instead of "I guess?" What would that make her?

Now simultaneously he gently nibbled on a nipple while stroking her below. Her back arched.

"Would you like to…make love?"

Her ardor evaporated.

She sat up.

"I wasn't raised like that," she said, aware of the incongruity, given her fierce enjoyment of what she had been experiencing.

"Are you a virgin?"

It wasn't a bad word, but she hesitated before applying it to herself.

"I know I'm old-fashioned, but I think intimacy should be reserved for marriage."

Deflated now, Will was annoyed. He could not say that she'd been a tease, a tease in the worst sense of the word, but he nevertheless felt as if he'd been teased. He didn't want to be angry with her, but he was.

He sat up and stared at the moon. Maybe if it had been full things would have gone better. Nonsense and he knew it.

"Let's go," said Will.

CHAPTER THIRTY-NINE

Roy Haugen arrived home late and after dinner sat with Amy in the living room. Since the kids were in the house, he kept his voice low.

He'd been on a routine launch site inspection when he got a call to report immediately to the missile wing commandant's office.

———

Colonel Nichols said, "At ease, Sergeant Haugen. Please take a seat.

"First of all, as you know, those grenades haven't turned up, but I'm thinking they may never have been on that Humvee in the first place so I'm looking into the men on duty at the armory that day who loaded the grenades into the vehicle. Anyway, that's just an update.

"I want to tell you about an incident recently that I don't know what to make of. A woman wrote me a letter. Let me read you a part of it. She's describing a visitor here."

. . .

'...the man looked around the room like he was in a daze. Not drunk, mind you, but in some sort of intoxicated state. He appeared frightened of looking at his hands which he kept under the table. He wouldn't look at me but at one point fluttered his fingers at me... It is an outrage that someone who could start World War III is taking drugs.'

Nichols continued. "The man she's referring to was a missile launch officer, at least that's what he told her. Now I don't know what to think. This is the lady people are seeing around town who's antimissile in the first place. Maybe she made this up, though I doubt it. Through my own sources I happen to know your wife is friendly with this lady. Do you know whom I'm talking about?"

"Yes, sir, I do."

"I'd like you to speak with her and find out what you can about the man, if there was a man. How does that sound to you, Sergeant?"

"Fine, sir. I'll get right on it."

"That O'Hare woman may be a nuisance but she sure as hell is right to get ticked off about drug use on base, not to mention drug use by a launch officer. I'm authorizing you to question anyone else on the base you think might be involved. That includes those with higher rank. Just tell them Colonel Nichols sent you. And if you think you've got the bastard, get a couple of MPs if you have to and search his place."

"Would you like a drink?" said Amy, seeing her husband's distress. This was a miserable assignment, sure to cause ill will, the identification of the airman probably impossible to discover unless O'Hare had failed to mention some distinguishing feature like an eagle tattoo on his forehead. He saw this assignment as punishment over the grenade loss, though he clearly had nothing to do with that.

"That's a good idea. Gin and tonic, please."

They drank together.

"I'll talk with her, too," said Amy. "Let me do it first."

"Please do. Get a description of the guy, but don't worry too much about identifying him. I'm going to question every single launch officer who was off duty that day. Maybe someone will be a bad liar."

But he got a better idea. After compiling a list of the thirty off duty launch control officers on the day of the visit, he also obtained their identification photos. He told his wife to scratch her visit to O'Hare. He'd go see her.

———

He wore his dress uniform, which like his other uniforms displayed the insignia of the 91st Missile Wing: an upright fist in an armored glove holding three bolts of lightning and an olive branch. Under the escutcheon the words, "Poised for Peace."

Before this moment he'd given no thought to how he knocked on doors. But an intense door-knocking could be frightening. He did not wish to frighten her. Nor did he wish to knock so gently that she didn't hear him. To complicate matters somewhat, this was a screen door. He knocked on the metal frame.

She opened the door and welcomed him in, assuming as he later discovered, that he was here to accept her open invitation to all the airmen on base to drop by for coffee and cake.

"I'm Edna O'Hare as you know. Welcome."

She held out her hand for him to shake.

"I'm Roy Haugen. I'd like to speak with you about the intoxicated visitor you had a while ago."

They sat at the dining room table.

"Colonel Nichols was as distressed as you by the thought that airmen may be taking mind-altering drugs. I'm going to show you some pictures."

Less than a third of the way through the photos she said, "That's the man."

It was as easy as that. Sergeant Haugen was in the security squadron and didn't know the launch officers well, if at all. This man was a stranger to him, but Haugen would soon discover who he is.

"We haven't proven that this man was on drugs, so the colonel would prefer you not talk about this with anyone else until we have the truth. It would look bad for the base."

"I've already talked with a few people about it."

Haugen wrinkled his nose as if smelling something bad. He considered asking her to talk with no one else about it, but thought he'd said enough.

"Are you going to make it public if it's true? I mean, that the missileers are using drugs?"

"You don't care much for the Minuteman, do you?"

"I don't care much for any ground-based ballistic missile. You might as well spray paint bullseyes on the silos. And if we scrapped the GBSD, can you imagine what a hundred billion dollars or so could do for our roads, schools, hospitals, and so on?"

"Is there much support for your position in town?" asked Haugen.

"No, not much, but I've just started."

"Thank you for helping out with the photos."

He had his hand on the doorknob, about to leave when she asked, "You're not related to Karen Haugen, are you?" As soon as she'd said it, she looked worried.

"You know Karen?"

She hesitated.

"We've met."

"Under what circumstances?"

Karen had approached her after reading one of the flyers, explained Edna.

"Has she been out here?"

"Yes."

"Why?"

"You'll forgive me for saying so, but this is beginning to feel like an interrogation."

"It's not an interrogation. Karen's my daughter. I was just curious."

Haugen asked several more questions but learned nothing more.

"Come back sometime if you want to talk about the rockets."

CHAPTER FORTY

On a Sunday morning, when Karen would ordinarily be at church with her family, she was driving to Edna O'Hare's along with Suzy whom she'd dragooned to go with her.

"I'm only doing this because we're friends," said Suzy. "But a team of wild horses couldn't drag me into the parade you guys are planning. Anyway, I don't think the city will give you a permit. Can you imagine Minot endorsing a protest against the air force base?"

"It's not against the air force base. How many times do I have to tell you that?"

"I know. I know. It's against the rockets. It's the same thing."

"It is not."

"Okay," said Suzy. "Let's talk about something else. How about Will?"

"I told you what he wanted to do."

"Yeah. He wanted to do it, that revolting slug. All he cares about in the world is possessing your body for his diabolic lust. I mean how disgusting can you get?"

"Just because I have different standards than you doesn't make me anymore a prude than it makes you a slut."

"I do appreciate that."

"I do this thing sometimes when I'm driving," said Karen, changing the subject. "Imagine that the car is not moving. Stare straight ahead and picture the highway—the whole Earth—is rolling toward you and under the car."

"Ooh. It's kind of scary," said Suzy.

"Yeah. Kind of hypnotic."

Five minutes later Suzy returned to the old topic.

"You're attracted to him, aren't you?"

"What kind of question is that? Do you think I would have let him…let him touch me, if I weren't?"

"You know, Karen, you said we have different standards and that's true, but I think you have your parents' standards, not your own. Do you think my parents would approve of my sex life if they knew about it? Do you?"

Karen tightened her hands on the wheel, while Suzy continued.

"How is intimate touching so different—morally different—from, if you'll forgive me the word—intercourse. With birth control, of course."

They maintained silence for the rest of the way to O'Hare's.

———

Two blue sofas, one longer than the other, and two blue armchairs composed the living room's rectangular sitting area, a coffee table the centerpiece, replete with coffee pot, cream pitcher, sugar cubes, cups, saucers, spoons, and cookies.

Edna and Rasmussen sat on the large sofa. Suzy and Karen on the small one and Will on one of the chairs. One chair remained empty.

"Are we expecting someone?" said Rasmussen, indicating the empty chair.

"No. Nobody else. Maybe my husband's sitting in it at the moment. He'd be happy to be here."

Suzy wondered what she'd gotten herself into, noting that Karen and Will looked anywhere but at each other.

Edna thanked them for coming but told them she just wanted to discuss an idea with them, that she didn't expect any commitment as participation might be dangerous. There wasn't much to discuss. Edna planned to walk north on Main Street, South starting at 2nd Avenue, South West.

"That's where we're most likely to be seen because of the shops. I won't be doing anything different, just handing out leaflets and talking to people, but I hope some of the college kids will join us. I contacted this girl Betty Carlson who works on the college newspaper. She's interested in joining and bringing along some friends. Do any of you think a march is a bad idea?"

"Are you going to ask for a permit?" asked Rasmussen.

"I imagine we won't be more than a handful of people. Do you really think it's necessary?"

"It would be good to have one," said Rasmussen, "and if you didn't you could march anyway, though you might get a fine."

Karen had already found the city's Event/Parade Permit request site on her phone.

"This looks easy," she said. "It doesn't even ask what kind of parade we're planning."

Karen filled out the online parade permit, unrealistically

overestimating, as it turned out, that twenty to thirty people would be marching.

"It would be nice to have something besides signs to attract attention" suggested O'Hare. "Some music maybe."

"I could play my recorder," volunteered Karen.

"You could play 'Semper Fi,'" said Will.

"This concerns the air force," said Rasmussen. "How about 'The Wild Blue Yonder?'"

"Let's not get too militaristic," said Edna. "No offense."

"I like 'El Condor Pasa,'" said Karen. Simon and Garfunkel did it as 'If I Could.' I already know how to play it."

"You've got my vote," said Suzy.

"Yes, 'El Condor Pasa' would be good," said Edna.

They decided to announce the parade with a small ad in the *Minot Daily News*.

March Against Land-Based Missiles it read, naming the time and place, and adding, as an added attraction, music by recorder. Karen did not wish to be named.

CHAPTER FORTY-ONE

The call came in the middle of the day.

"It's the lady with *breast cancer* again," said Nurse Axelson, rolling her eyes.

"Hm. Get her phone number," said Rasmussen. "Tell her I'll call when I get a chance, but it may take a while."

He didn't need the distraction of a mildly elevated heart rate—his—and its implications. He remembered his dream. He would not dash himself upon those rocks. Fortunately the concreteness and proximity of patients was all he needed to focus his mind.

At the end of the day, after everyone had left, he called her.

"Oh, Dr. Rasmussen, thank you so much. I'm sorry. I… I need to talk. Is there any way you could meet me in the lobby of my hotel?"

"Could you tell me what this is about?"

"It's about my mind. I think… I don't know. I just need to talk."

"Are you in any danger?"

"I'm depressed."

Rasmussen went through his well-rehearsed screening for suicidal thoughts, but she denied being in any danger, though he heard her muffle a few sobs.

"I'm sorry to have bothered you. I'll be fine."

"Wait a moment. I can't come over tonight," he said, adding tactically, "My wife is expecting me, but I can probably drop by tomorrow." He said this so she would not imagine the visit to be anything other than a doctor's house call.

"I'm so embarrassed. I don't want to be a nuisance. I'm fine. Really. Overreaction."

"I'll call you tomorrow."

She gave him her number.

———

At home that night, he was consciously demonstrative. He hugged Darlene. He kissed her on the lips, fleetingly, only because she disengaged. He wondered if he were trying to inoculate himself against an infectious thought.

She looked at him curiously but said nothing about this showering of affection.

Though she sat at the table with him, sipping a glass of wine, she'd already eaten.

"That O'Hare woman's little talk at the city council meeting raised some eyebrows," said Rasmussen, now recalling the run-in he'd had with Earnest Schmidt.

They'd met in the parking lot after the meeting, their cars next to each other's.

"That woman might as well be a Russian asset," said Schmidt.

"You watch too many spy movies," said Rasmussen.

"I'm serious. Maybe not on their payroll but think how she's affecting morale at the base. At least I got to the video guy before he posted her little propaganda piece."

"The meeting's not posted? You don't have the right to do that."

"You'd better watch yourself, Andy. That woman's a witch and she's cast a spell on you."

"Damn, Earnest. If it's not the Russians, it's witchcraft. Are you seeing the Devil, too?"

Schmidt opened his car door, got in, slammed it shut, rolled down the window, and leaned out.

"She can blow off steam on her own website. She's not going to use ours."

Dr. Rasmussen told his wife about the encounter.

"Earnest Schmidt is frightened that his contracting business is going to suffer just because his sister-in-law thinks the missiles are bad news and isn't afraid to say so. He's being ridiculous."

Darlene finished her glass and poured herself another.

"It's not completely ridiculous," she said. "Grumman can't be happy about it. What if they decide to send their business to some other contractor to make a statement?"

"A statement! That company is worth over fifty billion. They aren't afraid of a little old lady saying she doesn't like their wares."

"What about a well-known, well-respected physician saying he doesn't like their wares?"

From the moment he saw her this evening, Rasmussen's wife had seemed remote. More remote than usual? A subtle distinction for which he had little reserve energy or inclination to examine.

"So what if they don't like me. What are they going to do? Tell my patients to take care of their own sore throats or broken arms?"

"Are you really going to continue talking to people about that new missile?"

Rasmussen turned his attention to the meal, a tasty chickpea curry, averting his eyes from his wife. The silence seemed to fill the kitchen. Until now he'd thought he might make an amorous proposition later in the evening, breaking a very long moratorium on love making which she'd initiated, but it would certainly be rejected. And what's more, he had to admit to himself, he was no longer in the mood.

"I'm not only going to keep talking about the rockets I'm going to help organize more protests. Poor Edna O'Hare is pretty worn down by the nastiness."

"God! Andy! You've got to be kidding."

He shook his head.

"Why in the world…" she began before changing direction. "It's unseemly. You're a family doctor, not a politician or antiwar activist. You're above this sort of thing—or should be."

"I'm not above nuclear war."

"Oh, don't be melodramatic. Nobody wants a war."

Though fatigued Rasmussen maintained control of his frustration, of his tone of voice. In any case, he was not the self-dramatizing type.

———

The next day's schedule was packed as usual. Rachel Green, whose operation for pancreatic cancer had been completed six months ago, was in for a routine check-up. She had an oncologist and a surgeon, of course, but never felt completely reassured unless she saw Dr. Rasmussen. It was he after all who had made the diagnosis based on the subtlest yellowing of her eyes and an abdominal examination and then talked her out of her plan to treat herself.

Since her neuroendocrine tumor had been slow growing, she'd wanted to try natural healing, alternative medicine, before undergoing surgery to remove the tumor.

For several visits Rasmussen had gently discouraged her from this approach. "Alternative medicine," he explained, "means unproven." There were no studies to show that herbs, diet, and yoga were of any benefit, but she was too frightened of surgery to listen. Finally one day, sitting next to her, with his hand on hers, he asked if she knew who Steve Jobs was.

"He's the president of Apple," she said.

"The chairman, yes, one of the founders of Apple, a very bright guy, but he died of cancer in 2011."

"Oh."

"His tumor was slow growing like yours. In fact, it was the same kind of tumor you have and like you he decided to use natural methods to treat it. But it grew over nine months, and he did eventually need surgery, but by that time his cancer was incurable. Rachel, I respect your wish to try a non-surgical approach, but after reviewing your CAT scan with Dr. Rudolpho, I agree with her that surgery is your best chance of a cure."

She had placed her other hand on his and cried softly. A week and a half later she underwent surgery.

Here she was, smiling and bubbly again, showing him pictures of her first grandchild. A sense of well-being and gratefulness suffused him. How extremely fortunate he had been to have been able to become a physician. A Rachel Green every now and then was for him one of the world's most genuine and enduring highs.

Time slipped away. Again he was the last to finish up. When Margaret asked if he needed her, he said he'd be leaving in a few minutes.

He called Darlene. He'd be later than usual. Paperwork, he explained. He called Claudia Cummings.

———

The drive to the Grand Hotel was a short distance and his ruminations made it subjectively short as well. He arrived before he was ready. A house call for depression? Why had he agreed to this? He could have spoken with her on the phone.

A large chandelier hung in the hotel lobby. Where ceiling and walls met, a white cornice, like the ghost of a giant python, circumscribed the room.

Two heavy armchairs at the far end of the lobby faced the entrance over a wide expanse of nondescript olive carpeting. Claudia Cummings, in a long red skirt and short-sleeved baby blue blouse, stood to greet him.

After they demurely shook hands, she took her seat, relieving Rasmussen, who'd feared she was going to invite him to her room. The other sitting area was near the entrance, and there was no one at the reception desk, so though they were in a public space there was a semblance of privacy.

But she spoke is such a soft whisper that he had to lean toward her, elbows on knees, to hear what she said.

Handkerchief in hand, she thanked him and apologized three times for asking him to come over.

"I know you examined me, and I know I can get a mammogram and I'm planning to, but I think I'm going crazy with worry. I can't do my work. I can't think. I didn't want to be a bother at the office—oh, but now here I am being a worse bother. You must think me a complete fruit cake."

Rasmussen refrained from reaching out to touch her hand, merely nodding as she spoke. She still smelled of apples.

The elevator discharged a group of people, some of whom went to the reception desk, some to the other sitting area, some to the lounge.

"Oh, I'm so sorry. I'm afraid I'm going to cry. I can't do this here. You'd better go. We can talk on the phone."

Whatever he may have envisioned on the way over here, he'd not envisioned this, a thirty second hello/goodbye.

"But," he began and then stopped himself. He tried again. "You're suffering."

"Sometimes I can get control of it. I'm so ashamed. I think you should go. It's way too public here."

Was he surprised to hear himself say, "Perhaps we could talk in your room."

She dabbed her eyes with her handkerchief and smiled. "Oh, would you? That would be wonderful."

Instead of the elevator, they took the stairs. She had a suite, two queen sized beds, and a large sitting area of comfortable armchairs, even a little alcove for making coffee.

"Would you like coffee or tea?" she asked as he seated himself at one end of a plush sofa.

"Nothing for me, thanks."

"Oh, I insist. Something. Decaf, herbal, something. I have to feel I'm offering something."

He settled on an herb tea, which had a hint of bitterness so that he uncharacteristically added a half teaspoon of sugar. They sat at opposite ends of the sofa sipping their drinks.

"You know, I feel calmer already. Actually, I felt good for a few days after I saw you. I know this sounds crazy, but I think if you can reassure me one more time, I may be able to get it under control."

As Rasmussen asked Cummings questions about past history of anxiety, family history, and a little developmental history, he felt a blossoming calmness, which unfolded into a sense of well-being and lightness.

"Sorry," he said, "I seem to be losing my train of thought."

She scooted next to him along the sofa and put a hand on his thigh.

"Oh, that's alright. Why don't you examine my breasts one more time to let me know everything is okay?"

"Well... I... I don't know."

"Yes, you do." She stood taking his hands and pulled. When he resisted, she spoke more firmly, "Now please get up." He was euphoric, relaxed, his thinking vague, unfocussed. He arose from the sofa. Tingling inside, now, he was barely able to ask, "Did you put something in my tea?"

"Oh, just a little something so you wouldn't be so tense."

He felt too good to protest. She walked him to the bed.

"You sit here," she said.

She removed her blouse and bra, and lay supine, her arms crossed above her head.

He put his hands on her breasts but was kissing them the next moment. She cradled his head in her arms pulling him down. "Now suck on them." She pulled his head more firmly against her and cooed.

"Take your clothes off," she said shortly. He removed them as if they were on fire and stripped off her skirt, panties, shoes, and socks.

"Do it," she said unnecessarily.

Rasmussen locked her in carnal embrace but having been sexually deprived for so long and now so intoxicated and aroused, he was prematurely spent so after a few cycles the engine died. Claudia lying under him, patiently stroked his head and waited. In five minutes the machine's piston was firm, the cylinder lubricated, the road trip restarted, with renewed energy.

"Not too fast," she said. "Let's take a little longer to get there. Okay?"

The driver could not hold the throttle for long, but this time Claudia also arrived, groaning, at that special place, that candied paroxysm of delight.

"Ahhh."

And with the help of that potion, a third and longer journey was completed, this time by a horse and a rider, a configuration which Claudia, the rider, had arranged, with full cooperation of the supine horse.

In his car on the way home, Rasmussen, no longer intoxicated, thought about his ineluctable seduction. First the office visit, allowing him to see her voluptuousness for himself, so that a fantasy might develop. And second, how astutely she avoided inviting him up to her room, which might have frightened him off, instead appearing to be on the verge of a breakdown while unconvincingly saying she could handle it herself, so that he would make the suggestion. And third, doping him up with some almost magical aphrodisiac.

But he was not entirely innocent. He could have gone home. He'd wanted to go up to her room. God! He'd never been unfaithful before. He was guilty. He was fearful. And he was perplexed. Was he really so attractive that she had to have him? That didn't seem quite right.

The fling, if that's what it had been, was over, they'd dressed and amiably said goodnight. Without words of affection. Without a kiss. Without plans to be in touch. But as he was about to step out the door, she sighed, "God, that was good."

He nodded.

CHAPTER FORTY-TWO

In the parking lot, at the end of his day, he was surprised to see Claudia Cummings standing by his car. Grateful that there was no one else there to witness his blush or his awkwardness, or to sense what he experienced as guilt emanating from him as if he were radioactive. But it was Ms. Cummings who was radioactive.

"Hello, Dr. Rasmussen."

"Hello."

"I'd like to talk with you for a moment if that's alright."

"Uh. Really. Maybe it would be better if you made an appointment."

"Oh, I think we can take care of this now. It's about my anxiety. I…"

An uncomfortable warmth arouse from within him. Whatever she wanted to say this was not the time or place to say it. His mind raced. Would she say she loved him? God! Would she want him to leave his wife? Would she accuse him of taking advantage of a patient? Was she bringing a lawsuit against him? She'd seduced him, but he'd gone along with it, hadn't he? Yes and no. There was nothing to do but wait.

"I think I would be so much better if you weren't going to march in that little protest parade at the air force base. I wouldn't want my doctor to be accosted by an angry crowd. You know how violent some of those people can be."

Completely ridiculous but he'd best not say so. At least not in those words. He was frightened. This woman might be as dangerous as the character in *Fatal Attraction* who stalks the man with whom she's had a one-night stand.

"Listen, Claudia," he began, calling her by her first name though he would have preferred the distance—which no longer existed—that a surname offered.

"There's no danger to me, though I appreciate your concern. It's going to be a non-provocative short walk and that's it. I really do have to get going. I'm late for dinner."

"Well, I'll still worry my little heart out if I know you're exposing yourself to danger. Please don't go."

His fear now had a tincture of anger admixed.

"I'm committed to this. I have to go."

"But you don't really believe that nonsense about the missiles so you shouldn't back it up by appearing in that parade. You're well respected. People look up to you."

"What does this have to do with your fear of breast cancer? Or your having drugged me in your hotel room."

"Oh, sweetie, wasn't it good though?"

"Claudia, what's going on?"

Softly she answered, "I would be very upset if you marched in that parade. That's what's going on. Would you please tell me you won't go?"

"Don't you understand, I can't do that. Look, I have to go home." He removed his key fob from his pocket and pushed the button to unlock the car. The click seemed unusually loud in his ears. When he grabbed the door handle, Claudia put the palm of her hand firmly on the door.

"Dr. Rasmussen, I can't let you go until you promise me you won't march in that parade."

"This clearly doesn't have anything to do with your anxiety, does it?"

"It certainly does. My anxiety is so high that I might have to tell your wife about it. Maybe she would have some sympathy for me. What do you think?"

"Stay away from my wife, do you hear?"

"Of course, sweetie. I don't really want to talk to her. She might get upset given our friendship, and everything."

"You're blackmailing me." He was about to tell her he'd have to call the police, but he was certain she would call his bluff.

Dumbfounded he stood there waiting for inspiration, something to do or say. He could not just push her away and get into the car. If it hadn't been for his goddamn lust. No. He must not forget he was drugged. This woman was diabolical and would carry out her threat. But if he gave in to this, what might she ask of him next: Anything she wanted. She could even ask him to give it to her again, or else. He felt like sinking through the Earth. Right to its molten iron core. And staying there.

"Okay. I won't march in the parade."

"Thank you so much and one more little thing. I would really appreciate it if you wouldn't speak with anyone about the GBSD or let anyone quote you on the subject. I don't want to read any stories about you in the paper or see you interviewed on TV or anything like that. And no more speeches at the city council meeting. Are you okay with these things, sweetie?"

He cringed each time she used that meretricious endearment, a stubby dagger that wouldn't kill him, just make him bleed.

"All right."

She removed her hand from the car door and before he could react, deftly kissed him on the cheek.

"It was so good. Maybe another time doggy style?"

She turned and left. He watched as she walked, exaggerating the sway of her hips for his delectation? No. For his intimidation.

There went the Devil. Oh, but she was not the Devil. She was a succubus, and she might return in his dreams to haunt him, but that would come later. In the present, he had to calm himself down, gather his scattered wits, and rehearse in his mind how he would greet his wife tonight, so she would see no telltale expression on his face. He was deeply shaken.

CHAPTER FORTY-THREE

At 10:30 on a Wednesday morning, a small group of protestors met, as planned, on the corner of Main Street, South and 2nd Avenue, South West in front of Gideon's Trumpet, a Christian bookstore. Present were Edna O'Hare; Will; Karen; Suzy, and Betty Carlson, the student on the staff of the *Red and Green*, the college newspaper, who'd become a convert after doing some of her own research. They took turns with the one sign held overhead on its long wooden handle.

"Where's Dr. Rasmussen?" asked Karen.

"I'm afraid he can't make it," said O'Hare.

"Oh, no. Is he sick?" said Karen.

"Well, to tell you the truth he sounded sick at heart. He said something had come up and he wouldn't be able to work with us anymore. He wouldn't tell me what."

The despondency in his voice had taken over a little corner of her mind, but she would not say more.

"Not much of a turn-out, is it?" said Betty. "I talked to some people. A couple said they might show up. Enthusiasm wasn't that great. But I'm still going to take a few photos and write the article. Don't worry."

"It doesn't matter," said Will. "We know this isn't a popular idea."

"Let's get started," said O'Hare.

They entered the bookstore.

"Good morning," said the attendant.

"Good morning," said the group in unison, lending a mildly humorous air to the visit.

"How can I help you?"

At each encounter a different person would hand out the flyer, and answer questions, if questions arose. O'Hare thought person-to-person contact was as important as the volume of flyers distributed.

"We're concerned about the nation's security," said Karen. "Land-based intercontinental missiles are dangerous, and we want people to know about it. It's all here in this flyer."

The clerk, a young man with a black handlebar mustache, took the sheet in his left hand, glanced at it, and twirled a tip of his mustache with the other.

"Boy, are you going against the grain. But I'll read it."

"Thank you," said Karen," adding, not cynically, but for good measure, "and God bless you."

"God bless you as well."

Anderson's Bootery came next. This time Will was the designated spokesperson.

A woman, in fringed cowgirl outfit took the flyer.

"You an anti-nuke group?"

Though it was his turn to answer questions he turned to O'Hare.

"Not per se, no. We need a nuclear deterrent, but the

government is planning to spend billions of taxpayer dollars to replace missiles we don't need in the first place."

The woman looked at each of the demonstrators and lay the flyer down on the counter.

"You folks from around here?"

"I've lived here all my life," said O'Hare.

"Me, too," said Karen.

"I'm from Bismarck," said Betty.

"You?" asked the woman of Will.

"Born in Brooklyn, raised in L.A., college in Berkeley. Residing in Minot."

The woman laughed.

"You should get some boots to go with that hat."

"I'd like to," said Will. "I'll come back and take a look."

The group moved on to Inspired Interiors, Cookies for You, Charlies Main Street Cafe, Margie's Art Glass studio, Lien's Jewelry, Jason's Electronic Security, and further down the block, eventually visiting fifteen shops. It seemed that their message was best received in art, music, and bookstores.

Everyone was polite. None of the store people refused to take the flyer. Truth be told, this was the first time that the question of missiles had ever been raised with them.

In addition to the flyers distributed in the shops, an additional seven were given to passersby, who were drawn to the group by Karen's recorder rendition of *El Condor Pasa*, a tune everyone seemed to know. Only a couple of people waved them off without even looking at the flyer.

O'Hare invited her fellow protesters to lunch at Charlies, which, according to *USA Today*, prepared one of the best hot beef sandwiches in North Dakota, though at this time of day the protestors settled for soup or sandwiches or both. During the covid-19 pandemic the restaurant made no-contact deliveries, and further protected its customers by wearing masks and single use gloves. Dr. Rasmussen had consulted with them.

Avoiding nuclear war was a public health matter in his mind but now something had happened, and he'd bowed out, sounding on the phone as if someone had died.

Betty Carlson, along with the others was sorry that he wasn't going to be part of her story.

CHAPTER FORTY-FOUR

Edna, Will and Karen were on their way to Edna's truck, parked on 2nd Avenue, South West. The two-story red brick building, beside which she'd parked, extended for a city block, its only windows over eight feet above street level so nothing happening on the sidewalk was visible from within.

"Hey, Russkies, business not so good, huh?"

They turned to face Wayne and Baxter, who'd come up silently behind them. Tagging along behind them was Jack.

"Hi," said Karen in a forced friendly tone.

"Good morning, gentlemen," said Edna.

"Not much of a parade," said Baxter.

"You're right about that," said Edna. "Do you wish to join us?"

Wayne pulled the flyers from Edna's hand and threw them in the street.

"What do you think?"

"Jack!" implored Karen. But he stood unmoving.

"You jackass," said Will, stepping toward Wayne.

"No," said Karen, placing a hand on his forearm. "We should go. We can print up more flyers."

Will stood undecided.

"She's right," said Edna. "It's not worth it."

"Jack, please, tell your friends to leave us alone."

"Baxter," said Jack, "maybe we should go."

"What are you, pussy whipped?" said Baxter. "These guys are traitors."

Jack glanced at Karen and then at his shoes but said nothing.

"Come on, Will," said Karen. "Let's go."

As Will reluctantly turned to go, Baxter stepped forward, punching him in the back, below the shoulder, but above the flank over his kidney, a punch which would have ended things then and there. It hurt bad enough as it was but was not incapacitating. Will had been expecting an attack and had not lost his footing. The punch shook Karen's grip loose. Will backed three quick paces away from the assailants, whirled around, and walked back toward Baxter.

"You two had better pick up those flyers."

Baxter swung at Will's face with his right arm. Will blocked it with his left and hit him hard in the gut with his right. Baxter doubled over, placing hands on knees to steady himself, but remained standing. Wayne, apparently thinking that Baxter, weighing over two hundred pounds, would wrap things up by himself was unprepared for Will's barrage of punches to the chest and abdomen, and finally the face. He staggered away holding a hand over his bleeding nose.

Baxter partially regaining his breath, pulled a large folding knife from his pocket. He opened it and charged Will who drove him away with a series of intimidating high kicks aimed at the abdomen.

Karen and Edna began calling for help, but Baxter was exhausted and backed away too slowly from Will's last kick, which hit him at the belt line, so that once again he doubled over, but this time fell to the ground.

When several shoppers responded to the calls for help, Edna pointed to the knife.

"They attacked us."

They turned to go, the bewildered shoppers calling 911 so the injured assailants could be attended to.

Jack had disappeared.

In her living room after the parade, Edna listened to Will and Karen as they tried to cheer her up.

"No, it wasn't much of a parade, but we got some people interested," said Will. "And those two jerks were completely on their own."

"How do you know that?" asked Edna. "Someone may have put them up to it."

"I suppose," said Will.

Edna ran her fingertips over her temples, a gesture of thoughtful frustration.

"I have to admit I'm discouraged, and a bit worn out. Minot is just not interested in what I have to say."

"What we have to say, Edna," said Karen. "You're not alone."

Edna nodded weakly.

"And another thing," said Edna after a pause, "I don't want to put you two in danger. There have got to be more than just two hotheads in town. Without more support, I don't think I can keep this up. I've tried to keep my spirits up, but I feel exhausted."

CHAPTER FORTY-FIVE

Almost everyone on campus—staff, students and faculty—read Betty Carlson's article about Edna O'Hare's minimally attended street march, the ideas behind it, and the street fight that followed it. Not quite naive, but relatively new to the newspaper business, she was unconcerned about the possibility, which she had not even considered, that the paper could be sued for publishing unflattering, not to say incriminating, descriptions of the two young men who'd started the brawl.

Inevitably Baxter's father, Colonel Frank Nichols, 21st Missile Wing Commander, received a copy of the paper from his smirk-suppressing adjutant, whose own boys might not be on the football team, but who at least kept their noses clean, as the saying goes.

Alone in his office he read a bit, cursed, read a bit, and cursed some more. Baxter, he was afraid, was not only capable of doing what he was reported to have done, he most certainly had done it. That boy was out of control. Nichols's second wife Judy had frequently complained about his sassiness and now this, though it wasn't his first fight. But drawing a knife!

He briefly considered suing the paper, a reflex reaction to protect his indefensible son, but clearly no defamation was intended, and the story might even force some sense into the boy. Baxter was a high school senior who, unless he changed his ways, might see his prospects for an athletic scholarship at a good university slip from his grasp like a football covered in olive oil.

Nicholas needed to know what legal action if anything was planned.

———

"But, Dad," protested Baxter. "That SOB almost killed us."

"You drew a knife on him."

"It was self-defense."

"Two big football players against that kid?"

"Hey, whose side are you on? This bunch of commies are attacking the air force."

"The article says you struck the first blow. It was the Larrabee boy who was defending himself."

"That reporter is lying. He hit me when I turned to go."

"Enough, Baxter. Enough. You are not to use the car. And no allowance until I say so. And I don't want you seeing your buddy Wayne. Sometimes I wonder if he's the one who eggs you on. You've become a bully. I want it to stop."

"But—"

"I don't want to hear any more from you."

———

Engaged in a seemingly harmless conspiracy of silence, neither Amy nor Karen Haugen had mentioned the march or the fist fight, which occurred in downtown Minot three days previously. Amy, though, had only reluctantly agreed to keep the secret. When Roy Haugen confronted them with the *Red and Green* article in the living room after work they were embarrassed.

"You were hiding this from me," said Roy scowling. He held the copy of *Red and Green* out to Karen.

"No, Daddy, I wasn't."

"You don't usually read that paper," added Amy.

"You're in on it, too. Did you know our daughter was parading around town saying our own missiles put us in danger and their replacements are a waste of money?"

Foreseeing the possibility of a long engagement, Amy took a seat on the sofa, followed by Karen, but Roy Haugen remained standing, the paper now clutched in both hands behind his back.

"You seem more concerned about the beloved rockets," said Amy, "than you do about our daughter and her friends being attacked and with a knife, no less. God knows what would have happened if that boy Will hadn't been with them."

"That boy is part of the problem," said Haugen.

"What have you gotten yourself into young woman?"

"What do you mean what I have I gotten myself into?" said Karen.

Haugen harrumphed and began pacing in front of the sofa, whacking his left palm with the newspaper, which he'd rolled into a baton, occasionally raising it above his head.

Lilly came into the room, sat between Amy and Karen on the sofa, and addressed her father.

"Are you having a fight?"

"No, we're not," said Haugen.

"We're having an argument," said Amy. "It is kind of boring. Maybe you should go to the den and play."

"What are you arguing about?"

Sending Lily to another room in this house, would not have prevented her from listening, especially if her door was open, nor could her father demand her isolation without the whole family being troubled by the move, after all, she wasn't being punished. Haugen tossed the newspaper on a chair and said they'd talk about this later.

After dinner, without encouragement, Lilly left the room on her own to watch a TV program. The argument now continued, though at a lower volume and without the emphasis of a newspaper baton being waved about.

Until now Karen had not discussed with her father the depth of her newfound aversion for the underground rockets spread around Minot over thousands of square miles, nor had Amy mentioned, even to Karen, her own growing unease about these missiles.

"They don't do us any good, Daddy," said Karen for the third time. "We don't need them."

"Look," said Haugen reasonably, "you're not going to change my mind and I'm not going to change yours, but I don't want you going on any more marches. I'm going to leave a message with Edna and that boy to leave you out of the protests."

"Don't do that, Daddy."

"It's dangerous. There are people here who have very strong feelings about this."

"So they're allowed their strong feelings, but I'm not allowed mine?"

He would not mention it now, but the knowledge that one of the boys who attacked them was Nichols's son Baxter gnawed at him. He didn't know what to do with it.

"Roy, she has a point. You're allowing her view to be suppressed. What if I want to protest?"

"Damn! Sorry. Excuse me. That's all I need. Next thing you know, you'll have Lilly carrying antinuke signs."

"This isn't antinuclear," said Karen. "It's anti-land-based missiles."

"What does it look like when one of my children makes a fuss about our nuclear deterrent? I don't much care what civilians think, but on the base this sort of publicity is bad for morale. You may not know it, but sometimes those launch officers get a little down in the dumps."

"I'm going to see them. Edna and Will, I mean. I'm sorry, Daddy, but I'm going to see them."

"No more demonstrations," said Haugen, sidestepping the question of his daughter's friendship with these people. What could he do about that?

CHAPTER FORTY-SIX

It only took a few days before Will concluded that he'd rather be on the road than be forced to see Karen almost every day, now that she was committed to this work. Convinced of the arguments for the elimination of the ICBMs, Karen Haugen had pledged to help Edna promulgate the idea.

On a pleasant summer evening two days after Karen told Will, "That's not how I was raised," Edna had the two of them to dinner. For her it was simply a way to express her gratitude for their help. For Karen it was a chance to see Will again. For Will it was a chance to say goodbye.

They ate at the bright yellow kitchen table, Edna talked about her testimony at the city council meeting and of how Dr. Rasmussen had supported her, before mysteriously bowing out.

She did not mention how badly this had affected her and tried to keep her tone lighthearted.

"I'm glad things are working out for you," said Will.

"You've got people's attention and you're bound to get some volunteers to help you. You'll get all the help you need, or at least all the publicity. I've decided to get back on the road. It's still a long way to New York."

As he spoke, Karen's sadness over their spat—it couldn't be called a lovers' quarrel—turned to vexation. She'd told him she couldn't sleep with him, but she liked him, liked him a lot and he knew it. Yet it appeared that sex was so important to him, or maybe even the only reason he was interested in her, that now that he couldn't get what he wanted, he was leaving town. Well, fine, she thought. Fine. He could go satisfy his lust in New York. She suppressed the memory of her taking such pleasure in his caresses at the riverbank. To stop herself from crying she bit her lower lip.

Edna looked back and forth between them.

"Has something happened?" she asked. "Since you arrived here tonight, you've both looked—what should I say? Sad?" She paused. "Oh. Because you both knew Will was leaving, is that it?"

"I didn't know," said Karen, glowering briefly at Will, before turning away.

"My brother called again," he lied. "The family really needs my help and I'm not doing much here to help so—"

"And there's really nothing for you to stay here for, is there?" said Karen, interrupting him. Damn, she thought. She was wearing her heart on her sleeve.

"Needless to say, I'm disappointed," said Edna. "You've been a great help to me, but I am touched by your dedication to your mother. When do you plan to leave?"

Will hung his head. "I was thinking about tomorrow."

Abruptly Karen stood. "Excuse me."

She walked to the bathroom.

"She's upset," said Edna. "She must be very fond of you."

"The feeling's mutual," said Will.

"Is your mother in extremis?"

"No. No. Nothing like that. It's hard to explain."

"So she's not dying."

"No. She's just… She's just having difficulties."

"And your brother can't handle it. I'm sorry."

Could his capable, well-to-do brother, if he knew he had to, *handle it*? Will didn't want to discuss family dynamics with Edna. Family dynamics, though, was indeed useful in understanding why some families were unhappy or did hurtful things to each other, like flushing each other's medications down the toilet. Happy families didn't have family dynamics.

He asked about Edna's near term plans. She wasn't sure, and was reluctant to talk honestly about her discouragement, her diminishing energy, her dissipating hope. And she certainly didn't want to give him cause for guilt by telling him how much he'd bolstered her spirits and that she dreaded the idea now of working without him. Instead she said she'd been considering inviting interested people to her house, maybe to reconstitute the Missile Land Owner's Association.

"Though I really wonder if there are people in this town who are ready to stand up and be counted, if I may coin a phrase."

"I'm sure there are," said Will.

Karen was still in the bathroom when the explosion went off, blowing in the living room window, the shock wave felt thought the house.

"What in God's name—" said Edna.

"Get down!" said Will.

"But…but shouldn't we go look?"

"Now! To the floor," he commanded.

He took her arm and steadied her as she reached down for a soft three-point landing and then sat on the floor.

Moments later Karen came running.

"What happened?"

"Get down!" ordered Will so forcefully that she did so at once.

He crawled to the kitchen cabinet that housed the shotgun and removed it. He broke open the gun, exposing the breach and two shells. He snapped the barrels back into place and crawled to the switch to turn off the kitchen light.

"Call 911," he said. Karen dialed on her cell phone.

He crawled to the front door where, still on hands and knees he reached up to turn off the rest of the lights, including the porch light.

He flung open the door, and crouching, scuttled out on his feet and one hand, shotgun in the other. He rolled to the side, next to one of the four-by-four posts supporting the handrail. On his belly, he pointed the gun into the front yard.

The light from the half moon was sufficient to make shadows.

He saw the car about to leave the driveway and turn onto the road.

Standing, then springing from the porch, he ran, but the car was well on its way when he reached the road. He aimed and fired both barrels.

He went back inside. "You can get up now." He turned on the lights.

As Edna and Karen arose to take seats at the kitchen

table, Will replaced the spent shotgun shells and put the weapon back in the cabinet.

"I was wrong about this being a funny place for a shotgun. It's a damn good place."

"What is going on, Will?" asked Edna, her expression drawn.

He stepped behind her, squeezing her shoulders reassuringly.

"Everything's under control, so to speak. Someone threw a bomb onto the porch, but I think it was meant to scare us, not kill us."

"Not scare us. Me," said Edna. "And I'm not sure about them not wanting to kill me, either."

"Whoever it was could have thrown the bomb through the window but didn't."

"Why did you make us get on the floor?" asked Karen.

"Just to be safe. In my experience shooting sometimes follows bombing, at least it did in Afghanistan. Are you two alright?"

"Well, I'm a little shook up, that's all," said Edna, before she started to cry. Will remained behind her, massaging her shoulders.

"Did you shoot anyone?" asked Karen.

"I doubt it. They were too far away."

"They?"

"Well, I couldn't see but I assume there was the bomb thrower and the getaway driver."

"I'm alright," said Edna. She reached back to pat Will's hand. "Would you get me that." She pointed to a box of tissue paper. She blew her nose.

"Why would anyone do this?" asked Karen.

"To frighten me, like Will said. And they have succeeded but I feel better now. I must say it's nice to have a man around the house."

"I'm going to look at the porch," said Karen.

Will and Edna followed her.

A nasty-looking jagged hole, about the size of a dinner plate, had been blasted through the porch's wood floor. Deep cracks radiated up the wall.

"Who would want to do a thing like this?" asked Karen.

"A missile hugger," said Edna, managing a weak laugh.

———

Sheriff Andresen had been called at nine that night as was his wish.

"When an oddball or horrendous crime occurs, call me, day or night."

He had once chewed out a new dispatcher when she, uninformed about exactly which crimes fell under the categories of odd or horrendous, forgot to follow his wishes. He was never to be seen as ignorant if confronted by the public about one of these crimes: arson, occurring on average once or twice a year and murder, occurring on average once every other year. Not that he was uninterested in rapes, assaults, and burglaries.

Murder was the worst and most newsworthy crime, so naturally he was to be informed immediately.

As for his interest in arson, only his wife knew that once, at age ten, he had started a fire playing with matches. It had quickly spread across the empty plot, devouring an ample fuel supply of weeds and dry grass, reaching a familiar two story, clapboard house on the far side of the lot, which itself was soon in flames.

Terrified, he ran home to inform his mother that a house was on fire. He didn't mention the matches.

It was his great good fortune, not to mention the good fortune of the residents of the burning house, that the fire department arrived quickly. Their neighbor, alone at the time and temporarily wheelchair bound, toppled over in the living room in her rush to escape the building, but was not seriously hurt. She could have been burned to death.

He wasn't preoccupied with arson, until arson occurred. The explosion wasn't arson, but the dispatcher took no chances.

He arrived at O'Hare's before the firetruck, having far exceeded the speed limit, Officer Shirley Johansen, in the seat beside him, ordinarily a stickler for rules, wisely silent.

While Edna made tea, Andresen, and Johansen, with flashlights, followed by Will and Karen, walked around the house and out to the road.

Officer Johansen took a photo of a tire track on the dirt shoulder two car lengths away from the entrance to the house's driveway.

"If you'd been looking out the window, you might have seen the guy," said Andresen.

"The guy?" said Johansen.

"The person. The perpetrator," said Andresen.

"The son-of-a-bitch," said Will.

"That's charitable," said Karen.

———

The fire engine came wailing and flashing up the road. Though no one had mentioned fire, the crew was taking no chances. The medic spoke to the three of them. Another fireman determined that no gas line had ruptured. Indeed, other than lines from the propane tank outside the kitchen, there were no gas lines.

"We'll get them, Edna. I promise you," said Andresen.

CHAPTER FORTY-SEVEN

The next morning when Karen arrived, Will, kneeling on the porch, was prying something from the wall near the front door with a pocketknife. He kept his back to her as he worked, though he'd surely heard the car. This was the day he was to depart, but as she stood there watching him gingerly remove something from the wall and dropping it into a paper bag, she knew he'd changed his plans. The change, however, had nothing to do with her. He should stop mooching from Edna, she thought, and get a hotel room so she wouldn't have to see him when she came by or accompanied Edna into town on her campaign.

Will moved along the wall and began prying at a new spot. Karen moved closer, quietly as if stalking him. Her stealth ended as she climbed the front steps to see what he was doing. She really didn't want to talk with him and could have simply gone into the house, but she was too curious.

"What are you doing?"

"Collecting shrapnel."

He didn't sound angry with her, just businesslike.

She said, "A box of grenades went missing at the base. I should have thought of that last night."

Still on his knees, he now turned and looked up at her. Ironically she was disappointed in herself to be so happy to see him. They stared at each other briefly before he stood up. She kept a straight face. He held the bag out toward her and shook it. Metal shards tinkled. She'd read in a fairy tale how a wizard had bewitched a girl by ringing a magic bell in her face. The wizard too was a sex fiend, but the story only spoke of enchantment, of course. Her anger was re-awakened.

"I thought you were leaving today."

"I changed my mind."

"Playing detective?"

"I'm not playing."

"What about your poor mother?"

"You don't have to talk to me like that. I haven't done anything to you. I'm staying because Edna needs some protection."

Karen walked past him into the house, calling "Edna."

———

Edna invited Will to join them for breakfast and to make plans.

Addressing Will, Edna asked, "You don't think they want to kill me, just scare me. Is that right?"

Will nodded.

"Well, like I said, they have scared me." She hung her head.

"But who are *they*?" asked Karen. "We should make a list."

"I've thought about that," said Edna. "There's the business community, Grumman itself, our congressman and senators, and maybe some gung-ho weekend warriors, you know, fanatics, who don't just want to keep their AK47's but their hydrogen bombs, too. Thinking about it makes me sick. Anyway, we'll never figure it out."

She looked at Karen with sad eyes.

"Did Will tell you he was going to stay with me for a while? Sort of like a bodyguard. I'm embarrassed to say I like the idea. But I don't think you should be involved. It's too dangerous."

Karen choked on a piece of bacon, coughing. She covered her mouth with a napkin.

"Say something," said Will.

"You say something," she said angrily.

"I just wanted to see if you can breathe."

The coughing subsided.

"I want to work on your project, too, Edna. I want to."

"What about your parents?"

"Well, first of all, I didn't tell them what happened last night and I'm not going to. They will learn sooner or later but I'll face that when I have to."

Edna looked at Will.

"Looks like you'll have to be her bodyguard, too."

Will shrugged his shoulders.

Karen wanted to say "no", but she feared her voice would betray emotion.

"I don't think she wants a bodyguard," he said finally.

As they ate Edna talked about her plans to stay home this day to call some home security companies. She wanted to install one of those newfangled video surveillance systems.

"You can actually see who's hanging around the house and who shouldn't be."

"But there's that rally at the TV station," said Karen.

Edna frowned. "Frankly, at the moment, I don't feel up to that rally. I'm a bit ashamed to say this, but I don't feel like going out of the house for a while. Karen, I wonder if you'd consider standing in my place—"

"But—" began Karen.

"Just to introduce the speakers. People are coming mainly to hear Dr. Rasmussen, anyway. Oh, drat, I forgot. He's no longer working with us. But back to you. You're from Minot. That gives you some credibility and the fact that your father works on the base does too. I know. I know. You don't want him to find out about it, but you have to be realistic. Sooner or later he's going to learn that you're still protesting. What am I thinking! You shouldn't have anything more to do with me. It's dangerous."

"Edna!"

———

Eager for business, Jason's Electronic Security sent an installer out in the early afternoon. Will and Karen found themselves together following the installer around and asking questions as she installed a top-of-the-line system of video cameras, microphones, and alarms.

After the installer had left, Will looked over Karen's shoulder as she worked on Edna's undeveloped website, The Missiles of Minot.

Then Amy Haugen arrived. Forewarned that her mother was coming to get a scoop about the explosion, Karen had decided that rather than hide upstairs, she'd go for a long walk.

"You go with her, Will," demanded Edna.

"That's not necessary," said Karen.

"I'd feel much better if he'd go with you. Please."

The bitter criticism she'd experienced, the slander, vandalism, harassment, violence, and finally an actual bombing, had deeply dispirited her. She had put these young people in danger. Further demoralizing her was Dr. Rasmussen's unexplained withdrawal from participation.

———

They walked side by side, silently, both considering whether to speak but waiting for the other to speak first. They walked for over a mile, leaving the O'Hare property and climbing the gentle slope of a low, grassy hill toward a crowning copse of basswood before they stopped to look back.

Karen sat, crossing her legs, staring straight ahead.

"Tired?" asked Will sitting down beside her.

"No."

"About what I said—" began Will.

"About the explosion?"

"No. About leaving. I shouldn't have said that. I was just disappointed."

"That you couldn't have sex. I know."

He sighed.

She didn't want to talk. He'd been disappointed and pouted, cutting her off, planning to leave. Now he was trying to apologize but she didn't feel like forgiving him, making her feel ungenerous. But what would happen if she forgave him? What did she mean "happen?" Nothing would, nothing could happen now.

Not far from them, a rabbit, which had been hiding there in the tall grass all along, stuck its head up, sniffed the air, and dashed away down the hill.

She thought of *Alice in Wonderland*. Might she herself have fallen down a rabbit hole if she'd let herself? Entered a surreal world?

Like Alice, she gave herself good advice but unlike Alice, she usually took it. Nor did she tend to scold herself, or like pretending to be two different people. But the question that now occurred to her revealed the fissure dividing her into two selves: the seeker of truth, despite the risk of pain, and the defender of stability, despite the risk of ignorance.

"Did you have a condom with you that night?"

"Of course."

She uncrossed her legs, pulling them up to her chest, and wrapped her arms around her knees. She gazed straight ahead. Did being prepared mean he expected compliance? And if he did, what did that make her in his eyes? Or was being prepared just common sense? Respectful even?

A half hour passed before Will spoke.

"Edna's in danger. It actually would be best if she'd stop her protest."

"Well, she's already unnerved," said Karen, relieved for the distraction from rumination, "and she's close to giving up."

"You need to be careful. You're in danger, too."

Karen sighed,

"You know," said Will, "we're going to have to work together. I'm sorry I acted like a kid."

"I thought you weren't even sure the missiles were a bad idea. You want to keep protesting even if Edna can't?"

"They are a bad idea. I may be a slow learner, but I learned. It's just that I'm an ex-marine. I wasn't prepared to question this country's defense plans. Semper fi's the motto. But I am being faithful by confronting an idea that puts this country at risk."

"You should show the shrapnel to my father."

"Yes. I should. I will."

She felt herself softening. She'd never even thanked him for defending Edna against those bullies in the street the day of the march.

She turned toward him.

"Will, right after the explosion last night you were...you were...brave...you—"

"Don't. You're embarrassing me."

CHAPTER FORTY-EIGHT

How absurdly easy it had been to identify Calderone as the launch control officer who'd dropped in on Edna O'Hare that sunny Sunday. Sergeant Haugen had simply to assemble ID photos of those who had that day off and show them to Edna O'Hare for identification.

It was a bit awkward for a sergeant to grill a lieutenant, but Haugen had the authority directly from Colonel Nichols, indeed, Nichols had texted Calderone with the info. They sat in Haugen's office.

"Mrs. O'Hare said you were intoxicated."

"Well, I'd had a few beers," said Calderone. "It's not a crime."

"Not that kind of intoxicated. Your speech wasn't slurred. Your coordination was intact. You appeared to be seeing things."

"I wasn't drunk, but I'd urinated quite a bit and I think I was dehydrated. It was hot and I was lightheaded and as far as seeing things go, I hope Mrs. O'Hare wasn't claiming to see other peoples' hallucinations."

Haugen learned that Sergeant Caulfield and Airman Forster had been Calderone's drinking buddies that day. He would also be speaking with them. But further questions led nowhere. Sergeant Haugen felt defeated. The O'Hare woman had been convincing and though, in some indefinable way, Calderone had been less so, Haugen realized shortly that he was as likely to get the whole story from Calderone as he was to get him to enumerate his wife's shortcomings, if she had any.

"I figured it would come to this," said Haugen, "so I've drawn up a little document, which I want you to sign and after than I'd like you go to directly to the lab to get a tox screen drawn."

Haugen was ad libbing. Poker-faced, Calderone evidenced no telltale hesitation in signing the formally worded, but toothless document, a denial of the use of drugs other than alcohol.

After Calderone left the office, Haugen brooded about reporting nothing of interest to Nichols when an idea occurred to him. Yes, it was bold, but Nichols would back him up, he was near certain of it.

————

Calderone, Caulfield, and Forster sat at a small table in the cafeteria, having propped the fourth chair against the table to be sure no one would join them, almost as if they'd had a premonition.

"I don't know how that O'Hare woman learned my name, but she did and now Haugen has yours."

Caulfield shook his head in disgust and Forster moaned.

"Hey, I didn't want to be caught in a lie. All I said is that we were drinking buddies. And that's all you have to say when he comes around to talk. And there is one other little thing…"

"You know," said Caulfield addressing Forster, "I had a bad feeling about dropping acid in the first place, but you made it sound so good. Like the Devil sweet talking someone into lust or gluttony."

"You Catholics and your sins," said Forster. "You had a good trip and now you're trying to blame me because of Joe's snafu?

"Just a second. I didn't screw up anything."

"You sure as hell did," said Forster. "Going to visit the antimissile witch for a cozy little chat. How stupid can you get? Have you spilled the beans about any other little matter?" Then, speaking softer than he had been, "What about exam questions?"

Calderone shook his head.

Deeply involved as they were in this stressful back and forth, they did not see Haugen enter the room. He appeared at their table accompanied by a burly MP, who stood as if frozen, a disinterested look on his face, but a hand on his night stick.

"Gentlemen," said Haugen, "May I have your cell phones, please."

"What?" said Caulfield.

"On Colonel Nichols's orders. Your cell phone, please." He held out his hand."

Haugen had considered a number of preambles but dispensed with them. The shock value of being brusque might be helpful in scaring something from its hiding place.

"You can't do this," said Caulfield.

"I can. I'm doing it. I'm authorized to have you arrested if you refuse. Hand them over now, please."

Calderone should have seen this coming. It had gone too well in Haugen's office. He was shaken.

He and Caulfield handed over their phones. When Forster hesitated, the MP tapped Forster lightly on the shoulder with his baton. They provided the passwords as well.

Pleased with himself, Haugen left the room with three cell phones in his pocket and the codes to open them.

Calderone, Caulfield, and Forster stared at Sergeant Haugen and his MP as they left, not wishing even to look at each other while those two figures were visible.

"I'll bet it was the witch told him," said Forster. "It's got to be her. We've got to do something about that woman."

"What the hell are you talking about?" said Caulfield.

"Nothing. I'm just pissed off, I guess. And anyway, Washington goes out to see O'Hare. I wonder if she ID'd you?"

"How could she do that?" asked Calderone. "She wasn't there when I visited O'Hare."

In his little office, Haugen made himself a pot of coffee, arranged a notebook and pen on his desk, and opened Calderone's phone. If he'd acted less quickly, he was certain, all incriminating evidence would have been erased. As it stood, a hundred phone numbers many text messages

—some with photos attached—were still there for all to see. All who had access anyway.

Of interest: Calderone and Forster had exchanged texts as had Caulfield and Forster, but Calderone and Caulfield had exchanged no texts between them. Furthermore the few photos Forster had sent to Calderone and Caulfield were not of pin-up girls, but of sheets of blotter acid, divided into thirty-six tabs, each tab decorated with a tiny likeness of the Mad Hatter from *Alice in Wonderland*, his eyes pinwheels, holding a tab of acid in one hand, a clock striking 13 in the other. A tab cost $35, which was a little steep, but this was an air force base, not a college campus, so that acquiring the psychedelic was more difficult than it might otherwise have been. All this Haugen pieced together from individual texts over the course of several hours.

Forster had exchanged texts, crudely coded so their meaning was not too difficult to discern, with Batman, as the sender called himself, if it was a him. Envelopes, drop-off sites, money were the topics. So Batman was the supplier.

CHAPTER FORTY-NINE

Dr. Rasmussen had cared for Karen Haugen since she was a baby, but his pediatric practice had morphed into a family practice over the years. Karen was so grateful that she would not be shuffled off to an internist just because she had turned eighteen. She was comfortable with him.

In making the appointment she had refused to tell his receptionist why she wished to see the doctor.

"So what seems to be the matter," asked Rasmussen.

Karen was embarrassed by the reason for her visit, and she was a little afraid. Although she was now an adult her father would nevertheless breath fire if he found out, inflexibly opposed as he was to premarital sex. In this sense he was not her mother's domesticated lion but rather Karen Haugen's personal dragon, guarding his gold, in the person of Karen Haugen.

"This is all confidential, right?" she asked.

"Yes, you're an adult and your medical record cannot be shared with your parents without your permission. That's what you had in mind, isn't it?"

"How did you know?"

"Let's just call it intuition," said Rasmussen.

"Do you know why I'm here?"

"No. You tell me."

She felt the heat in her cheeks and became aware of her heart beating in her chest. She felt as if she'd had way too much coffee.

"I'd like to have birth control, maybe an IUD, if you think that's an okay way to do it."

"Karen, may I ask you a few questions?"

She nodded.

"Are you sexually active?"

"Oh, God, no!"

Rasmussen leaned back in his chair.

"Do you plan to become sexually active?"

"I'm not planning," she said, knowing this was not strictly true. "I just want to be ready if anything should come up."

She paused now as her cheeks flushed even more because of the unintended, off-color pun. She probably learned to think 'dirty' from Suzy. Now she recalled her last date with her boyfriend Jack, whom she'd known since middle school. They were friends even as children, rode their bikes together, went frog hunting and collected crickets, played card games in each other's kitchens. As their bodies changed with maturity so did their relationship. They no longer played together, though Karen would have liked to. She maintained an interest in the natural world. He less so. They went to movies together or to parties. When they could get away with it, that is when they found a way to be alone, they necked. But Karen had put limits on the geography of their touching. She wondered, sometimes, if he

270

really liked her. Her father must have had his suspicions. Jack thought so.

"I swear, I wouldn't be surprised if he was tracking us by GPS," he'd said, "and you know what, when you were in your room getting ready, he asked me if I'd ever been in trouble with the law. Man! But what really gets me is your —I don't know—being so… prudish. You kiss me like I'm your brother or something, or a Chinese paper cut-out you're afraid of getting wet."

"You want to French kiss."

"You're damn right, I want to French kiss."

Because of Jack's pressure and her reluctant acceptance that she, too, had a sexual appetite, she'd long ago started thinking about making this appointment, but when Jack failed even to try to stop his friends from harassing Mrs. O'Hare, she could simply not tolerate the thought of sleeping with him or, for that matter, even with holding his hand.

When he asked why she was breaking up with him, she forced herself to tell him the painful truth, painful to him, and painful to her. "You're a coward."

———

"Karen," said Rasmussen, interrupting her thoughts, "you say you're not planning?"

"No…I mean what if I had a boyfriend and what if... You know. I'm not planning, but what if…" She felt the blush growing over her entire face. What if the doctor knew? What would he think of her? But, no, she didn't have a boyfriend. And nothing was going to happen, just what if?

Rasmussen asked a few more questions about her health,

examined her, and then gave her a pamphlet entitled Sexual Health and Hygiene.

"Margaret will be here in a moment to help you with the insertion. If you have any questions later, feel free to call her or me."

As she waited nervously for the nurse, she thought about Will. Was it possible that she was ready for intimacy with someone she hardly knew? Though the idea was brand new to her, she now disliked the notion that women must be the passive ones, the ones who waited.

———

When, at the dinner table that night, her father asked what she'd done during the day, she almost fumbled over her answer: she'd gone downtown to look for a dress she'd seen advertised.

"That all?" said Roy Haugen.

She attributed to her father an uncanny ability to detect any funny business. Did he know about the visit to the doctor? The very word IUD, spoken by one of his daughters, would probably make him choke on his food.

"I window shopped," she said.

Roy Haugen turned to Lilly.

"I went to Molly's to play," said Lilly. "She has a swimming pool. A kind of pool made with plastic. It isn't very deep but it's fun."

"Her parents were home, I take it."

"Roy," said Amy, "you know I wouldn't let her go to someone's house if a responsible grown-up wasn't present. Really."

"Her mom," continued Lilly, "told us a funny story

about seeing a witch downtown, with a pointy hat and everything. But she's not a real witch, is she?"

"That was Edna O'Hare," said Amy, "and she's not a real witch. I wrote an article about her. She's protesting the replacement of the Minuteman missiles for new ones."

"Her again? And you're going to give her publicity? You know she's invited my airmen to drop by for coffee? That woman is a troublemaker."

"Don't worry too much," said Amy, "I think it's unlikely that Wilburn will publish it. He said, and I quote, 'One off kilter protester does not a story make and besides the Grumman team is in town and we don't want them to feel unwelcome.'"

"What about your day, Daddy?" said Lilly.

On the base it was business as usual except they hadn't found the lost grenades yet. And as far as he knew nobody had gone to drink coffee with the troublemaker. He'd started asking, which struck Amy as an invasion of privacy.

The talk turned to a possible winter vacation someplace warm. Minot was rough in the winter. They discussed the possibilities. As they said on the base, freezin's the reason.

Later that evening, Karen knelt beside her chest of drawers, opened the lowest drawer and, from underneath the neatly folded clothes, pulled out one of O'Hare's flyers. Why had she kept it? She'd read it so many times. Her father would have seen it as dangerous contraband smuggled into the house.

But nothing as dangerous as the pamphlet entitled, The Kleerwand IUD, Usage and Care.

CHAPTER FIFTY

There was no way Brad Wilburn could reject Amy's article about Edna O'Hare, after all, the woman's house had been bombed.

Mysterious Explosion Threatens Local Woman

Two nights ago, while Edna O'Hare of Ward County was entertaining guests, an explosive device detonated on her front porch. No one was injured. Sheriff Bjorn Andresen would not speculate about a possible motive.

Ms. O'Hare, a well-known figure in Minot, dresses as a witch to bring attention to her campaign against replacement of the aging Minuteman missiles with the new Ground-Based Strategic Deterrent (GBSD). She believes that a deranged individual is trying to frighten her into silence, though most observers consider her crusade quixotic and fruitless. On the other hand her attire as a witch may have disturbed an already unquiet mind.

There are no suspects.

. . .

Amy had written a longer, more detailed article, including O'Hare's reaction to the bombing, her arguments against the GBSD, and the reactions of people she'd spoken with about it. She had also mentioned the likelihood that a grenade, stolen from the air force base, had been used. Wilburn cut the article down to a nubbin, which appeared on a back page of the paper. Nevertheless, such drama and intrigue drew wide attention through town.

Some people who, despite their residence in Minot, had never heard of the GBSD were now expressing their opinions like nuclear war planners. Rumor had it that Dr. Rasmussen, a popular family physician, supported O'Hare, arguing that it was a question of public health as there was no conceivable medical response to a nuclear war, which land-based ICBMs made more likely. But when he was approached, he denied having an opinion one way or another, which seemed odd since he'd spoken against the GBSD at a council meeting.

After she'd read the article three times, Ellen Conklin called Claudia Cummings to her suite in the Grand Hotel, which housed the visiting Grumman entourage.

"Have you read the article?"

"Who hasn't?" said Cummings.

"I think that O'Hare woman is basically a harmless crank, but someone obviously doesn't think that. A bomb! Can you believe that? There is a nutcase under every bush. I actually feel sorry for the woman. I wouldn't want to see her hurt. She's a human being, no matter what she says. In any case she's powerless, but I do have one concern. What if someone influential starts talking up this nonsense? I know it won't stop the project, but it may sour community relations. Do you think I'm a worry wart, Claudia?"

"Which influential person do you have in mind?"

"Andrew Rasmussen," said Conklin.

"And?"

"And I don't know. You're the public relations expert. I'm just blowing off steam, I guess. There's nothing anyone can do."

"Let me think about it."

Claudia Cummings felt no compunction to talk about her coup. Dr. Rasmussen would not present a problem. Besides, Conklin was a bit straight-laced and might not have approved.

CHAPTER FIFTY-ONE

The large wall clock read 9:47 a.m. and Joe Calderone had yet to say more than a few words. Washington assumed it was just a bad mood, a headache, or a family squabble and refrained from asking him about it until now. They'd already gone through the morning routine, checking the status of each of their ten missiles and attendant monitoring devices and silo systems.

Calderone sat morosely at his console, thumbing through a code book.

"Hey, Joe, something bothering you?"

Without looking up he said in an uncharacteristically curt tone of voice, "None of your business."

This must really be bad thought Washington, best to stay out of it.

"But now that I think about it," he added, "maybe it is your business after all, goddamn it."

He looked up at her.

"This *sergeant*—can you believe that—dropped by for a visit with two of his MP pals on the order of Colonel

Nichols. He sat me down in my own living room while one MP stood by the door and the other in front of the hallway. Scared my wife to death. They wanted to know if I were using drugs. I said no. This sergeant apparently had spoken to that crazy lady who's running around town like Chicken Little but if the sky is falling, it's falling on me. She told them I was acting funny when she saw me. It was a hot day. I was dehydrated. A little light-headed when I stood up. No drugs. I told them no drugs.

"They asked if they could search the house. What am I supposed to say? They were pretty damn thorough. They even found a *Playboy* I'd hidden in the basement. They took my computer. I had to give them the password.

"You know, maybe they were just looking for drugs, but I got a little lecture from the sergeant about keeping fit for our mission. What did he mean by that, I wondered? Doing well on the tests? You haven't mentioned anything, have you?"

Washington hesitated. She had yet to tell anyone— beside her father and mother and Edna O'Hare—about the cheating. But keeping this a secret was grating on her. She had planned to do so soon, risking both her career and any acceptance on the base. As a newcomer to Minot, she'd have few people on her side.

"No. But to be honest, I've been thinking about it. Not naming you, of course. Just…just. I'm not sure what I'm going to say or how."

The conversation ended at 9:49 a.m.. Washington sat flanked on her left by three columns of drawers of elec-tronics and on her right by a printer, a screen, and numerous switches, nobs, and dials. She faced a console labelled Missile Group Status Board with a row of ten square white buttons aligned under a row of ten thimble-shaped red lights.

At 10:03 she began a routine check. As she pushed the white buttons, the corresponding red lights went out, all but one, accompanied by a soft whistling alarm at her console.

"I've got a warhead alarm on number 8."

"Flick it with your finger," said Calderone.

When Washington tapped the red light, it went off. She expelled a puff of air.

"Allow reset," said Calderone.

Washington pushed a toggle switch. The computer screen now showed the number 8 rocket, viewed from below before the camera scanned the missile from bottom to top.

A klaxon sounded. Loud. Jarring. Insistent. Then, over the loudspeaker, a man with a sober, amplified voice spoke.

"Sapphire, this is Moon Rock with a Blue-dot knife-edge message in two parts. One. One. Blue Dot. Alpha."

Oh, no thought Washington. They'd never run drills without warning that one might be in the pipeline in the next few weeks. She took a deep breath and exhaled.

"Stand by to copy message," ordered Calderon. They opened their respective loose-leaf notebooks to a transparent red plastic envelope covering a page with designated spaces for codes. They wrote on the plastic with felt tipped pens as the disembodied voice continued: "Blue-dot. Oscar. Tango. Alpha. Lima. November. Romeo. Romeo. Alpha."

Washington had a fleeting urge to look at Calderone, but the voice was still providing code.

"Authentication follows: seven seven five five zero Blue-dot."

As he stood Calderone said, "The message is valid. Stand by to verify."

"I agree with verification," said Washington, also rising from her chair.

This didn't feel like a normal drill, but maybe the cheating had been discovered and someone planned this little shake-up drill. Yes, that had to be it. This was to shake everyone up. And it sure was shaking her up.

They moved to either side of a double-locked red steel box affixed to the wall.

Washington turned the dial on her combination lock to clockwise to 15, back one full turn to 25, then clockwise to 6. They opened their respective combination locks almost simultaneously.

Calderone lifted the lid. From the box, each took their respective credit-card-sized verification cards, their biscuits. Washington returned to her chair, snapped open the plastic biscuit, and compared the code on the card with the one they'd just received. They matched.

"Enter launch code," ordered Calderone.

"Joe," called Washington. "This is a strange way to run a drill. What do you think's going on?"

"Hell if I know." said Calderone. "Enter the launch code."

"Entering launch code," called Washington as she began typing it on her keyboard. The screen now read, LAUNCH ORDER CONFIRMED.

"My God!" said Washington softly before continuing. She sat stiffly staring as the screen, reading aloud the phrases as they appeared.

"Target selection complete."

Of course, neither she nor any launch control officer

knew what the targets were. They were certainly military targets, but Moscow was surrounded by such targets. Twelve and a half million people.

She continued reading from the screen.

"Time on target sequence complete."

"Yield selection complete."

"Begin countdown," said the speaker voice. "T minus 60."

"It's that time," said Calderone. "Insert launch key."

Simultaneously they inserted their keys.

"Launch key inserted," said Washington. A six hundred pound Bengal tiger about to attack her could not have released more adrenalin into her blood stream than was now being released.

"On my mark," said Calderone, "turn launch key to set. Three. Two. One. Mark."

The loudspeaker called, "T minus 50."

Washington pictured blast doors sliding open over silos spread across vast stretches of the upper Midwest. She saw hundreds of nosecones shining in the sun. She saw U. S. AIRFORCE stenciled on the rockets.

"Enable missiles," said Calderone after reexamining the screen for a moment.

The loudspeaker called "T minus 40."

She should have talked with Tyrone. She should have told him she loved him. Did it take the end of the world to make her realize this? What had the Russians thought before they launched their missiles? Had they wanted to speak with their loved ones, too?

Like an automaton, though incongruously trembling, Washington began flipping switches, "Number one enabled. Number two enabled. Number three enabled... Number eight enabled. Number nine enabled. Number ten enabled. All missiles enabled."

Overcoming her machine self, she blurted, "I want to call wing command."

"That's not in the protocol, Lieutenant."

"I'm not going to kill millions of people until I'm sure this is for real." She dialed the phone number but got no answer.

The speaker called, "T minus 20."

"I don't get anything. It's not working," said Washington.

"They've probably all been had. We've got to do this now. On my mark turn launch keys to launch."

She grasped her key. She stiffened as if electrified as a panoply of visions raced through her head. Her mother singing a lullaby. Her father running behind her as she wobbled along on a two-wheeler. Tyrone in the water below as she shows off on the diving board...

The Chicxulub crater marked the collision of an asteroid in the Yucatan sixty-six million years ago that dimmed the skies with dust, cooling the earth and killing the dinosaurs. A great many more craters were about to come into existence and hundreds of towering firestorms smothering the firmament with unearthly quantities of black soot.

CHAPTER FIFTY-TWO

The young officer at the reception desk in Colonel Nichols's anteroom displayed no discernable expression when he asked Lieutenant Washington to take a seat. She had only a few minutes to wait before a buzzer went off and the colonel asked through the intercom that the lieutenant be shown in.

Nichols, a vigorous fifty-two-year-old, short-tempered man, compensated for frontal baldness with a walrus mustache thick as fur. He was stocky but quick on his feet. Washington sat in a heavy wood chair placed directly before his desk, where he sat, hunched forward as if eager to get at her.

"Is something wrong with you?" asked Nichols as soon as she was seated. No greeting. No return salute. "Are you sick? Death in the family or something?"

"No, sir."

"Do you know why you're here, Washington?"

"I think so, sir."

"You're here because you failed to follow launch protocol."

"It was a false alarm."

"You didn't know that. It looked like the real thing, didn't it? It wasn't aborted until the last few seconds."

"Yes, sir but—"

"Are you arguing with me?"

"No, sir. Of course, not."

"You breached protocol. You will receive remedial training. You are dismissed."

Washington was smoldering. What kind of madness was this? She was being reprimanded for questioning what was indeed a false alarm. Reprimanded for not wanting to start World War Three.

"Sir, did anyone else breach protocol?"

"I can't discuss that, Lieutenant."

She spoke more firmly now, having rehearsed the words in front of a mirror. She was fully at ease with her decision, and given Nichols's attitude, she was going to get some personal satisfaction from it.

"I request transfer out of the launch control service, sir."

Nichols, who'd been sitting back in his chair, moved forward, leaning his elbows on the desk. He looked worried. And his attitude did a summersault.

"Now, just a minute, Washington. You're a good officer. You've never scored less than a hundred percent on your proficiency exams. There is probably no need for remediation. I just called you here to ask if there was anything I could do for you."

"Thank you, sir. You can transfer me to the 91st maintenance group. I cannot fire those missiles at millions of innocent people."

———

Nichols assembled the 91st missile wing's operations group, maintenance group, and security group, eleven squadrons in all, sixteen hundred persons, including enlisted airmen, officers, and civilians.

Only childlike naïveté would allow one to believe that word of the false alarm could be kept from Minot or, for that matter, from North Dakota, from the country, from the world. And yet Nichols, far from naive, felt obliged to caution the assembled about how to speak of the error, never referring to it as a near catastrophe.

"I know some of you will wish to talk about the error," said Nichols, "and I'm not saying you shouldn't, but I want to remind you to tell your listeners that the 91st has again won the Omaha Trophy making us the best missile wing in the country. And remember to emphasize that we found the error and corrected it. The public was never in danger."

Washington swallowed hard. The public was never in danger? Bullshit. All of humankind had been in danger.

Nor was Washington the only one taken aback by this statement. Many of the launch control officers on duty that day had seen their lives flash before their eyes moments before the attack order was aborted.

Colonel Nichols did not explain the source of the error: that a foreword station in Greenland had bounced radar waves off the moon coming up over Norway, interpreting the signal as an attack by dozens of Russian missiles. The last time the Russians had fired nuclear armed missiles at the United States they'd been a flock of geese.

Inevitably, however, the truth oozed its way out. Washington was one of the first to learn about it and immediately planned to tell Mrs. O'Hare.

CHAPTER FIFTY-THREE

Compared to the end of civilization, cheating on an exam dwindles into insignificance, except if one makes a connection between the two. An inadequately trained officer, a higher up, making a mistake. Did the generals have to take an exam? What if they cheated? Washington's dilemma was unresolved, though she'd gone over it again and again, until she decided she must act, or she'd get sick.

———

Washington and Calderone were on duty together again. Calderone was reading a book in the late afternoon after all the systems checking had been completed. The tone of her voice alone told him something serious was on his mind.

"Joe, I need to talk with you."

He lay the book down and swiveled in his chair to face her.

"What's up?"

"I have to tell Nichols that there is cheating on the exam. I'm not going to mention any names even if he threatens me. I wanted you to know so you wouldn't be surprised if he discovers your one-time indiscretion."

He felt the onset of a stomachache. Indeed, he briefly placed his palms over his abdomen, before clasping his hands together and resting them on his lap. He only very briefly considered trying to reassure her that it had all ended, but that was untrue and, just as bad, he hadn't worked up the courage to tell the kingpin of the test *coaching* business, that the jig would be up soon.

"When are you going to tell him?"

"In a couple of days. I need to get some sleep first."

"Make it three days. I want to speak with my wife about it."

"Three days it is. I'm glad you didn't try to talk me out of it this time."

Calderone nodded gloomily.

———

Soon after arriving home the next day, Calderone told his wife he had something important to discuss with her.

"I can make you a cup of coffee. We can talk in the kitchen."

He started talking while she was still standing at the machine, meticulously measuring out the coffee and adding it to the filter.

"You know how important that monthly exam is, well I fell behind in my studies... And I... I got the answers to the test ahead of time and used them. Just once."

Despite her care with the coffee Maria had been listening closely. She closed the machine and pushed the start button before seating herself at the table across from him.

"You cheated on the exam?"

"Yes. I was worried I'd mess it up."

"But Joe, that's not like you."

"It really isn't. I regret it and I'll never do it again but it's too late. Nichols is going to find out about the cheating, that it's going on. He won't be given any names. I don't know how he'll find those who cheated. There are a lot of us."

"Oh, he'll find a way. Who's going to tell him about the cheating in the first place?"

"Washington."

"Oh. How did she find out?"

He was embarrassed and frightened enough without revealing that she'd seen him looking at his not-so-smart watch.

"I don't know, but she told me she'd seen someone with a crib sheet during the exam. She wouldn't tell me who."

"When is she going to tell him?"

"In three days."

"Joe, one way or another Colonel Nichols is going to get the names of everyone involved and it's going to go down hard on them. You've got to see him as soon as possible—today—and confess. Tell him as much as possible about the scheme. Do it before she does. In fact, tell her you're going to do it so she doesn't. Your confession looks better that way."

She got up to pour them both cups of coffee.

"Are you mad at me?" he asked.

"I'm disappointed. I'm sad. I'm worried. But I'm not mad. I don't know why I'm not. I guess I look at it like you had an accident."

He would do as his wife recommended. It was wise. But first he'd have to speak with Forster. He'd have to be fair to Forster the way Washington had been fair to him.

———

They met at a pizza parlor on the base, sitting as far as they could from the short line of customers in front of the cash register. Calderone wanted to break the news to Forster in a public place. Why? He wasn't sure. Forster's temper? Maybe.

"Don't you want a pizza?" asked Forster.

"Maybe later. I need to tell you something first."

Calderone took a deep breath, exhaling fast, a puff, and then he did it again as if he'd been out jogging. He'd come here with the intention of giving Forster a heads-up about his imminent revelation to Nichols of widespread cheating on base, but given that Forster had organized the whole scheme, he was at risk for a much greater penalty than a one-time cheater. He'd be furious.

So instead he said, "I'm not doing drugs anymore."

"We had to come here for you to tell me that? Hey, it's no skin off my ass. What's wrong? You don't look so hot."

"Oh, Maria and I had an argument. It was her idea I quit, and I've hardly even started."

"Well, if you change your mind."

"I won't."

———

The apple-cheeked young officer in Nichols's anteroom asked Calderone to sit. His appointment was for four and at exactly four he was told to go in.

Nichols was seated behind his desk. Calderone saluted and thanked the colonel for making the time for him.

"All right then," said Nichols, indicating a chair.

Calderone had two serious offenses he should admit to, but he just couldn't bring himself to reveal both. He'd admit to the more serious of the two. If it were later discovered that he'd used drugs on a few occasions, so be it.

But what was he going to say about the cheating? Nichols would ask from whom he'd gotten the answers. He'd be a snitch if he told, but what he really feared was Forster's anger. He was a hot head.

"Sir, I am here to confess to cheating on a proficiency exam. It pains me to say so, and I'm sure it will pain you to hear it, but there is widespread cheating on these exams because poor grades, maybe even one poor grade, will block career advancement."

Nichols scowled like a prizefighter hit below the belt, and remained silent for an inordinately long time, as if recovering from the blow.

At last he spoke. "Tell me about your cheating."

"What do you want to know, sir."

Calderone explained in detail as much as he knew about it, including Forster's role in organizing the scheme and collecting a hundred dollars per exam. A specially encrypted website had the answers so there was no incriminating email to be found on people's computers. Other than Forster,

Calderone knew of no one else who cheated, though he understood that many did.

"What about your duty partner, Washington?"

"She doesn't cheat."

"How do you know? Have you discussed this with her?"

"She learned about the cheating and was going to report it, but I beat her to it."

CHAPTER FIFTY-FOUR

Rasmussen's call to O'Hare had been brief. He apologized for not being able to go on the march. Somberly he said he'd be unable to participate in further demonstrations nor could he express support for the anti-GBSD program. Phrasing it differently three times, she asked what the matter was. And three times he awkwardly evaded any semblance of a satisfactory answer.

So Edna was surprised when he accepted an invitation to a Sunday afternoon cup of coffee at her place.

"I didn't think you would come," said Edna.

"I didn't think so either," said Rasmussen, putting a couple of lemon cookies on his plate and pouring himself another cup of black coffee strong enough to keep him awake for a few days. "But I thought I owed it to you."

"Something has happened, but you're unwilling to talk about it. Is that it?"

"Correct. And I assume you've put truth serum in my coffee."

"Never crossed my mind. Didn't think you'd need it," said Edna.

"Thank you for the vote of confidence. You know, Edna, I really would like to confide in you. Confession is good for the soul, but I don't want to burden you with this. Honestly, though, I'm not as concerned about my soul or about burdening you as I am about my marriage…"

"Oh," said O'Hare.

"It would have helped legitimize your argument if a well-known, well-respected physician backed it publicly. Well, that physician was about to do so when something came up. Edna, I feel a bit foolish asking you, but can you keep a secret?"

"Sounds like it's a marital issue, so yes I can."

"It's not really a marital issue. Okay, here goes."

He told her about Cummings' first office visit, how she essentially offered the sight and feel of her breasts for his admiration. He admitted that three or four times in his career he'd been strongly attracted to one of his patients, but he'd never acted inappropriately, nor had he done so on that visit. He felt foolish to have believed her story of anxiety, but she was utterly convincing.

Then came the panicky call from the hotel. Might he not have gently held his ground with another patient, insisting on an office visit. After all, half the patients seeing a general practitioner were there because of psychological problems, or so the research indicated, and he was as comfortable prescribing antidepressants as he was prescribing antihypertensives.

But he went to the hotel and she'd played her cards so well that it was he who suggested they go to her hotel room. Had she invited him to her room, now that he thought about it, he might have demurred. He might have realized what she was up to.

Sitting here with his confessor, he spoke of his long-standing interest in pharmacology. What had Cummings put in that tea he'd asked himself repeatedly? A potent tranquilizer to weaken resistance to suggestions coupled with a stimulant and some other psychotropic? He considered barbiturates, amphetamines, THC, and almost certainly sildenafil or a similar drug. He'd rapidly become euphoric, suggestible, and aroused.

"It was the perfect aphrodisiac. So you know where this is going."

"And there's a risk your wife will learn of your indiscretion?" said Edna levelly.

"Yes. If I make a peep about the GBSD."

"Oh, my God. Grumman put her up to this?" O'Hare shook her head, puzzled.

"It does seem odd, doesn't it? A fifty billion dollar aerospace giant, which has already won the contract, worried about me. If I weren't scared, I'd be flattered."

"Do you suppose she wanted to seduce you and then thought of an additional benefit?"

"No. Edna. I appreciate it, but I'm not that desirable."

"Too bad you can't find out what was in her head?"

"I'd ask but I'm too frightened to go anywhere near her."

"You know, Andrew, when we marched, we passed a specialty shop you might be interested in."

And then she outlined a way he might learn more about her machinations. And maybe even throw a clunky monkey wrench into the machinery. But could he be that bold?

———

Rasmussen called Claudia Cummings on a Tuesday afternoon, stepping out onto the street to use his cell phone. Would she meet him in the lobby of her hotel at 7:00 p.m.? She readily agreed.

She awaited him in the same spot as last time. Her hair was pulled back in a short French braid. She wore tight maroon slacks and a snug but frilly white blouse.

She arose to greet him. "Good evening, Dr. Rasmussen." She extended her hand. He took it briefly. They sat.

He wore khaki slacks and a blue short-sleeved shirt, a pocket protector holding a pen and a mechanical pencil.

"I haven't talked about it," began Rasmussen. "I haven't gone to any meetings. I even cancelled going on a parade. I just wanted you to know."

"I've never had any doubts, but you could have just said this on the phone. I would have thought that after our little get together, you wouldn't want to see me again. Hmm. Maybe I was wrong? Would you like to come up to my room?"

She smiled and shifted her shoulders so her breasts moved lasciviously. Rasmussen clasped his hands on his lap, staring at them in the endearing attitude of a small boy who wants something from the candy counter but is ashamed to ask.

"I'd like to, yes, but not tonight."

"Why not tonight? "said Cummings.

"I don't know. I didn't think you'd... I don't know."

"You didn't think I'd want to?"

"Perhaps."

"Let's go upstairs," said Cummings.

Rasmussen looked up at her. Then looked around the lobby.

"You go first," he said. "I'll be up in a minute."

"You'll definitely be up in a minute. I'll see to it."

––––––

"Can I get you something to drink?"

"Yes, but not that stuff you doped me up with last time. I've never been so intoxicated. I couldn't think. You could have gotten me to do anything. What was in that stuff?"

"You sure you don't want some more. It may have knocked out your will power, but it sure didn't knock out your performance."

"Well, I might try it again sometime. You can't blackmail me twice for the same drug-induced seduction. No offense."

"Well, if it's blackmail, it's blackmail in your own interest. You can't go around saying bad things about those missiles without riling up some people. I just have your best interests at heart. I really wouldn't want to have to tell your wife."

"Will Grumman give you a bonus?"

She laughed.

As she was preparing him a high-ball, minus unusual pharmaceutical additions, Rasmussen's phone rang.

"What? He won't go to the emergency room. Oh. Okay. I'll be there shortly."

"Ms. Cummings," said Rasmussen. "I've got to go." He stood abruptly. "A difficult patient. I've got to make a house call."

"You don't mean it. A house call. I thought those weren't done anymore."

"You'd be surprised."

"Well, then goodnight, Dr. Rasmussen." She approached to give him a kiss, but he stepped back.

"Good night, Ms. Cummings."

"Good night."

CHAPTER FIFTY-FIVE

Before Will could arrange to show Roy Haugen the tinkly bag of twisted shrapnel ribbons and tags, Haugen called O'Hare to make an appointment.

Will met him at the front door, letting him in, and called for Edna who was in the back of the house somewhere.

"Good morning, Mrs. O'Hare," said Haugen as she entered the room. They shook hands.

"I'd like to speak with the two of you about that explosion."

"Yes, please take a seat. I'll get us some coffee."

"That's not necessary," said Haugen.

"Well, I need a cup in hand to settle my nerves although most people would choose a drink. May I get you a drink?"

Perhaps it was an indication of how disturbed he was by this whole matter, but he'd been tempted to ask for a shot of whiskey.

"On second thought, a cup of coffee would be good," he said. "Thank you."

"You too, Will?"

"Yes, please."

Wishing to fully include Edna in the exchange, Will waited until she returned with the coffee before handing the bag of telltale metal fragments to Haugen.

"I pried these out of the wood on the front porch. Karen told me grenades had gone missing on the base."

"When was that?" said Haugen.

"When was what?" said Will.

"When did she tell you?"

"The morning after the explosion."

"Where did she tell you. I mean where were the two of you when she told you?"

"Here."

An uncomfortable silence followed, but finally Roy Haugen turned away from Will.

"Mrs. O'Hare, may I put the cup on the table so I can use the saucer for something?"

"How thoughtful of you to ask, Sergeant Haugen. Yes, you may."

He shook out the shrapnel fragments onto the saucer. A few retained some olive green paint.

"I think they're from a grenade, but I'll get an ordnance expert on the base to be sure. Does anyone else know your suspicions?"

"I wanted to speak with you first," said Will. "I haven't told Sheriff Andresen yet."

"I'll be talking with him, but I'd rather the grenade idea didn't become public while we're investigating. It would put the creeps who did this on alert."

The three sipped coffee simultaneously.

Unnecessarily, Haugen told them to be careful, hesitating before mentioning that he'd rather his daughter not take part in any protests.

Will and Edna glanced at each other.

"She's your daughter," said Edna, "and I understand your concern. At the moment I'm too demoralized to do any more protesting but if Karen wants to protest, I hope you don't expect me to say no. I can't do that."

Haugen could say nothing to that.

———

Andresen motioned Haugen to an heirloom sea captain's chair with a worn black leather cushion, a sign of how happy Andresen was to see him.

"Between you and me," he said, "I haven't gotten anywhere with this thing so I'd appreciate any help you can give me."

"Actually I'm here to ask for your help," said Haugen.

He gave the bag of shrapnel to Andresen, explaining that an ordnance expert had identified the pieces of a grenade that had gone missing on the base.

"I'm trying to find the person who took them, but would like to keep my investigation secret for now otherwise—"

"Otherwise," interrupted Andresen, "you'll tip off the mad bomber."

"That's about it."

"You will tell me the minute you find the bastard, won't you?" said Andresen.

"This loss of grenades is a bit embarrassing. Colonel Nichols would like to keep it quiet, but I don't see how that's possible, so yes, I'll let you know."

"Good."

"There's something I'd like from you," said Haugen. "Another embarrassment. Someone is dealing drugs on the base. I have the telephone number of the dealer but not the name. Can you find out who owns the phone?"

Andresen pulled a pad of paper toward him from across his desk..

"Shoot."

Haugen gave him the number.

"I shouldn't have any trouble getting a warrant to find a drug dealer, but sometimes the phone company takes its time," said Andresen.

"This probably won't be much help, but the dealer goes by Batman."

CHAPTER FIFTY-SIX

As soon as Rasmussen got to his car, he called Edna.

"You're timing was perfect. If you'd called a little later, I wouldn't have had a good excuse to walk out on her, except for cold feet, I guess."

"Have you listened to it yet?"

"Not yet. I'd like to make a copy before anything happens to it."

"I don't suppose you'd let me hear it."

"Why, Edna, your interest's not salacious, is it?"

He patted his new pen in its plastic pocket protector.

"Hm," mused Edna. "Let me think about that, but for the moment I'm just curious how damning it is, and whether Grumman will give a damn."

———

Ellen Conklin was resting in her hotel room at around three in the afternoon, when her phone rang.

"Good afternoon, Ms. Conklin. This is Andrew Rasmussen."

"Hello. Yes. What can I do for you?"

"I wonder if you'd be so kind as to meet me at the Lucky Strike Restaurant for a cup of coffee this afternoon. It's less than a quarter mile north of your hotel."

"May I ask what this concerns?"

"A matter that will interest Grumman, I'm pretty sure."

"Why don't you just come over here?"

"I'd like to be discreet."

She didn't like the sound of it. Rasmussen was no friend of Grumman. It hadn't been long since she'd actually spoken to Claudia about him.

———

The sound of the bowling balls rolling down the alleys and the muted thunder of the falling pins easily penetrated the restaurant, though their booth offered some buffering.

"It is rather a noisy place for a meeting," said Conklin after some preliminary talk about the difference between North Dakota and Virginia summers.

"Yes, well, it was close by your hotel and the background noise just makes our chat all the more discrete."

By unspoken agreement neither of them raised the subject of that chat until coffee arrived.

"Now that Boeing has dropped out of the competition," said Rasmussen, "the contract is in the bag, isn't it? You are going to build the GBDS."

"Well, yes. There's no one else competing and Northrup Grumman has built rockets for the air force since 1954: Atlas. Thor. Titan I and II. Minuteman I, II, and III. Peacekeeper and Small ICBM." She'd slipped into saleswoman mode.

"It sounds to me," said Rasmussen, "that the company should feel about as secure as can be."

"It does, of course."

"Then why did the company feel it necessary to black mail me?"

"I assure you, Dr. Rasmussen, I don't know what you're talking about."

He placed upon the table the digital audio player to which he'd transferred the recording from his spy pen.

"I'd like you to hear this."

Conklin sat transfixed, as the recorder began to play:

———

"Can I get you something to drink?"

"Yes, but not that stuff you doped me up with last time. I've never been so intoxicated. I couldn't think. You could have gotten me to do anything. What was in that stuff?"

"You sure you don't want some more. It may have knocked out your willpower, but it sure didn't knock out your performance."

"Well, I might try it again sometime. You can't black mail me twice for the same drug-induced seduction. No offense."

"Well, if it's blackmail, it's blackmail in your own inter- ests. You can't go around saying bad things about those missiles without riling up some people. I just have your best interests at heart. I really wouldn't want to have to tell your wife."

"Will Grumman give you a bonus?"

Laughter.

———

By the time the recording ended, Conklin looked as if she'd just been scratched by a cat.

"Your public relations person," said Rasmussen, putting the small device back into his pocket, has threatened to tell my wife about the episode if I talk about the new missile or the old ones for that matter."

"Grumman had absolutely nothing to do with this."

"Ms. Conklin, rather than argue with you, I'd like to ask you to dissuade your employee from ever speaking to my wife about what happened. If she does my marriage will be severely damaged as will Grumman's reputation when the news reports appear. 'Grumman employee blackmails local physician into silence after drugging him into indiscretion.' Oh, it won't stop you from getting the contract, but it might slow down the approval process in congress. The people of Minot are good people. They will speak to the national press about this."

The sound of tumbling bowling pins comforted Rasmussen.

CHAPTER FIFTY-SEVEN

Ellen Conklin met with Claudia Cummings in a small hotel conference room shortly after Rasmussen revealed Cummings' blackmail plan.

"Is it true?" asked Conklin. "Did you drug him?"

"I wouldn't put it that way exactly. He was completely awake." Had Conklin not appeared to be so irritated, Cummings might have smiled at just how fully awake he'd actually been.

"He knew what he was doing."

"I don't think you understand," said Conklin. "How do you think the public would react to Northrup Grumman blackmailing people? Blackmailing people about anything. Threatening his marriage. Slipping drugs into his drink. Leading him into adultery. Holy mother of God, Claudia!"

"Weren't you worried about him making a fuss and turning some of the town against the missiles? I thought you'd be pleased that he'd decided not to talk and anyway his story sounds so far-fetched that no one would believe him anyway. He didn't want to screw me. Oh, no. He had to be drugged."

"Claudia! Let's not be vulgar."

"It would be his word against mine and no matter what people believed his reputation would be ruined."

How had Conklin become VP of the Grumman GBSD team, wondered Cummings. She was so small-minded.

"Northrup Grumman does not operate by ruining people's reputations."

"What do you want me to do?" asked Cummings, becoming angry. After all, she'd taken some risk to silence the troublemaker.

"Tell him that you've been forbidden ever to reveal to his wife or anyone else what happened. You're to tell him the company had nothing to do with what you did. And you're to apologize. And all of this as discreetly as possible. On second thought, I'll tell him. You stay away from him."

"So you're not as worried about him as you appeared?"

"Claudia, I'm more worried about him now than I was before he told me about this. If you tell his wife what happened, everyone will learn about your little love potion and blackmail scheme."

Cummings shook her head. "They won't believe it."

"They'll believe it when the transcript of your confession appears in the news."

"Transcript of my confession?"

"He recorded your last conversation with him. A nice crisp recording."

Claudia felt her throat tighten. She swallowed.

Conklin spoke. "As I said, I'll do the apologizing. I don't want you to have any contact with him whatsoever. Promise me that."

Cummings nodded.

"I promise."

He'd outsmarted her. She felt a keen bitterness, but could she accept defeat? Re-examining their last meeting, she saw that pencil and pen in his pocket. So that's how he did it. She should get one of those, she thought.

———

Almost everyone on campus— staff, students and faculty— read Betty Carlson's article on O'Hare's minimally attended street march, the ideas behind it, and street fight that followed it. She went so far as to publish the names of the attackers and of the marchers.

CHAPTER FIFTY-EIGHT

Of course, even in summer, even if all she grew were sunflowers, even if her hired hands still showed up when they were supposed to, there was always work to do on the farm. Edna mended fences. Repainted the front porch. Straightened up the woodshed, did some canning.

To say she was racked with guilt would be to exaggerate, but she blamed herself for not having the fortitude, or was it just thick enough skin, to continue with her protests. Few people showed any concrete interest in the GBSD. Calling their door-to-door visits in the business district a parade was ludicrous. Then they were attacked and finally someone had set off a bomb on her front step, endangering Will and Karen.

Yes, she was energetic for her age, but she was frightened and depressed. And now Will was again beginning to talk about going to New York. She hadn't realized how much his mere presence meant to her, how it made getting up in the morning easier and coming home in the evening easier as well.

Will's mother had called again.

"Can you believe it? Tom hid my phone from me; that's why I haven't been able to call. Where are you anyway? Why don't you call? When are you coming out here? Oh, damn, I shouldn't be talking on the phone in the first place." She lowered her voice. "You know what I mean." And then again loudly, "I need your help. They're going to lock me up. You know that will kill me. Will, what do I have to do to convince you? Jump from the Brooklyn Bridge?"

Edna's protest had fizzled so Will doubted his presence was particularly significant, if it had even been so in the first place. After he told her he was on his way, he began questioning himself? What would he do when he got there? Was his goal to keep her out of a psychiatric hospital because that's what she wanted? Was he antipsychiatry? Was he doing what she wanted because he'd always done what she wanted? Why was he so conflicted about this?

The same day Will's brother called.

"No. I don't think she'll get violent. But she blows up and Grandma is at her wits end. And now she's bringing in stray dogs, but she doesn't walk them. Her hygiene is godawful. She's been arrested again for shoplifting. I know a psychiatrist who'll help get her committed. I'm calling just so you'll know what's going on. I know you're on your way out here, though what's so fascinating about Minot, North Dakota is beyond me. A healthy corn-fed Midwestern girl? Anyway, there's no rush."

Fortunately Will procrastinated.

While Will was out checking over his car, Dr. Rasmussen came over to see Edna.

"Hello, Will."

"Oh, hi Dr. Rasmussen. Long time no see. Are you okay?"

"Never felt better."

As usual Edna needed coffee to fortify herself.

"I wanted to tell you in person that I'm ready to get back into the parade and flyer business, Edna," Rasmussen said.

"Oh, my goodness. What about you-know-who? What happened?"

He began the tale in a measured pace, but the words eventually began tumbling out like a load of smooth round stones from a wheelbarrow, their clatter indefinably pleasing. Best of all, besides imagining Cummings' chagrin, of course, was Ellen Conklin's face-to-face apology and assurance that he was free to say anything he wanted without fear of being—how did she say it—compromised.

"And I don't just want to march. I want to give speeches. But we need you. And people are asking where you are."

"That's sweet of you but I don't know if I'm up to it. Nobody seems to be listening and even if they were I know this whole protest business is quixotic. Besides it puts people in danger. A bomb! Can you believe it?"

"From what I've heard it wasn't meant to kill anyone."

"Listen, Edna, I've been reading up on this ICBM business ever since you opened my eyes to the danger. I see plenty of suffering in my practice, but that suffering is like a grain of sand compared to the Everest of suffering, death, and desolation of nuclear war. And as I've said there is no medical response possible. These missiles could be launched by mistake. I'll take your flyers if you're not going to use them. Your sign, too. I don't blame you for taking a break, but I can't. I'm even cutting back on the time I spend in the office."

"Well, Andrew, I don't think I can put people at risk and I'm not telling you anything you don't know if I say I'm down in the dumps. I think I've had it."

"I understand. I hope you won't mind if I ask for your flyers and signs. I'm going to work on this. You can always let me know if you change your mind."

———

His having avoided marital catastrophe by his own daring was a pick-me-up, one with ramifying effects.

He spoke to his colleagues about cutting back his work hours and taking no more new patients. They'd considered adding another partner to their practice for years. Now was the time to start interviewing.

"What's up, Andy?" asked Rich Kovacs.

"I'm going to sound like a politician who's dropping out of a race, but I just want to spend more time with my family."

To avoid sounding like a fanatic, he made no mention of a prolonged campaign against the GBSD.

But he had not lied about wanting to spend more time with his family, by which he meant his wife, whom he'd come close to losing by neglect if not by revelation of his sin. He now routinely arrived home in time to eat dinner with her.

Earlier in their marriage they had regularly read aloud together. He suggested they do so again, mentioning *The Girl With the Dragon Tattoo*. One would read, the other would cook, and they'd rotate duties.

"You'll cook?" asked Darlene. "Every other day? I want it in writing."

He suggested that after dinner each night, they watch a Netflix series together, maybe the one about the unflappable, stoic Wyoming Sheriff Longmire, who rode the range in his Ford V8 Bronco.

"It's not too violent," he assured her. She accepted.

After ten days of newly established domesticity, she still rejected his intermittent, amorous approaches, her bitterness over years of neglect not easily assuaged. His patients and his colleagues had always come first.

But despite her bedtime coolness, he continued coming home on time, cooking, sitting close to her in front of the TV. And his mood was more upbeat than it had been in years.

They even began going on walks together.

Rasmussen was at peace with himself. On weekends, he went to Edna's for an hour or two. Occasionally Darlene went with him. But at bedtime she remained aloof until one night, after he'd gotten into bed, she appeared at the bedside in a new, pale blue, baby doll pajamas. In her palms she cupped her breasts, their nipples visible through the gossamer material.

"What are *you* looking at?" she asked in a teasing, little girl voice he could not remember ever having heard.

He rolled over in bed to grab her, but she moved a few steps back.

"I know what you want to do, you naughty boy."

When she didn't move, he swung his legs over the side of the bed and lunged for her, but she was too quick and moved to the foot of the bed. He pursued her around the bed, but she sprang onto the bed and over it, so she was still out of reach.

"You really want to stick it in, don't you?"

"Darlene!"

In turn he sprang across the bed to the other side, but she was already at the foot again. He was out of breath, but Darlene, summer jogger, winter skier, was inexhaustible. He was now as excited as he'd been on that drug. Again he lunged for her and again she eluded him, moving to the other side of the bed, quick as a rabbit. He followed but again she sprang onto and over the bed.

"Come on, Andy. Don't you want to do it to me?"

But she wouldn't let him catch her. In half an hour he really was both exhausted and exhilarated. Hands at his sides on the bed, he hung his head, but kept his eyes on her feet. When she was in range he pushed off the bed with both hands and tackled her, landing on top, but she struggled against him, laughing.

He pinned her wrists over head with his left hand, wedged himself between her legs, but pressed against her rocking body, the excitement was too great. He released his grip and lay atop her, quiescent as was she.

"I love you, Darlene."

"I love you, too, Andy."

In seven minutes they stood and got into bed.

"Please don't run off again," said Rasmussen.

"And don't you either," said Darlene.

The second grinding of the mill was entirely satisfactory.

Surprised by his ardor and pleased with her response, she finally asked, "What's going on with you, Andy? I like it but I don't understand it and I'm afraid it's not going to last."

"At first my protest against the new missiles was purely intellectual. I thought it was, anyway. But fearing the mistakes that could lead to nuclear war jogged loose other feelings and made me finally examine the life I was leading. You know I like my patients, but, God, I don't love them. I realized, though, that I was too fond of them loving me, or maybe just adoring me. Real ego boost. And if my partners asked me to cover extra time for them, or fit in that extra one, two, or three drop-in patients, I said, 'Sure, I can do that.' I was too fond of hearing their gratitude and praise.

"I love you and Robert, and my siblings, and some of my friends and—sorry, this sounds corny—I love humanity, which is in danger of annihilation. I needed time to play my bit part to stop that and I needed time to be with you. That's the long and short of it."

CHAPTER FIFTY-NINE

The several protests, flyer distributions, newspaper articles, and rumors had lent Edna O'Hare a certain notoriety and even respect, so when Karen, Will, and Rasmussen spent a few days distributing her new flyer announcing a rally to protest the GBSD, more than the handful of people were curious. The big attraction, though, was not O'Hare—who in any case was dispirited and house bound—but Andrew Rasmussen, probably the physician of record for half the people who'd attend.

Rasmussen was a man who demonstrated daily his caring and concern for the town. He'd volunteered for the Minot Area Homeless Coalition, Habitat for Humanity, the Feed the Children's Foundation, and United Blood Services. Indeed people wondered how he managed his practice, volunteered his services, and still managed to be a good husband. No one suspected that for years now he and his wife might read in bed or sleep in bed, but not love in bed.

Announcement of the time and place appeared in Minot State's *Red and Green* and in the *Minot Daily News*.

Rasmussen had called the media, promising a big story. Betty Carlson and Suzy emailed friends and placed a notice on their Facebook pages.

By doggedly calling various newspaper offices, Rasmussen had managed to obtain a not quite iron-clad commitment from Ben Grossman of the *Bismarck Tribune* to attend the rally, though it meant a two hour drive to get there. Amy Haugen would be there for the *Minot Daily News*, and Betty Carlson from the *Red and Green*, of course, but what really excited the Committee for a Sound Nuclear Deterrence, as they now called themselves, was the chance that they might appear on local TV since they were going to hold their rally in front of the KMOT TV station near the corner of 16th Street S.W. and 18th Avenue S. W. In the parking lot to be specific.

Rasmussen built a sturdy one-foot-tall wood speakers' platform—essentially a box—broad enough for a person to stand on. To get the lay of the land, the featured speaker visited the venue, a one story studio building, nondescript except for its dazzlingly tall transmitting tower.

On the morning of the rally the sun rose before the first of the protestors appeared. The building faced east so, with their backs to the sun, the demonstrators faced the studio. Studio manager Tina Nilsen, a patient of Rasmussen's, agreed to video part of the demonstration, and produce and air a news clip if more important events didn't take precedent.

"More important than safe nuclear deterrence," said Rasmussen smiling. "Like what, Tina?"

"Be grateful for what you get. There are people who are going to want to scalp me after this thing airs, believe me."

He flinched at the word scalp, remembering that there

was another speaker, John Silverhawk, a man that Will had met in a diner in Grand Forks, who might object to that phrase.

Fifty-three well behaved men and women, several with signs, watched as Karen, with Will and Rasmussen at her side for assistance, stepped onto the platform.

"Good morning and thank you for coming. My name is Karen Haugen. I've lived in Minot my whole life. I'm one of the founding members of Edna O'Hare's Committee for a Sound Nuclear Deterrence, whose goal it is to tell people of the danger, pointlessness, and wastefulness of replacing the Minuteman missiles with the new GBSD missiles, which stands for ground-based strategic deterrent. I only have a few words to say before I introduce the first of today's two speakers.

"A Russian intercontinental ballistic missile can reach the United States in about thirty minutes so if our missiles are fixed targets there's little time to verify that a warning is real before launching them. And firing the missiles by mistake, leads to nuclear war. I know I'm a broken record but this needs repeating. Nuclear war could lead to the deto-nation around the world of thousands of nuclear warheads with the destructive power of 100,000 Hiroshima bombs."

She spoke for a while longer before introducing the first of two speakers.

"Hello. My name is John Silverhawk. I own an auto shop in Grand Forks. As you probably guessed, I'm a descendant of the first Americans, specifically I am Sioux. Now I am not here today pretending to represent the Sioux nation. I am here as an American citizen with a Sioux heritage. But because of that heritage I am sensitive to the value of the land in a way that is not the same as the real estate value of the land. And in this I *can* speak for the Sioux, the Mandan, the Hidatsa, and the Arikara Nation. The Chippewa and the Sisseton-Wahpeton Oyate Nation.

"I am here to talk about the danger to the land. And about warnings ignored. There have been many warnings, and oil spills despoiling land and water and killing wildlife. Many oil spills. The last one was an hour's drive from where I live. Hundreds of thousands of gallons covered half an acre of wetlands. It could take years for the wetlands to return to their normal state.

"Warnings ignored. Damage done.

"And now again warnings about the danger to the land. The U.S. government has turned the upper Midwest into a bullseye target for Russian atomic bombs. I know what the government says. The rockets are here to protect us, but they do not protect us. In official descriptions the land has been described as a rocket sponge to absorb hundreds of atomic-tipped rockets from Russia. But unlike years for an oil-soaked wetlands to get healthy, a radioactive wetland may stay radioactive for thousands of years.

"North Dakota has about one hundred fifty missiles in underground silos and many of them are in danger of flooding as happened to one of them a few years ago. The missile had to be pulled out and inspected.

"To spend a hundred billion dollars to replace these rockets is much worse than foolish spending.

"I have said I am not here as an official representative of my tribe whose members have their personal travails, but I will be speaking with them and with other tribes. If you believe these rockets put you in danger, you too must speak up. Remember there are people in this country who don't even know these missiles exist.

"Thank you for your attention."

After he was applauded, Rasmussen climbed the little platform, the morning sun in his eyes also.

"Good morning. My name is Andrew Rasmussen. I'm a family doc her in Minot and I know many of you—"

"Most of us," called someone from the crowd.

"Well, most of you here and a lot more who aren't here. I've been blessed with the chance to go to school, study medicine, and practice in this fine town, where I've worked most of my professional life. My son was born here, graduated from Magic High, and attended Minot State University. My wife was born here in Minot and has family here.

"I care about this town and am here today to talk about an issue whose importance it's hard to overstate. But before I do, I want to tell you about a few cases that have stuck in my mind over the years.

"Some of you will remember the Frederickson fire, the pictures of that inferno. One of the children was ten years old, Carol. She'd run out to the barn to save Brownie, the family's horse, but got trapped inside briefly by the fire but not so briefly as to escape severe burns over her face, arms, and legs. I saw Carol before she was transferred to the University of Colorado burn center by helicopter. I'm pretty good at finding professional distance but I had some bad dreams about that little girl, who, as you know died in the hospital.

"I was furious at Stanley Frederickson for starting the fire. He'd been smoking in the barn and got distracted by a bat. He doesn't remember what he did with the cigarette butt. He made a mistake.

"Intelligent, careful people make mistakes.

"I saw a young woman whose case made the newspapers. Her name was Debra Fisher. She worked in a lab at the university studying the effects of low levels of methyl mercury on enzyme function. She wore gloves, a mask, and used a fume hood. Everyone who knew her said she was meticulous, yet one day, while using a micropipette to make a dilution, a tiny drop of the solution landed on her gloved hand. Over the next several months she developed some slurring of her speech and clumsiness, then difficulty walking, muscle weakness, poor hearing. She died after five months. Her death due to a mistake. People make mistakes.

"Some mistakes are worse than others. No matter how diligent people may be, how alert, attentive, concentrated, they still make mistakes.

"Think about the recent false alarm of a Russian missile attack. We have all heard about it. Radar surveillance appeared to show dozens of missiles heading toward us. This is not the first time a ground-based or satellite surveillance system appears to have shown an attack.

"Submarine captains and airplane pilots have some time to assess the quality of the warning they are receiving, but commanders of ground-based intercontinental ballistic missiles, the Minuteman missiles all around us, have little time because if they delay too long in a real attack, their missiles will be destroyed. You can't call a missile back once it's fired.

"And the same is true of the missiles the government wants to replace them with. But a mistake would lead to nuclear war and as a physician I am telling you there is no medical response possible and the suffering, loss, grief, and deaths is too horrible to try to imagine. Just think of millions of ten-year-olds incinerated. You don't want to? Of course not.

"We are gathered here to protest the replacement of these missiles. We have more than adequate deterrent might in our airplanes, cruise missiles and submarines.

"But what of the business that may be lost if the Minuteman is not replaced? I suppose this is not just a theoretical question, but how much potential business will be lost is unknown. And how the government may be able, through support of the air force base, to make up for some loss is also unknown. People must ask themselves, are we going to continue gambling that there won't be a catastrophic error so that we can receive contracts with the government? And remember that, should the GBSD project be cancelled, there will be either refurbishment of the Minuteman or its removal, both of which will bring work to Minot."

"I invite you all to join me as we picket in front of Minot Air Force Base. The time and date are on the flyer that is going around."

Rasmussen stepped off his little platform as the crowd was still applauding. A woman stepped up to him.

"May I say a few words?"

"It's a free country," said Rasmussen before having second thoughts, but so what if she spoke in favor of the missiles. This was a supportive group. She couldn't do any harm.

"My name's Makenna Washington. I work on the base. I just want to tell you all that the rumor of a false alarm almost launching the missiles is true. Just thought you should know."

And with that she stepped down.

CHAPTER SIXTY

Rasmussen, Karen, and Will provided quiet but undeviating encouragement. With a day or two more to think about this after Rasmussen's visit, Edna was ready to go again.

A dozen new adherents joined their next march, triple the number they'd had on their first, but Rasmussen was dissatisfied.

"I think what we need next is something newsworthy, dramatic, like a sit-in. Now ideally that would be done on the base, but I don't think we can manage it."

"We could do it right outside the base," said Karen. "There's a big sign there for the photographers to use as a backdrop. We could protest across the street. It's just farmland there, I think, but they might make us move before the newspaper or TV people show up."

This time there was organizing to do. Rasmussen and Edna would contact out-of-town radio, television, and newspaper offices to see if they were interested in sending a reporter to witness a protest.

Karen said they would reconnoiter and surprised Will by asking if he'd drive out to the base with her.

At Minot Air Force Base on US 83, they parked at the edge of a grassy field directly across from the Missile Avenue entrance. A low, wing-shaped brick wall read 5th Bomb Wing. 91st Missile Wing.

The sun was overhead. At 1:00 p.m. there was little to see as all the commuters to the base had long since arrived.

"I guess I didn't think this through," said Karen. "We've no idea what the traffic is like in the morning or in the evening either. It's still light at six, so we could also demonstrate then."

Eventually it was too hot in the car, even with the windows open, so they got out, and sat on the grass facing the entrance to the base. A hundred yards behind them ran a stand of leafy trees parallel to the highway.

An hour passed while they waited to see if anyone would object to their presence. Karen found herself talking about her plans to be a pediatrician, while Will listened.

"What about you?" she asked.

"My plans? I don't have any plans."

"You're going to New York to help your mother. That's a plan."

"Well, I'm not going to medical school while I'm there."

"Be serious," she said. "What do you want to do?"

He didn't answer immediately. She waited, forcing him to speak.

"I thought about physics but I'm not that smart. I majored in chemistry. Working in a lab might be enjoyable. But you know, I did think about medical school at one time, before everything was thrown off kilter, but I don't want to bore you."

"Will, if there's one thing you're not, it's boring."

"Nice of you to say."

Again silence intervened before he began talking about having to drop out of college because his mother had spent his college savings, his time in the Marines and disillusionment with the war. And now about his confusion about why he was really going to New York.

"At this pace I'll never get there."

"At least you're your own man," said Karen. "It's your decision. In my house, plans have to pass muster with my father first, he's such a control freak. I even have to get permission to sleep over at Suzy's. Can you believe it?"

"So what would he do that's so terrible if you just asserted yourself?"

"He'd scold me. He might even ground me?"

"Ground you? You're eighteen. Is he going to tie you up and lock you in your room?

"He'll be very angry. He might even throw me out."

"I thought you loved each other."

"We do."

"And he'd still throw you out?"

"I really don't know."

———

At 2:15 p.m., they decided to come back in the morning to get a sense of traffic.

"I have an idea," said Karen. She turned away from the entrance, pointing. "What if we camped out in those trees.

Then we could observe the entrance from early in the morning."

"But we could just drive out early in the morning," said Will.

"I'd have to explain why I was getting up early. It would be easier to say I was spending a night with Suzy."

"You really want to do this, don't you?"

"No. No. Not so much, if you don't want to."

"We'll be in the same tent, sleeping next to each other. What if I lose control of myself?"

"Okay. If you don't want to, that's fine."

"I didn't say I don't want to. I think it would be fun. Do you have the equipment?"

"I have everything. Family stuff. The works. But I have to figure out how to get things out of the house with no one catching on. I'll call you."

The logistics were a little trickier than Karen at first had thought. She had to enroll Suzy in her plan.

"You're going to spend the night with him in a tent?" said Suzy. "Wow! And what if he gets rambunctious, to use a word that doesn't rhyme with corny. You know just because he stopped when you said no last time doesn't mean—"

"I'm bringing a can of mace."

"God, Karen!"

Karen burst into a heaving fit of laughter, followed, after a brief hesitation, by Suzy.

"You got me," she said after catching her breath. "For a second I thought you were a complete idiot. Are you up to what I think you're up to? Oh, my God."

"I am but I'm nervous."

"Well, of course, you're nervous, but are you prepared?"

"My mother had this old recording of a math professor who wrote and sang funny lyrics. One was about the boy scouts. She wouldn't play it when Dad was around, but she let me listen to it. It's kind of bawdy. I still remember some of the lyrics. She began to sing.

If you're looking for adventure of a
new and different kind
And you come across a Girl Scout who is
similarly inclined
Don't be nervous, don't be flustered, don't be scared
Be prepared!

"Wow, Karen, you are full of surprises. Unbelievable."

———

To be sure that Suzy's parents would not inadvertently give the secret away, Karen told her parents she was going for a sleep-over at Suzy's, neglecting to mention that on that date Suzy's parents would be out of town.

When Roy Haugen was at work and Amy out shopping, Suzy came over to pick up the tent, sleeping bags, flashlights, etc., and then transferred them to the trunk of Will's car.

On the big night Suzy picked up Karen at 9:00 p.m., dropping her off a few blocks away where Will picked her up.

They had earlier noticed what might be a surveillance camera facing the entrance to the base, so they boldly drove onto the base, parking in a small visitors lot, and without going through security, carrying their gear, they walked back out to US 83, where they turned left. They walked for a quarter of a mile before crossing a field to the line of trees. Once screened, they walked back toward the base entrance, where there was essentially no traffic.

They set up the two-man tent on small expanse of grass, well hidden by trees from the highway and the Missile Avenue entrance. They unrolled the sleeping pads and bags inside the tent and exited to lie on the grass and look at the stars.

As the twilight dimmed, the stars began to reveal themselves.

"This is great," said Will. "You can really see the Milky Way. There's too much light pollution in the Bay Area for that."

"Do you know the constellations?" asked Karen.

"Only the Big Dipper." He pointed.

"Yes," said Karen pointing. "It's part of Ursa Major and that bright star is Serius."

"So you're an astronomer."

"Well, everyone's interested in the stars, aren't they? Do you know which star is closest to the Earth, other than the sun."

"Alpha Centauri."

"Karen said, "I'll bet you can't point to it."

"Of course not. It's in the Southern Hemisphere."

"Oh, very good for a city boy. Do you know how many stars there are in the Milky Way?"

"A hundred billion, more or less," said Will.

"That's right, more or less."

"Do you know how stars get their energy?" asked Will.

"Everyone knows that," said Karen. "Nuclear fusion. Hydrogen nuclei being mashed together into helium nuclei."

"I thought you wanted to be a pediatrician, not a nuclear physicist."

"We're not exactly talking deep physics here, are we. More like crossword puzzle clues."

"You know, you're pretty smart for a girl," said Will.

In a wink, they were laughing, and simultaneously worrying they might be heard at the entrance gate down Missile Avenue, though the distance was greater than a football field. Karen muffled her laughter with a palm held over her mouth—Will by using the crook of his elbow.

Neither dared speak because every thought seemed funny enough to trigger a new outburst.

"Maybe we'd better go in," said Karen after a few minutes.

"I'm going to the men's room first," said Will, disappearing into the stand of trees. Karen went in the opposite direction.

———

Inside they sat back to back while changing into pajamas, brought without prior discussion. They each had a flashlight.

"You know we can zip these together to make one big sleeping bag," said Karen. "There's actually more wiggle room that way."

"I'm all for wiggle room," said Will.

Practiced, Karen joined the sleeping bags and opened a flap. Will got in, then Karen. She zipped up the double bag. They lay on their sides, facing each other.

"You know, the top of my father's head would blow off if he knew we were out here together in the same sleeping bag. Even if I told him you were a perfect gentleman, which you are."

"You've made your wishes clear," said Will.

Karen put a hand on Will's shoulder. "If my wishes changed, I'd want you to be very gentle and slow.

"What are you saying?"

"You know," said Karen, "in London during the blitz, when everyone feared they were going to die, people didn't want to be alone at night, which lead to a lot of love making between people who'd never have slept together if it weren't for the night time bombing. Do you know what the doomsday clock is?"

"No."

"It's a symbol, a metaphor for how close we are to doomsday, midnight on the clock, a global catastrophe worse than anything mankind has experienced, a nuclear war. A bunch of nuclear scientists started it in 1947. Right now it's set at 100 seconds before midnight. Since starting this project with Edna, I've had a couple of really bad dreams about it."

She moved closer to him, letting her hand rest on his shoulder.

"I want you to make love to me."

"I… I can't," said Will, startled.

"Oh."

"I'm not prepared."

Karen chuckled.

"It's not funny," said Will. "Not a bit funny."

"You don't have to be prepared. I am."

"You are?"

"Yes. I have an IUD. But I want to be in charge here, do you understand? I want you to do it the way I tell you to."

"Karen, I don't want to be teased again like that time in the park. Do you understand? It actually hurts."

"I'm not going to tease you. I just want to slow things down."

"You can't slow things down much more than this. Nothing's happened yet."

She lay on her back pulling his head down to kiss her. Despite her wish to slow things down she was quickly aroused, her tongue darting as animatedly as his. Gently she pushed him away, hands on his shoulders.

"Just a minute," she said. She unbuttoned her pajama top.

His lips held a nipple captive. She clasped his head in her hands, as if fearful he'd stop what he was doing. Braced on his left elbow, he roamed over her belly in widening circles until the fingertips of his right hand periodically brushed over that nubbin of her delight.

"Oh, God. I'm ready. Wait."

She unzipped the sleeping bag and got her flashlight out.

"I've been struck stupid with lust."

Still amazed by this real life fantasy, Will said nothing.

She dug into her pack.

"Baby oil. Here."

He reached out for it.

"And this." She handed him a towel.

He removed his pajama bottoms and then hers. He anointed himself and moved over her, touching but not entering.

"Slowly," she said. Their bond deepened until she said, "Ooh."

He stopped. "You alright?"

"Hurt a little. Not bad."

"You're sure?"

"Yes. You know what's wonderful? I can talk to you. Even doing this. More."

He didn't move.

"Deeper."

He didn't move.

She wrapped her legs around him, placing her heels on his buttocks, pulling.

"Don't tease."

"You want more?

"Yes. Don't tease. That's mean."

"Okay, now we're even."

They moved in a rocking synchrony, moaning into each other's ears, heightening their excitement. Karen embracing him like she'd never embraced anyone before. After a while she felt that deep, focused sweetness begin to rise within her, the wave now carrying her away.

"Yes!"

Will, to this point, trying to avoid depletion, visualized himself on a chain gang, breaking rocks with a sledgehammer, but now released himself.

———

As they took down the tent and packed their things, they made no reference to the night before, at least not initially. As well as they could, they hid their belongings, which they would carry to the car when their reconnoitering was over, but there wasn't much reconnoitering to be done. Only now did they realize that this, being the visitor's entrance, and hence the fancy signs, was not the base entrance that most people would use, which was on Bomber Avenue further south, indicated by a modest green highway sign.

"It doesn't matter," said Karen. "It's better here with the big signs and anyway we're going to let people know where to go."

On the way back to town, Will asked, "Did you dream up that camping idea so we could be alone?"

"Would you think I was a slut if I did?"

"You can't be a slut if you're a virgin. And anyway don't you think it's unfair to have a word like that for a woman who likes it, but not for a man, unless you think the word satyr is the same, which it isn't."

"I think I'll leave the question unanswered, if that's all right with you."

"Karen, I haven't done much camping in my life but overnight it's become my favorite outdoor activity."

"I don't know when I'll be able to go camping again. It was tricky to make the arrangements. If my parents ever find out about this they'll have seizures, at least my father would. I keep saying that, don't I?"

Will wondered what had changed her from prudish to passionate and whether it was possible she was only interested in his body, the thought striking him instantly as so ludicrous he had to laugh.

"What are you laughing at?"

"I think I'm just happy," said Will.

"I am, too.

CHAPTER SIXTY-ONE

Chubby, energetic, Marvin Martin, a quirky but talented producer of documentaries, spent hours on the internet fishing for hints of much larger stories, which swam around under the surface like marlins. Marvin's marlins he liked to say.

Finding such hints, he might go so far as to fly out to the location and start doing what he was good at, interviewing people, to see if there really was a marlin of a tale to be told. His soft-spoken, even a little awkward at times, style was disarming. Indeed, many saw him as a sad sack, inept, and clumsy, though these characteristics tended to put at ease those he interviewed.

He could, indeed, uncover important stories and make popular and well-reviewed documentaries, but despite this he always needed reassurance and encouragement that what he did was good.

This was his sister Sarah's role. She felt protective of him because, despite his success, he was delicate, vulnerable.

He repeatedly asked, "Let me list you as a co-producer." But she always refused.

"Any kind of notoriety at all would screw up my life," she'd tell him. "Don't ask me again. The answer is no. This is your show, okay? We've been through this before."

Despite his sensitivity to criticism, he pursued controversial stories, which ensured that he would be criticized.

He'd found an article in a little North Dakota newspaper that piqued his interest. A small group calling itself The Committee for a Sound Nuclear Deterrence was actually attacked by two young men on a downtown street in Minot, North Dakota.

A separate article described a bomb attack at the home of Edna O'Hare, a seventy-eight-year-old woman, the head of the organization.

Minot was also the site of the air force base from which a box of grenades had disappeared.

All together this didn't suggest any particular story but was certainly interesting. About the GBSD he knew nothing, but the replacement of all the Minuteman missiles was going to cost a lot of money and these people were saying it was unnecessary.

So he made a reservation to fly out to Minot.

Shortly after booking into the Grand Hotel with his crew, he called local reporter Amy Haugen, who was initially suspicious, until she googled his name, which she did as she spoke with him.

He wanted to interview as many people as he could.

CHAPTER SIXTY-TWO

Edna had become fearful of participating in public demonstrations, not simply for her safety, but also for the safety of those around her, especially for the safety of those around her.

She was the red-haired witch drawing the ire of unknown assailants, or in the case of those two boys, of known assailants.

But she was comfortable meeting with Rasmussen, Karen, and Will, to discuss tactics.

Marvin Martin found her easily and she agreed to speak with him, with the proviso that he leave his film crew outside in the van until she decided whether or not she would allow herself to be filmed.

She was gratified that Andy Rasmussen, Karen, and Will wanted to be present to hear his presentation.

After introductions were made, they sat in the living room, Edna serving coffee, naturally, but there were no cookies.

"So what I have in mind," said Martin, "is an investigative documentary about the GBSD controversy and the people involved.

"If it were just heated arguments among the citizens of Minot about the missiles it would be a dramatic enough story, but someone actually threw a hand grenade at this house. That makes for real drama.

"I plan to get both sides of the story, I mean, to interview as many people as I can who want the Minuteman replaced and as many as I can who don't want it replaced."

Martin fumbled with a pen and pad he was holding on his lap, which he moved from hand to hand until the pen dropped. He put pen and pad on the coffee table.

"Frankly, Mrs. O'Hare, as I see it, the story revolves around you."

He took sips of coffee, his hand mildly tremulous, the cup rattling on the saucer before it was safely back in place, but not before he'd spilled a few drops on the table, which he quickly dabbed with his napkin.

"Of course, if you don't wish to participate, you'll still be an important part of the story, maybe still the focal point, though there'd be no interview of you in the film."

He dabbed his lips with the napkin, crossed and uncrossed his legs, and picked up the pen and pad again.

"I'd like to assure you that I would do my best to respect your time and your privacy, but I might have to come back from time to time to ask more questions."

"And all of that goes for Dr. Rasmussen, Ms. Haugen, and Mr. Larrabee.

Rasmussen spoke. "What if we changed our minds about having our interviews included after they'd been filmed?

Perhaps because they were edited in way that put us in a bad light."

"I can show you the interview immediately after it's videotaped. You could veto it then or have it redone, but once it's in the complete documentary, you couldn't take it out because that would affect the entire narrative."

CHAPTER SIXTY-THREE

Now settled in at the Grand Hotel with Olga, his videographer, and Benson, his sound and lighting man, Martin began to make phone calls, finding people surprisingly willing to talk with him, both those for and those against the replacement of the Minuteman.

With a list of interviewees-to-be in his pocket or, more precisely, in his moleskin pocket notebook, Martin filled in his filming calendar. Edna O'Hare was first, of course. He asked her a few preliminary questions about who she was, how long she'd lived here, and how long she'd been interested in missiles.

"How long I've been interested in missiles? Since I was a sophomore in college. A couple of things happened that year. We had the Cuban missile crisis, and I met my husband-to-be, James Hashimoto, who was born in Hiroshima."

"Your husband was born in Hiroshima?" said Martin. "My goodness. That explains a lot doesn't it."

"Yes, it does."

"You kept your maiden name? Why?"

"Mr. Martin, you're a little behind the times. Many women prefer to keep the names they've grown up with."

"You're right. Tell us more about your husband."

"He was two years old when the bomb went off. The family lived just outside of town on a small farm. Their house was damaged, but the family survived. After the war they moved to Los Angeles where James's father had a brother who'd been interned during the war but had managed to keep ownership of his small strawberry farm. James and I met at the University of California, Davis."

On wooden chairs on the front porch, they sat facing each other, a dish-sized area of fresh, unpainted wood between them.

Martin only asked a few more questions before jumping into the topic that would interest the most viewers.

"So someone is so upset with you about your protest that they bombed your house."

"It appears so, yes."

She had been instructed to ignore the videographer and sound man, but though they tiptoed around her, she couldn't ignore them, and they added to her anxiety. The publicity was good, but the very idea that she might be viewed by thousands of people was an idea she tried unsuccessfully to squelch.

Martin pointed to the spot between them.

"And that's where the bomb went off?"

"It was a grenade."

"A grenade?"

"Yes, from the air force base."

"From the air force base?"

His tone was that of feigned disbelief. Would he ask a

question each time she answered the previous question? He was managing to draw her attention toward him and away from his assistants.

After a pause that a later reviewer of the documentary would dub "pregnant," Martin asked, "It would be truly shocking if someone from the air force had done this, wouldn't it?"

"I'm not saying anything like that, only that the grenade was from the base."

"Hmm. Well let's get back to your husband. He was two years old when the bomb was dropped on Hiroshima. Did this affect him, I mean physically?"

Edna nodded. "He'd been vaccinated but came down with covid anyway.

"The doctor had wondered if anyone had ever been concerned that his immune system was underperforming. In fact, since childhood, when he caught a cold, it was always a little bit nastier and longer-lived than expected. We both wondered if radiation exposure in childhood had a lingering effect. Who knows?"

"I see."

Martin paused, then picked up the thread. "Review for us your arguments against these missiles."

"Before I do that," she said, "I'd like to show you some pictures of what Little Boy did."

"Pardon me," said Martin.

"Little Boy, the name of the Hiroshima bomb."

From a short stack on the floor next to her chair, she picked up a green folder, removing a black and white photograph from a magazine and displaying it to the videographer.

"This is the shadow of a person with a cane sitting on

the steps of the Sumitomo bank. He or she was vaporized by the heat of the blast. Nuclear bombs are not like ordinary bombs. They don't just cause a blast. In Hiroshima anyone within sixteen hundred feet of the explosion was vaporized in an instant.

"Here is the shadow image of a child jumping rope. Speaking of children, almost all of them under ten years old developed thyroid injury from radioactive iodine leading to physical deformities and mental impairment. Some responded to thyroid hormone treatment.

"And here's one that's particularly hard to look at, a seven-year-old girl with third degree burns on half her face and neck.

"I'm talking about the Hiroshima bombing before talking about the GBSD because I want people to know that nuclear weapons are not ordinary bombs, as I've said. They do not just blow away buildings. The burn and irradiate people. They cause generations to suffer from excess cancers and birth defects. Firestorms would cloak the atmosphere with soot blocking out much of the sun's light. We'd have a nuclear winter so that crops would fail and there'd be mass starvation. A nuclear war between the United States and Russia would lead to the end of civilization.

"If we can reduce the risk of an accidental war, we must. That's where ground-based missiles come in…"

———

With his office mates' permission, Dr. Andrew Rasmussen allowed Marvin Martin and his two person crew to film him in an examining room, though the videographer had to station herself in the doorway, and the sound man outside the office, having provided Rasmussen with a lavalier microphone.

Rasmussen sat in his chair by the small desk, Martin in the chair next to the desk, ordinarily the patient's chair.

Martin introduced the doctor, described his participation in Edna O'Hare's protest and his high standing in the community with the consequence that his opinions would more likely be respected, or at least considered, than would those of an ordinary citizen.

"How did you become involved in this protest?" asked Martin.

"Mrs. O'Hare convinced me that—and it's no exaggeration to say this—land-based missiles threaten humanity. There is no plausible medical response after a nuclear war so it's a public health question, a question of prevention. I couldn't live with myself ignoring what is staring us in the face—concretely here in Minot."

"And do other doctors feel the way you do?

"Some, yes. And I'm glad you asked because there is a national organization, Physicians for Social Responsibility, which is concerned, in addition to global warming and economic inequality, with nuclear disarmament. The board of directors asked me if I'd be interested in establishing a North Dakota chapter. I think I'm going to do it but I must say my main focus will not be on nuclear disarmament, but on stopping the replacement of the Minuteman with the GBSD."

"I learned," said Martin, "that Mrs. O'Hare's protest must have angered someone so much that they bombed her house. Has anything like that happened to you? Have you been threatened?"

The videographer, it would later be noted, had not simply set up her camera on its tripod and let it run. She'd paid close attention to Rasmussen's face. When Martin asked if Rasmussen had ever been threatened, she zoomed in, as Rasmussen frowned and then smiled weakly. A full ten seconds passed before he spoke.

"My truck has not been vandalized. My house has not been bombed, but, yes, I have been threatened. I was told I would be hurt if I continued speaking against the GBSD. I'm sure it would interest the viewers of this interview to know what I was threatened with, but I can't tell you."

"Why can't you tell me?"

"I knew the person who threatened me and was able to do something about it. I just can't say anything more."

———

Initially reluctant to be filmed by Martin, Earnest Schmidt eventually convinced himself that someone had to counter Edna's blathering. And now here he was. A woman with an industrial-sized camera and a man with a light reflector wandered around his living room before suggesting where the interviewer and interviewee should sit.

"Mrs. O'Hare is your sister-in-law, is that correct?"

"Yes, she is," said Schmidt with evident distaste.

"What do you think of her?"

"I thought we were going to be talking about the missiles. What I think of Mrs. O'Hare is not relevant."

"Oh, but it is. Didn't you pay a local therapist, Ted Swenson, if I'm correct, to write a piece suggesting that Mrs. O'Hare might be dangerous."

"I don't know where you're getting your information.

The only theoretical danger she presents is if people believe her and I assure you that the people of Minot do not believe her. The Ground-Based Strategic Deterrent will not only continue to protect us, it will bring jobs and business to this city. I'm a proud member of the chamber of commerce, which is fully supportive of the replacement plan."

"What do you think of her argument that because it is on hair-trigger alert a Minuteman missile might be fired by mistake?"

"The air force doesn't make mistakes."

Schmidt's naïveté, simple ignorance, or conscious dissembling—everyone makes mistakes, and this was Schmidt's—irked Martin, so that he now departed from his usual one-question-after-the-other style to read from a long list of mistakes the air force has made, including the loss of atomic and hydrogen bombs over Spain and the explosion of a Titan missile in Damascus, Arkansas.

"It was topped with a nine megaton hydrogen bomb. If that had exploded—."

"These things happened a long time ago," said Schmidt, recognizing his error. "Technology has much improved. This town trusts the airmen of the Minot Air Force Base. It's an award-winning operation."

"It is indeed an award-winning operation, a fine operation. We all support the men and women in uniform, but they are only human."

"It seems to me that you've picked a side in this fight, Edna's side. I want that to be clear to anyone watching this. And I want to repeat that the people of Minot look forward to the installation of the GBSD."

Martin decided not to mention Edna O'Hare's other

arguments against the GBSD, but rather to ask Schmidt about the attempts to intimidate, or even kill her.

"Do you have any idea about who might have thrown a bomb at Mrs. O'Hare's house?"

"There are lunatics in any city," said Schmidt. "I'm sure our police department will find these evil people."

Shortly thereafter, Martin thanked Schmidt and left Schmidt's home.

Martin had concluded that there was no point confronting him with the latest mistake, the near launching of four hundred fifty missiles because a radar signal bouncing off the moon was interpreted as a full-scale Russian attack on the United States.

Because word was out that Martin's documentary might shine a positive light on Edna O'Hare and her arguments against not only the GBSD but against the Minuteman as well, Colonel Nichols reluctantly agreed to be interviewed.

"She means no harm, of course, but appears to ignore counter arguments."

"For example?"

"Missile sponge. Our one hundred fifty Minuteman missiles, plus the same number at Warren and Malmstrom Air Force Bases, force the Russians to send at least nine hundred missiles against them to ensure their destruction and so to use a significant number of their missiles."

"They need at least two missiles to destroy each of ours? Aren't global positioning systems becoming extremely accurate? What if they needed only one on one?"

Almost successfully hiding his annoyance, Nichols told him that the Russians wouldn't take the risk.

"So," said Martin, the upper middle of the country is sacrificed to draw off some of the Russian missiles."

"On the contrary, this is one of the legs of the deterrent force."

"Very well. Another one of Mrs. O'Hare's arguments, given that our ICBMs can't move to avoid being hit, is that there is little time to decide if a warning of an attack is accurate, but I don't want to ask about that. Is it true that a number of the missile launch officers on base have been using mind-altering drugs and if it is true, doesn't that make them less capable of using good judgement? They are, after all, in charge of the most destructive weapons ever made."

"A small group has been identified using marijuana when off duty. I'm afraid this generation of young people has a rather nonchalant attitude toward marijuana. As I said, they were not on duty and remember it takes two missile launch officers to launch a rocket. The public has never been in any danger whatsoever."

Martin shook his head and leaned forward.

"Colonel Nichols, former Secretary of Defense William Perry was interviewed on NPR in 2018 about the danger of false alarms. He was asked if it terrified him. This is what he said." He read from his moleskin notebook.

PERRY: It does terrify me. In fact, what really terrifies me is that people don't understand this issue. They don't understand the problem we have today—the problem of starting a war by mistake is probably greater today than it was during the Cold War because the things that can cause that false alert are not just a single person making the wrong judgment. It's not just a machine here. Now we have the possibility of malicious hacking into the system either by a malevolent individual or by an unfriendly government. So the problem today is much greater than it was during the Cold War.

"So, Colonel Nichols" said Martin on finishing, "does it scare you?"

"I have full confidence in the U. S. Air Force."

CHAPTER SIXTY-FOUR

From a somewhat reluctant Roy Haugen, Captain Andresen received the telephones confiscated from Calderone, Caulfield, and Forster. Haugen had considered the benefits to himself were he the one to expose the drug supply line. But marijuana and LSD were not what most people considered hard drugs and he worried that his airmen, specifically Caulfield and Forster, bad boys as they were, would suffer punishments out of proportion to their crimes. Calderone, a missile launch officer, because of his responsibility was another matter. Who knows how he might be disciplined?

Andresen quickly established that Forster's telephone was the most littered with coded messages and that Batman was the sender and receiver of most of these messages.

The telephone company, with a court order to do so, unmasked Batman as Wayne Smedberg.

When Andresen and Officer Shirley Johansen arrived at the Smedberg's front door, Johansen allowed playful visions of battering rams to dance in her head. When Harriet Smedberg, Wayne's mother, puzzled but relaxed, welcomed the officers in, her visions of battering rams evaporated.

Introductions made, Andresen said he'd like to speak with Wayne.

"He'll be home soon," said Harriet Smedberg. "He's out skateboarding but he's always on time for dinner." She added hopefully, "He's a good boy."

Mr. Smedberg, who'd been out working in the garage, soon came in.

As of yet Andresen had not mentioned the purpose of their visit, but now with both parents present, he decided to tell an abbreviated version of the story. The Smedberg's were attentive.

"...so I'm concerned your son is, forgive the expression, a drug dealer. Not heroine or methamphetamines, that is, not the most dangerous drugs."

Dinner delayed, the four waited in the living room for Wayne to return.

When he did, skateboard in hand, the adults stood.

"Wayne," said Mrs. Smedberg. "This is Captain Andresen and officer Johansen. They'd like to speak with you."

"Yeah, sure. What about?"

He remained standing.

"Do you know a man named Charlie Forster?" asked Andresen.

"You haven't told me what this is about."

This was Andresen's business, but Johansen was reminded of a nasty cousin of hers who was always disrespectful.

"We think you're selling drugs to people on the base," she blurted.

Andresen shook his head.

"Okay, officer, I'll take it from here." He smiled at her so she would not be too offended.

"I want to speak with a lawyer," said Wayne.

They were still standing.

"Wayne!" said Mrs. Smedberg appalled. "What do you mean a lawyer?"

"That's all right, Mrs. Smedberg," said Andresen, taking an envelope from his back pocket. "He does have a right to remain silent."

He took a sheet of paper from an envelope and handed it to Mrs. Smedberg who shared it with her husband. The words "search warrant" could not have been printed any bigger or bolder.

"Excuse us," said Andresen. He turned, followed by Johansen, to face a staircase. "I take it the bedrooms are upstairs."

"Yes," said Mr. Smedberg, as dismayed as his wife.

A hallway ran along the second floor. Wayne's room was easy to identify, given an unmade bed, a couple of t-shirts on the floor, a desk laden with plastic figures representing various characters from an online shooter game.

Andresen on one side, Johansen on the other, examined the bed, not overlooking pillows, mattress, and then the underside of the bed frame.

Each searched one half of the desk. In the rear of the bottom left hand drawer under some Batman comics, Johansen found a blotter of acid, divided into squares, each printed with a likeness of the Mad Hatter.

"Bingo," she said, displaying the blotter, held at a corner between thumb and index finger. "He's not too concerned about anyone finding it."

Mr. and Mrs. Smedberg stood in the doorway.

"What's that?" asked Mrs. Smedberg.

"LSD," answered Johansen.

"Oh," she said, perplexed.

Mr. Smedberg disappeared from the doorway, returning as Andresen began going through Wayne's closet.

"He's gone," said Mr. Smedberg. "Took off just like that. It's going to take a while for me to process this. Wayne's a good kid."

Wayne's attitude had disturbed Johansen, though for her being a good kid might have consisted of instant contriteness, admission of guilt, and an offer to polish her car.

"Possession of LSD is a crime in all fifty states," she said.

Down on hands and knees and halfway into the closet, Captain Andresen passed articles of clothing, sporting equipment, board games, books, magazines, and shoes to Johansen, who placed them aside.

A cardboard box containing something heavy, was the last object on the closet floor. Within it was a single 40mm high-explosive NK 18 grenade.

Andresen picked it up and whistled.

"That's not a grenade, is it?" asked Mr. Smedberg, shocked.

"I'm afraid so," said Andresen. "We're going to have to arrest the boy when we find him. You understand?"

Wayne's parents agreed they would call the police when their son returned home, which Andresen was fairly confident they would.

On the way to their patrol car, Johansen said, "I wonder if he will go home. This is deep shit, if you'll excuse my French."

"It sure is. One of these grenades exploded on Edna O'Hare's front porch. But he's just a kid, not even finished with high school. He probably doesn't have a place to go."

"How about his friend Baxter."

"Good idea, though I don't like the idea of barging in on Colonel Nichols."

"He's not your commanding officer, if I may say so."

"You're right, Shirley. You're right."

———

On the base, the Nichols family lived in a well-manicured tract of similar two-story, white houses with ample driveways and garages, and modest, but sufficient, front and back yards. Most Americans would be happy to live in similar pleasant, if uniform, neighborhoods.

Not expecting to find Wayne Smedberg at the Nichols home, Andresen and Johansen nevertheless drove from Minot north to the base.

"We're going to have to speak with Frank Nichols sooner rather than later," said Andresen.

"He won't be home at this time of day," said Johansen.

"I know."

———

Judy Nichols had not seen her son's friend Wayne for at least a week, which was not out of the usual. He seemed perfectly normal.

"We'd like to speak with Baxter," said Andresen. Obligingly, Mrs. Nichols immediately called him on her cell phone asking him to come home. After a little back and forth in which she explained that the police wanted to speak with him, she hung up.

"He's playing touch football with some friends. He'll be home in twenty minutes."

Only now did she ask what the matter was.

By the time Baxter arrived, they had explained the situation. Mrs. Nichols had been concerned that they were here about the fight at Edna O'Hare's protest. They weren't.

Introductions made, the four sat in the living room. Baxter was subdued and polite.

"My husband Frank will have wished to be here, but we know better than to bother him when he's at work. So much on his mind these days."

"Wayne is a friend of yours, right?" said Andresen.

"Yeah. He is."

"Does he use LSD?"

Baxter frowned.

"Yeah. I guess. He has."

"You guess? Have you ever had LSD with him?"

Baxter looked at his mother. He was already in trouble with them both for the fight and now this, but he could face another parental scolding. How serious a crime was use of LSD? It couldn't be that bad? He saw no point in lying. Not yet.

"Yeah. I have."

"We'd like to search the house, but we have no warrant. Would you permit us to?" asked Andresen.

"Yes, of course." said Mrs. Nichols.

Baxter shrugged.

They limited the search of the house to Baxter's room, which was much more ship-shape than Wayne's had been— military influence doubtless.

Next they searched the garage, if a bit haphazardly, Helen and Baxter tailing them. The garage's rear door lead into the back yard in which sat a small red garden shed not much bigger than a van.

Johansen walked over and tried the door.

"It's locked."

"That's funny," said Mrs. Nichols. She went back into the garage for the key.

Wayne sat on the floor cross-legged, head hung. He sighed and stood up.

"You're under arrest," said Andresen.

Irate that his son could be caught up in such a mess as drug dealing, Frank Nichols refused to get Baxter a lawyer when Andresen threatened him with arrest.

Under questioning in a bleak grey room at police headquarters in Minot, Baxter, offered clemency if he cooperated, admitted driving the car to Edna O'Hare's home, where Wayne had thrown the grenade onto her porch, because she was a Russian sympathizer. Baxter swore he didn't know what Wayne had been up to when he asked for the ride.

Wayne had received two grenades from some guy on the base in exchange for a blotter of acid and eight ounces of marijuana.

Whatever might be said about their delinquency, Wayne Smedberg and Baxter Nichols were not hardened criminals, as newspapers sometimes described those with multiple felonies.

Wayne admitted to several crimes: drug possession, drug sale, accepting stolen property (grenades), and malicious mischief, having convinced everyone that he had no intention of hurting anyone when he threw the grenade onto the porch. He just wanted to frighten Will Larrabee.

"Larrabee?" said Andresen. "Not Mrs. O'Hare?"

Tears ran down Wayne Smedberg's cheeks.

"The son-of-a-bitch beat me up. I thought about it day and night. My nose hurt so much. I wasn't doing anything. I was just watching him fight with Baxter. And then he beat me up in front of those people and just walked away."

He was sobbing now.

As far as the grenades, he swapped some blotter acid and marijuana for them. His grenade supplier, a guy named Charlie on the base, though they never met on the base.

Wayne went to Ward County juvenile detention.

Andresen and Haugen reviewed the case. Charlie had to be Charlie Forster.

CHAPTER SIXTY-FIVE

The Committee for a Sound Nuclear Deterrence, headed by a red-haired old woman dressed as a witch, was enthusiastic to have Mr. Martin in town making a documentary about the ICBMs. And while enthusiasm might not be the word to describe Minot's reaction, there was excitation if not excitement.

This could be nothing but a good thing for Edna, thought Will. Her aim, after all, was to raise consciousness about the plan to replace the Minuteman with the GBSD and now her arguments might be heard by a national audience. No matter that the air force's arguments would be heard, too.

This was the time for Will to complete his trip to New York, to keep his promise to his mother.

———

When Will told Karen he had something he wanted to talk with her about, she suggested they take a stroll along the river walk.

They stopped on a bridge crossing the Souris, leaning their forearms on the railing. The water was covered with a blanket of green algae.

"I've been thinking that this might be the time to go to New York."

"Oh," said Karen.

"Edna has made an impact. People are going to hear her arguments."

Karen looked at him and nodded glumly.

"So I was thinking, why don't you come with me?"

"Oh, Will. What a wonderful idea, but... I couldn't possibly do that."

"Why not?"

"You know why not."

"You like the idea though."

"Yes. Very much."

"So tell your father. I mean if you're old enough to have a lover, you're old enough to go on a car trip with him, not that I would put it that way to your family.

"We'd only be there for a week max. I'm going to lay all responsibility in my brother's lap, which I think he wants anyway. It will be easier on him if I keep my promise to my mother. She won't be able to use me against him. Come on, Karen. What's the worst your father can do?"

"I don't know."

"I want to be there when you tell him you're going with me."

Karen laughed.

"You want to, though, right?" asked Will.

"Yes."

"So ask him and see what he says. You can do that for me, can't you?"

They turned back to stare at the green river.

———

To Karen's surprise, when her father heard that she wanted to discuss an important matter with him and wanted Will to be present, he invited Will to join them for dinner.

"I hope it's not about the missiles," said Haugen. "I'm not changing my mind about that and I'm not going to be interviewed by that Martin character. I'd rather house one of the missiles in our garage than mug for that guy's camera."

At dinner, Amy said, "We have ice cream for dessert."

"Yea," said Lilly, though it was no surprise as Roy Haugen's one vice was addiction to ice cream after dinner, summer, winter, spring, or fall. Still, Lilly never tired of saying "Yea."

When all had empty ice cream dishes before them, Roy said, "So what's on your mind, Karen?"

"Maybe Lilly should go watch some TV while were talking," said Karen.

"I want to listen, please," said Lilly. "I won't say anything."

"Is this an adult subject?" asked Roy.

"Well, no," said Karen. "Not exactly."

Karen's hesitancy signaled that maybe it was indeed an adult subject or had adult subject implications.

"Lilly, please respect your sister's wishes," said Amy. "She wants some privacy."

Lilly made a face and left the table.

"I hope when I have kids, they're as well behaved as Lilly," said Will.

Roy nodded.

"All right. What's the topic, adult or not?" said Roy.

To everyone's surprise, it was Will who spoke.

"I'm going out to New York to visit my family for a few days, a week at the most, and then coming back to Minot. I'd like Karen to come with me."

"It was my idea," said Karen, thinking that little white lie might make the trip sound innocent.

Roy scowled but before he could say anything, Amy asked, "Why do you want to go?"

"For the fun of the road trip."

"And to be with Will?" added Amy.

"Yes, of course."

"I'm planning stops in Madison, and Cleveland. We'll have separate rooms, of course."

"I'm sorry," said Roy, "but I don't approve."

"Why not, Dad? I'm eighteen."

"I shouldn't have to answer that question, but I will. Because it's just improper. What kind of lax parents do you think we are? Can you imagine me letting my daughter go off for days with someone we hardly know? I mean no offense to you, Will. You understand my position, I'm sure."

Probably because he'd put his foot down so firmly, he did not object to Will and Karen taking a walk after dinner.

"You know, Karen, every time you talk about your doing something he doesn't like, you say he'll have a stroke, or a seizure, or the top of his head will blow off. But you don't mean that literally. You mean he'd be very angry. Extremely angry. Inappropriately angry, if you ask me. You know what you should do? Tell your mother we've slept together."

"What?"

"The opportunity for intimacy is the thing he's worried about, but it's already happened. Ideally you'd tell him, but if you tell your mother she'll tell him. He can blow up at her."

"I don't want anyone blowing up at anyone."

"Then you're not going with me, is that it?"

"I really want to go."

"Well then."

"I don't think I can. Leaving him so upset."

Will left without going back inside to say goodbye, nor did he kiss Karen goodnight.

Just after she'd changed into pajamas, her mother came into the room and sat on her bed.

"Can we talk for a while, sweetheart?" she asked.

"Of course."

"What's your relationship with Will?"

"We're friends, Mom."

"Like boyfriend girlfriend?"

Karen hesitated. Should she now say 'just friends' or should she acknowledge that they were indeed boyfriend and girlfriend, which would lead to the next fateful question. She remembered what Will had prophesied. "If you tell your mother, she'll tell him."

"Yes, like boyfriend and girlfriend."

Amy took her daughter's hand.

"How close are you?"

"As close as you can get."

Well, she'd gone this far.

"I have an IUD. It was my idea, believe me. Not his."

In stunned silence, her mother continued holding her daughter's hand.

———

Ordinarily a discussion like the one they were about to have would take place in their bedroom after the children had fallen asleep, but Amy was uncomfortable with the idea.

Instead she told her husband,

"I want to talk with you about something. Let me invite you out for a drink. I'll buy you a mai tai at the Outrigger."

"You know, Amy, this makes me nervous. Why can't you tell me here? You're afraid I'll blow up. That's it, isn't it?"

"I just want to talk with you away from the kids."

At the Outrigger, they had a booth to themselves, but in a public place Roy was less likely to roar when he heard what Amy had to say.

She waited until he'd almost finished his second drink, though he was impatient from the moment they were seated, oblivious to the Polynesian decor, burning torches affixed to the walls, the fishing nets hung from the ceiling. He wanted to get right down to business.

"Roy," she said finally, "our daughter is a woman."

"Tell me something I don't know."

"She and Will have slept together."

He sputtered, "What the fuck! I'll kill the son-of-a-bitch."

He stood to go.

Although she thought she'd been prepared for his reaction, she was mistaken. Somehow it felt to her that he'd discounted her parenthood entirely, discounted feeling, opinion, judgment.

She surprised herself by grabbing his wrist. "Sit down," she hissed.

Before he could yank his arm free she pulled forcefully so that he sat.

"I was just going to talk with her, damn it," he said. "And maybe track down that bastard."

"Are you also going to remove her IUD?"

"What are you talking... Don't tell me she has an IUD."

"I just told you and it was her idea."

"I don't believe it. She wouldn't."

"She has. She did. Are you going to ask her to remove it? Come on. Are you?"

She spoke with a vehemence that startled him.

"Look, Amy, this is so—"

"Are you going to ask her to remove the IUD?"

"Stop that," demanded Roy.

"I will not stop it. Answer the question."

"Did she tell you she was going to do this?"

"No. It was as much a surprise to me as it was to you. Are you going to ask her to remove it?"

"No. Of course not. I'm not a total idiot."

"Are you going to kill Will Larrabee?"

"Amy, what do you want?"

"I want you to give your blessing to her trip with Will to New York."

"What am I, a priest that gives blessings?"

"She doesn't want to upset you. She wants your okay."

He ordered another drink.

————

They sat together at the dinner table the next day.

"About your trip to New York," said her father with a hitch in his voice, "I want you to call me every day."

Karen stood, went around the table, and hugged him. "Thank you so much."

"Don't thank me. Thank your mother."

CHAPTER SIXTY-SIX

Netflix purchased Marvin Martin's documentary and the New York Times reviewed it.

While this country struggles to knit up a fraying social safety net and revitalize a public health system that had delayed in stopping the covid-19 pandemic, it simultaneously plans to spend many billions of dollars to replace four hundred fifty aging land-based Minuteman ICBMs with new missiles around air force bases in Montana, Wyoming, and North Dakota.

Marvin Martin documents the fierce debate over whether such a replacement is necessary or, as Minot resident Edna O'Hare, campaigning against the replacement insists, land-based ICBMs are inherently unnecessary, costly, and dangerous. Dangerous because they're on hair-trigger alert with little time to determine whether radar reporting a missile attack on the United States has instead located a flock of migrating geese.

So heated had the debate become that not only did young men attack participants in a protest march, vandalized Ms. O'Hare's car, but actually bombed her house with a grenade stolen from the air force base.

The Missiles of Minot is a short course in America's nuclear deterrent policy. Should land-based missiles be replaced, or should they be removed? America's and the world's destiny may depend on the answer to this question.

The *New York Times*'s article was reprinted in smaller news-papers around the country, including, to the chagrin of numerous champions of the GBSD, in the *Minot Daily News*.

Along with many in congress, Steve Jones, in his capacity as chairman of the Congressional Armed Services Committee, began receiving calls from constituents asking if the red-haired woman they'd read about was, as some of them put it, "for real?"

Additionally, numerous arms control groups and a significant segment of Democratic Party officials, pressed for hearings. Saving billions of dollars on unnecessary ICBMs, allowed responsible spending on new submarines, for example.

For its newsworthiness, Congressman Jones invited Edna O'Hare to testify, though she was not what might be called an expert witness, or was she?

CHAPTER SIXTY-SEVEN

With the invitation to speak before congress came the realization that her testimony would be national news, which, in turn, meant that millions of Americans would learn about the monstrous danger posed by land-based missiles.

Knowing this, her two-ply shame shriveled and disappeared: the shame of having done nothing for months to honor her husband's wishes and the shame of therefore having been emotionally unable to visit his grave.

Now she knelt on the grass, placing a bouquet of sunflowers before the headstone, having picked them because they were cheerful and because they'd come from their farm. Then she made herself comfortable on a small bright orange, yellow, green, and blue Mexican blanket, which they'd purchased on a trip to Mexico City.

"I'm sorry I didn't come until now." She knew she would cry, knew she had to cry, knew she wanted to cry. With a half dozen fresh handkerchiefs in a basket-like handbag, she'd come prepared.

"All those people you wanted to hear about it, are going to hear about it now."

THE END

—————

Don't miss out on your next favorite book!
Join the Melange Books mailing list at
www.melange-books.com/mail.html

AUTHOR NOTES

Chapter One

The US maintains 450 missile silos around air force bases in Montana, North Dakota, and Wyoming. Fifty of these silos are empty, but for simplicity's sake this story refers to 450 missiles, 150 around each base. Colorado and Nebraska house some of Warren Air Force Base's missiles.

Hans M. Kristensen & Matt Korda (2020) United States nuclear forces. Bulletin of the Atomic Scientists, 76:1, 46-60, https://www.tandfonline.com/doi/full/10.1080/00963402.2019.1701286

Chapter Four

Daniel Ellsberg. *The Doomsday Machine: Confessions of a Nuclear War Planner.* New York, London: Bloomsbury, 2017

Chapter Ten

Though the Minuteman III is capable of carrying multiple independently targetable reentry vehicles, the new Strategic Arms Reduction Treaty limits the number of warheads per missile to one.

Chapter Fourteen

Normile, Dennis. 2020 Aftermath. *Science.* 369:6502
   On the aftermath of the Hiroshima bombing.

Chapter Seventeen

This test question is from Thompson M. 2014. Are You Smarter than a Nuclear Control Officer. Feb. 13 *Time Magazine*

Chapter Eighteen

Wellerstein, Alex. Website *Nuke Map*. https://nuclearsecrecy.com/nukemap/

Chapter Twenty

Air force fires 9 Commanders in Nuke Missile Cheating Scandal. March 27, 2014

CBS/AP   https://www.cbsnews.com/news/air-force-fires-9-commanders-in-nuke-missile-cheating-scandal/

Chapter Twenty-Five

Snyder, Ryan. 2018 The Future of the ICBM Force: Should the Least Valuable Leg of the Triad be Replaced? *Arms Control Association. Policy White Paper*. March

Chapter Thirty

Most of the discussion is a transcription of an actual meeting of the House Armed Services Committee.

https://www.congress.gov/committees/video/house-armed-services/hsas00/IUm4qXTQFNs

Chapter Fifty-One

This chapter largely taken from the opening scene in the 1983 film *WarGames* directed by John Badham. With Matthew Broderick, Ally Sheedy, John Wood, Dabney Coleman.

Chapter Fifty-Two

A radar station did indeed once misinterpret the rising of the moon over Norway as a Russian missile attack. Stevens, Matt. Mele, Christopher. The New York Times. Jan. 13, 2018

Chapter Fifty-Nine

The number 100,000 Hiroshima bombs is from Blair, Bruce. 2007 Rebuttal of US Statement on Operational Status "A

Rebuttal of the U.S. Statement on the Alert Status of U.S. Nuclear Forces" Bruce G. Blair President, World Security Institute October 13, 2007

Chapter Sixty

Lehrer, Tom. *Be Prepared*

ACKNOWLEDGMENTS

For their reading of the text and their commentary, I'd like to thank Emma Rous, Bruce Amundson, Steve Harvey, and Dave Strauss.

I am grateful to Dr. Ryan Snyder for discussing with me his article on the third leg of the nuclear triad.

My publisher, Nancy Schumacher, has again made the production of a book as painless as possible, though not eliminating pain entirely.

And without Ingrid's support and criticism, there would be no book at all.

THANK YOU FOR READING

———

Did you enjoy this book?

We invite you to leave a review at your favorite book site, such as Goodreads, Amazon, Barnes & Noble, etc.

DID YOU KNOW THAT LEAVING A REVIEW...

- Helps other readers find books they may enjoy.
- Gives you a chance to let your voice be heard.
- Gives authors recognition for their hard work.
- Doesn't have to be long. A sentence or two about why you liked the book will do.

ABOUT THE AUTHOR

Peter J. Manos was voted one of Seattle's top doctors seven years in a row by Seattle Magazine. After retirement he attended a summer session of the Iowa Writers' Workshop. His books include: Care of the Difficult Patient: A Nurse's Guide (with Joan Braun, R.N.); Lucifer's Revenge, a novel of magical realism; Dear Babalu: Letters to an Advice Columnist illustrated by Toby Liebowitz, which was a finalist in the Next Generation Indie Book Awards competition (2017); and a young adult sci-fi novel, A Girl Named Cricket. Flash Fiction Magazine published his story Gamma Rays and the Kitchen Sink in June 2020.

A member of Washington Physicians for Social Responsibility, he takes an active interest in the threat to humankind of nuclear weapons.

ALSO BY PETER J. MANOS

WITH MELANGE BOOKS

Published by Fire & Ice Young Adult Books, an imprint of Melange Books

A Girl Named Cricket

Made in the USA
Coppell, TX
23 October 2021

64534779R00225